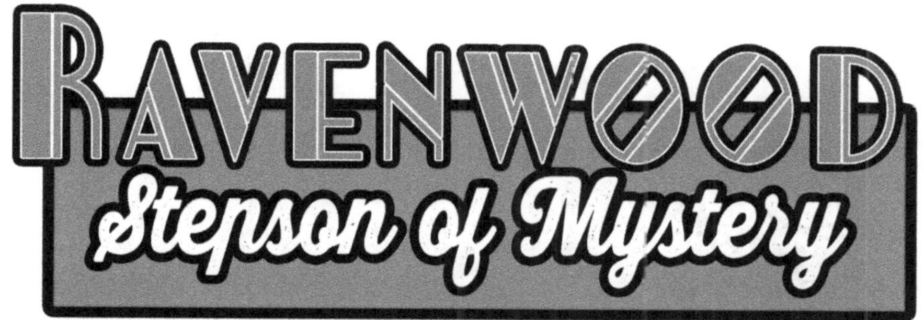

Volume Five

Airship 27 Productions

Ravenwood Stepson of Mystery Volume 5

An Airship 27 Production
www.airship27.com
www.airship27hangar.com

Editor: Ron Fortier
Associate Editor: Jonathan Sweet
Production designer: Rob Davis
Marketing and promotion: Michael Vance

ISBN: 978-1-953589-77-4

Printed in the United States of America

10 9 8 7 6 5 4 3 2 1

VOLUME V

THE DERVISH IN THE NIGHT

by Dexter Fabi

The first murder was at 12:15 a.m. according to the wife.

The second murder of the same man was at 1:42 a.m., an hour and twenty-seven minutes later, according to the son.

The third murder of the same man was at 3:11 a.m., an hour and twenty-nine minutes later, as witnessed by the daughter.

After this night, the Cevikbas family, fortunate and of the distant land of the Turks, would never be the same, and their fates were felt across town by the man with the chameleon eyes.

Ravenwood, his iridescent eyes misty, a medley of blue, green, and gray, picked up the phone in his penthouse at Sussex Towers after the first ring.

"Hello, Inspector Stagg," he answered into his phone in a hushed tone.

The gruff voice of Inspector Stagg had carried on the line with a mixture of surprise and annoyance.

"You and your hocus again! How the bloody hell did you know that I was about to call?"

To this, Ravenwood, the Stepson of the Nameless One, remained calm.

After some brief silence, Inspector Stagg had spoken more about why he had contacted Ravenwood, the most renowned detective of the uncanny and the occult, an investigator of mysteries that were threaded with the veil of what was hidden beyond the sight of regular mortals.

"There has been a death at Hughleigh Garden Towers. A Turkish gentleman who is the head of his family. They've been here in Manhattan for some time already. I've had most of the department already look into it. We're not in the habit of resorting to your kind of carnival fortune telling and hooey, you know."

"That is fine, Inspector. May I add that you can't make any sense of the matter so you have called me to investigate, as you have before. Inspector Stagg, we will never get along, and I harbor no ill will toward you, nor will I ever. I am beyond such ephemeral feelings in this mortal plane. It is all part of *Maya*, the Hindu word for this world. The least we can do in *Maya* is use our methods to create a more livable place."

From Inspector Stagg's heavy grunt on the line, Ravenwood sensed Stagg's skepticism and closed-mindedness more than ever.

"As you say," he tossed into the phone. "Be here immediately."

There is a corridor in the far rear of Ravenwood's elegant penthouse apartment that leads to a world away from the Western spheres and modes of thought. At the end of this corridor is a door that opens upon a room, an ethereal, dreamlike room, containing Ravenwood's stepfather, the Nameless One.

No one but Ravenwood was ever allowed to enter this room. Checking himself before a mirror in his modern library, his red tie impeccably folded on his spotless white shirt, his expensive suit tailored to an athletic figure of regular height, the outline of his hidden Luger was prominent. He focused his mind in projecting from the Western methods of thought, which he was born with, to the mystical Eastern modes of thought, two systems that clashed in the unique mind that was Ravenwood's.

Opening the door to the Nameless One's secret room, he stepped into a fragrant and otherworldly gloom. Within this very room, the hectic paced Western way of life was relieved. Tranquility pervaded within this chamber and reigned supremely. Peace was to be had in this room locked away from Western observance.

Here in this room was a savant whose powers exceeded Ravenwood's own unearthly capabilities.

Seated in a cross-legged meditative position, the Nameless One was motionless in the murkiness, his venerable head pointed in the direction of the floor, a flowing beard floating across a thin frame, the very picture of peace. The Nameless One's ancient eyes shone with the light of stars on a night with a cold moon. They glanced at Ravenwood with an automatic understanding, the wisdom of centuries accumulated from the land of India ablaze in his stare.

"My son, beware of the illusions of *Maya*! Beware of the god of justice and death, Siva! He that findeth not will seek himself. The soul that is lost is saved alone!"

Ravenwood answered in Hindi, the language of India.

"Most enlightened sire, I fear that Siva the Destroyer is about. Siva's justice only knows the answers to the Cevikbas family and the murder of the patriarch of this family. Siva possesses the light of the truth, and it is beyond my grasp at the moment. I see three deaths of the same man, yet this does not make sense."

The Nameless One remained still, though internally he was moving with the motion of thinking from the timeless East.

"What my eyes see, you shall also see, my son. See thou with my vision. What my ears hear, your ears shall also hear, so listen thou with my hearing, my son. As the sun sets upon this sordid world and plunges the world into darkness, so the person who is perseverant in his quest for the truth shall find it. The discovery will enlighten the discoverer."

"I call upon you, dear father, to open the ways of wisdom for me regarding the murder of Aladogan Cevikbas."

Ravenwood next looked on the diagram of worship, the *yantra*, on the wall beside the Nameless One. The *yantra* served as a guide for the worshipper to attain union with *atman*, the eternal self. Glancing at the *yantra*, he immediately felt his arcane senses expanding since he had envisioned the Cevikbas murder an hour before.

"There is vast confusion, my son. Death has struck and the hour of vengeance has perhaps already arrived. The patriarch was hated by all three of his family, and yet there is more than just their rancor toward him. There is a city with two identities and of two minds, and in this city is illumination that Siva wants you to find. Seek this family and question them in your search for the truth."

Ravenwood was held fixed in a hypnotic gaze peering into the seer's shining sight.

"As all that exists in threes flourishes, just as the Trimurti of Brahma, Shiva, and Vishnu hold the balance of all, three murders of one man must be understood in order to bring peace from chaos, in order to prevent this world of *Maya* slipping into chaos. A man who dies more than once sets the gods in motion to seek out those guilty. Be alert, my son! Be wary of the gods' vengeance upon vengeance!"

His kaleidoscopic eyes straining to see beyond the mortal veil as the Nameless One did, he stood there still bewildered.

The eyes of the Nameless One closed, signaling to Ravenwood that the insight of the holy man before him was all he could gather for the moment. A silence then conquered the room where the savant sat isolated away from the world, and Ravenwood quietly exited to enter his library.

Ravenwood was the son of an American father steeped in the ways of Eastern philosophies and a British mother. Fifteen years ago all three of them were living in India, Ravenwood having spent his childhood in that country, and Ravenwood's father was on a hunt near where Burma and Tibet shared a boundary. It was during this hunt of his father's that Ravenwood would first encounter the Nameless One, and forever would his life change as a result.

They had pitched camp near the mountainous crags of Burma, and had designated periods of vigilance between them because of the threat of tigers in the area. While enjoying this expedition, Ravenwood's father suddenly heard a tender sound on the trail. At once he held up his rifle expecting to see a wild beast, but he looked in puzzlement at the figure of a holy man.

A hoary-headed man, blessed in his presence, was following Ravenwood's family on their hunt, apparently having come from the direction of Tibet. His hands were empty, his steps stately and patient. The area was devoid of any human settlements for untold miles, and therefore there was neither food nor shelter. The mountain nights were growing increasingly cold, piercingly so. The blessed man's eyes shone with the wisdom of a sage.

While locked in this mutual stare, the reflexive fear of tigers had suddenly sprung into being. Ravenwood's father distinctly heard in his mind the word "Tiger!" and he couldn't place where the thought had entered. The deadly beast leapt toward the snowy-bearded holy man, and with lightning reflexes, Ravenwood's father fired the shot that saved the life of the robed wayfarer. He had not moved, even during the rifle shot, as the extended claws of the beast fell mere inches from his feet. The tiger fell immobile and harmless by the shot that rang in time.

The blessed man had lifted his luminous view upon his savior, Ravenwood's father, and moved his view to a stunned mother and son. In his native tongue of Hindi, in a voice as gossamer as the reverberating whispers between mountains, the Nameless One had said to the entire family:

"Always the Nameless One will guard you and your flesh."

Ravenwood heard this in a state of wonderment and admiration. As inexplicably as he had appeared, the Nameless One had vanished. Since then, it was impossible for Ravenwood to forget this mystifying being whose life his father had saved.

Some years later young Ravenwood had first felt the preternatural power which was the result of the encounter with the holy man. It was at this time when he first felt his powers drawn from beyond the mortal coil that a plague was ravishing the settlements in Burma. Ravenwood had then seen both his mother and his father perish in torturous fevers on the same night.

With his father's last breath, it was then that Ravenwood first perceived the fluent spiritual voice speak in his mind: "I am coming, my son."

It was then that the Nameless One had appeared to Ravenwood to fill in the void left by the absence of his parents. Versed with a familiarity beyond the grasp of Ravenwood's mind, the savant had returned to fulfill his promise.

Years and years of training with the Nameless One had stretched Ravenwood's natural-born, impatient Western mind to become patient and full of the mysticism of the Yogic and Vedic traditions of India. Immersed in the teachings of Yoga, the Vedas, and the writings of Upanishads, he was further honed with the knowledge given by his master. He had found every movement of his master and newfound father to possess layers of meaning and the wisdom of centuries upon centuries. It was during these formative years with the Nameless One that he discovered that learning and knowledge were the true treasures that could never be taken away, that there was a balance in all things that existed or are currently existing. Through the discipline of applying himself to the Tantric traditions of Indian spiritual thought, Ravenwood more and more was able to call upon abilities that regular humankind could not clasp. In mastering the dharma, the ways of India, he found that his mind was a battling clash between his inborn ways of the West and the patient, introspective ways of the East. As Ravenwood gained his Far Eastern gifts, his eyes had changed to become as iridescent as shells from the sea, his eyes constantly displaying a change from green to blue to gray and back again.

The venerable Nameless One had accompanied the shimmery-eyed Ravenwood to his home country of the United States three years ago. The frantic pace of America's largest city could not intrude upon the temple that the Nameless One had created within the secret space at the end of the corridor in Ravenwood's apartment. Instead of the frenetic and hectic, here prevailed serenity, encompassing the Nameless One in this secreted temple between heaven and earth. Without cease, he had assured Ravenwood of his promise, a daily reminder to Ravenwood that the Nameless One would always protect him.

The Sussex Towers where he lived with his manservant Sterling and his spiritual guide and stepfather the Nameless One were the most fashionable apartment buildings in Manhattan. Preparing himself for his arrival at the crime scene, he looked yet again at his appearance in the full-length mirror of his tastefully furnished library and study: a strikingly handsome young man, barrel-chested, a handkerchief decorously placed in the suit pocket near his left lapel, his wavy, thick brown hair and dazzling stare reflecting back. In the vestibule, he grabbed his elegant cane and his fine Homburg hat from the fully mundane Sterling, placed the hat upon his head, and dashed to the silent elevator that brought him swiftly to where his supercharged roadster was near the marquee of the Towers.

Now with the wheel in his hands after he kicked the starter, he toed the gas pedal deeply. He drove at an impetuous, reckless speed to where the Hughleigh Garden Towers were located, racing past a sight of the twinkling Brooklyn Bridge, his motor roaring, lion-like, as he passed through Times Square, people of the night wondering who was in the roadster. His mind in a meditative state, his Western temperament still urged with the impatience of the city, a complex mixture of East and West that was his.

There were several uniforms from Inspector Stagg's team waiting for him in the sophisticatedly appointed lobby. They had briefed him on the importance of the Cevikbas family of the now defunct Ottoman Empire. They were a wealthy family from Istanbul, the nexus between the Europe and Asia, who had ties to the Ottoman Empire by way of marriage. Though they could not be considered royal in the fullest sense, the Cevikbas family still had familial ties to the last Ottoman Sultan, ties that were as slight as a finely lined strand and yet still legitimate.

Stagg's men had informed Ravenwood further of the murder victim, the patriarch of the family. Aladogan Cevikbas was renowned in the occult book market in Istanbul, having opened an underground book trade not only in Istanbul but also in Ankara, the new capital of his country, and in the city of Bursa as well. Aladogan's trade had prospered so well that he was able to become the proprietor of a secret book shop in Istanbul's famous Grand Bazaar, a market containing thousands of shops trading in myriad goods, among them being Iznik pottery, clothing, gold, silver, and zultanite gemstones that were native to Turkey. The Gizli Kitap Carsisi, known in English as the Secret Book Bazaar, was in an area of the Grand Bazaar that some rumored sprang up in the middle of the day, only to vanish when those not in the network of Aladogan's book trade approached.

It was in this way that Aladogan Cevikbas was able to keep him and his family affluent, so much so that he was able to move his family to America. It was here in the Hughleigh Garden Towers that he maintained a personal collection of his most valuable and cherished esoteric books, the books that he would not allow to be on display in the Secret Book Bazaar, and felt that by bringing them an ocean away he would keep them secure in his possession.

Arriving to the upper level of the Hughleigh Gardens with Stagg's officers, he entered the apartments of the Cevikbas family. In one room, a room even in Ravenwood's esteem had been as tastefully furnished as his own, were sitting the three remaining members of the Cevikbas family. It was here that Inspector Stagg, his portly body sitting in an Ottoman-styled chair, his deep-set eyes shining distantly with innate skepticism, had his face turn red from seeing his prey, Ravenwood.

Not bothering to get up on Ravenwood's entrance into the spacious and graceful room, he blurted out gruffly:

"Well, Ravenwood, I can't hang this murder on you this time, though I would like to. Have a try. It's more in your area of voudou or what on earth it is you practice."

With that, Inspector Stagg got up from the room, not even looking Ravenwood's way. Ravenwood knew he was free this time from the clutches of the cynical and disbelieving Inspector Stagg since he was not in the area of the Hughleigh Gardens at all this evening, having checked into the newspaper office of the *Dispatch* that he was fond of being at. He had signed out of the newspaper archives at 3 a.m., having been granted personal access by his friend to stay till then. It was then that Stagg had learned that Ravenwood could not possibly be involved with the murder of Aladogan Cevikbas, all of Ravenwood's whereabouts accounted for this strange evening.

Ravenwood's mind, which was neither entirely Western nor Eastern but a personal admixture of both, heaved a sigh of relief while the Eastern half of his mind maintained an unruffled serenity at Stagg not having his hooks in him this time. Ravenwood was free to conduct his investigations without the bumbling cynical interference of the inspector.

On the couch was an elderly matron attired in the expensive modes of the city, her face with a look of frightful unease and her cheeks stained with the tear-mixed mascara that ran down her face. Standing next to a fire was a young man in a worn sport coat that looked as if had been used many times but wearing expensive trousers. On the couch across from her mother was the young daughter of the family, arrayed in splendid zultanite and gold jewelry, and having a look of dread and alarm.

All of them looked at Ravenwood, seemingly waiting for him as if they were weary of Stagg's skeptical presence.

"It can only be the Albasti," said the young son as he turned around to face Ravenwood. The son did not have a look of alarm or distress, having already settled with the murder of his father in the night.

"And what may be the Albasti?" asked Ravenwood as he doffed his hat politely and put his cane on a table exquisitely decorated with inlaid mother-of-pearl in a Near Eastern pattern.

"A spirit that seeks vengeance on guilty souls. It is from Turkic folklore, Mr. Ravenwood," said the matriarch of the family. Her English was elegantly accented though perfect, while the English of the son was pure American since he had been brought to the city during his early years.

"How can we know it is the Albasti? Has any one of us here committed something to arouse the wrath of the Albasti?" replied the distressed young daughter, also in unaccented American English.

The young man, his good-looking features seemingly unruffled, went to sit next to his sister.

"One of us or all of us are guilty of the death of our father," he said to his sister.

He then looked to Ravenwood, who stood there absorbing their remarks, taking in all of the information.

"We three of us all hated him."

After inspecting the bloodstains on the carpet in the adjoining study where the crime occurred, and going over what his senses could detect, he discovered that there could only be one murder of the same man. He felt murder to have occurred in the room. The imprint of murder was there and he could sense it. He took a quick scan of the books, the black sorcerous books that lined the walls of the expansive room. He read the titles, some of them in Sanskrit and Devanagari, hand scripts of India, others in Turkish, some in medieval Latin.

Nonchalantly he went back to join the Cevikbas family, noticing a fuming Inspector Stagg there still waiting in the hallway, holding a snifter of brandy, as if to wait for Ravenwood to trip on something that would provide a reason for Stagg to haul him in to the station.

"Now, I will take each of you into a private room while Inspector Stagg will be keeping company with the rest of you. I want to interview each of you about what has happened tonight."

They all quietly assented while Ravenwood brought Inspector Stagg into the room. Ravenwood thought this to be an advantageous arrangement in that Stagg would be out of hearing range during interrogation of each member of the family and also out of meddling range as well.

Ravenwood wanted to interview each in chronological order, deciding to question first the matriarch of the family, Hande Cevikbas. After Hande, he would then examine the recollections of the son, Ahmet, and Kelebek, the daughter.

Ravenwood had seated both him and Hande Cevikbas in a room far removed from where Stagg, Ahmet, and Kelebek were located. With this necessary privacy secured, Ravenwood proceeded to question Hande.

"Why do you hate your husband, Mrs. Cevikbas?" he asked.

She could only peer into the kaleidoscopic vision of Ravenwood as they moved from gray to blue to green.

"Zultanite eyes. You have eyes of zultanite," she whispered, barely audible, though Ravenwood discerned her words.

"Zultanite is a gemstone in your land of Turkey, isn't it? A gemstone that also possesses many colors, its color at any moment depending on the light that strikes it."

"Yes, you are right, Mr. Ravenwood. May I call you the Man with the Zultanite Eyes?"

Ravenwood was amused even though Hande seemed to be in a sedated state, still buffering herself from the shock of the death of her husband.

"If you wish, Mrs. Cevikbas. Now, please, tell me all that you can. And answer my question as well: why did you hate your husband?"

Before she began her side of what had befallen her husband in the night, she took out a cigarette and poured a glass of raki, a cloudy drink from her homeland. Soon the atmosphere held her fear, her hands trembling the glass as she began to recount.

"We all hated him. All he cared for were his ancient, forbidden books and cared not at all for us. He brought us to America to simply put us away from where he really wanted to be, which was at the secret book market he was conducting in the Grand Bazaar in Istanbul. He had put us in great surroundings and made sure there was no lack of material things. But you see, Mr. Ravenwood, material things are not a substitute for having a husband and a father for your children. If you ever become a parent, I think you would understand. He was never there for me and my son and daughter. When he was here in New York, which was rare, he barely said a word to any of us and indeed shunned us. Before he started his book market we all knew him to be far more attentive to us, a caring and dutiful husband and father, but it seemed as he uncovered some hidden knowledge in one of those books of his that he started to become withdrawn and haggard, always pacing back and forth all night in his study with his arcane collection, intoning peculiar words in the night. It was then that he completely avoided us, even to the point of removing all three of us out of his will.

"Soon, for no reason that we could find, he only appeared here in these apartments once every six months, preferring to stay in Istanbul. After a while, we were on our hands and knees begging for his financial help, for among the three of us left here in America, we found that rent on this apartment was only provided for the next six months. And then what was to become of us? Where would I take my dear son Ahmet and my lovely daughter Kelebek?

How could we even afford passage to Istanbul to find him once the money ran out?

"There was a noise in the passageway next to my bedroom that he no longer visited. I looked at the clock and it was fifteen minutes past midnight. I robed myself and went to see what the noise could possibly be, and followed all the way to his study, still flooded with light.

"At the time I entered Aladogan's library, I could not see the front of an unknown figure, but by his clothing I can identify him. He was garbed in the clothing of a whirling dervish! I am sure you have seen depictions or heard descriptions of the famous whirling dervishes of the Turkish Mevlevi order. They are very famous for their rotations as a group, whirling in tandem while in deep meditations. They are known the world over, and have been popularly filmed and described. Yet this whirling dervish in the night had clothing in all black, as was his cone-shaped cap, all black. The whirling dervishes are of the mystical Sufi branch of Islam, yet this dervish was definitely not of their order, the Mevlevi Order being based on love and tolerance. It was a masquerading of the order, using the dervish appearance and clothing as his disguise.

"A knife flashed in his hands, and while seemingly waiting till I entered the room, he plunged this knife many times into the chest of my husband. I swooned right then and there, and the next thing I knew I was in my bed. I was awoken by the screams of my daughter around 3:20 a.m. and I and Ahmet rushed into her room. She then described exactly what I saw earlier.

"And that is all I can tell you, Mr. Ravenwood."

It was then through the ether that a voice came to Ravenwood, the voice of the Nameless One through the avenue of nothingness:

"Beware of the deceits and the hidden truths of Siva, my son!"

Ravenwood assisted a bereaved and frightened Mrs. Cevikbas back to the room where Stagg was waiting.

"Wait till you hear the next two, Ravenwood. There are some real horsefeathers happening here and hang it, if you can't get to the bottom of it, I will charge you for it all."

The stepson of mystery said nothing and continued with putting questions to Ahmet to obtain his account of the proceedings of the night.

"Why did you hate your father? Please tell me all."

"I first knew my father as a protective and very loving man. He found fortune in Istanbul with his traffic in illegal and banned books that held, shall we say, an occultish nature to them. These were evil books that I dare not touch. I am a wide reader, and have read some of your works, Ravenwood, on topics of Far Eastern mysteries and philosophies. I abhorred having my father's evil library here, the most evil selection of the underground book trade in the Near East. These most malevolent of malevolent books were shipped here to Manhattan where my father in his younger days put us up in absolute wealth. Something along the way in his inquiries into the occult caused him to change. He of a sudden lessened his appearances here in America to be with us. Soon it became worse for us in that he wouldn't even be there for our birthdays. He was never there for Ramazan, the Holy Month, or there for support or guidance when I needed it. My mother started to become wrecked with worry. Yet that room, that infernal room, was always shut and bolted tightly so none of us three could see what had changed his behavior towards us. Soon he became paranoid and took us out of his will along with cutting off the funds we needed to maintain the lifestyle that he had put us up in. I am not a spoiled person, Ravenwood, I am the exact opposite. I am industrious and ready to put up with the real world, for I know that most people do not live like this. The money soon stopped and we were left to fend for ourselves with no support and no means of a safety net. Soon we were to be left out on the streets and all three of us knew it."

Ravenwood did not interrupt Ahmet's disclosures.

"In some months we were to have no money, and we tried to contact him. I tried to send him letters and he finally did respond with a letter that he was coming soon. After a space of almost a year, he suddenly shows on the doorstep here in Hughleigh and had a terribly haggard and worn face, seemingly twisted with the unholy. My mother and sister were frightened as we sat for a dinner that he had called for us.

"We ate some traditional cooking from Ottoman times for dinner, and he served a fresh round of tea, of which we had all taken. None of us could look him directly in the face, it was so menacing. I could see the shivers that ran through my sister and the trembling of my mother as we sat, all four of us, in silence."

Ahmet then dipped into a period of silence himself. After a while, he too started to show some strain, and took out a cigarette and poured himself a smidgen of brandy.

"What happened then? Was there anything else unusual about the dinner?"

"I am not sure, Ravenwood. I did dare to look at my father, though it took all of my strength and I was prepared to flee in extreme fear. My father had the face of a demon, sickly, contorted, bent. It was then that I fled from the room, and my mother and sister also fled as well.

"I shut and bolted the door to my room and had placed my drawers and

"...that infernal room, was always shut and bolted tightly..."

couch to guard my door even more. I assume my mother and sister did the same

"I had surprisingly fallen into a deep, untroubled sleep when I awoke to a sound, a sort of growl, at 1:42 a.m. I had looked at my watch and I was still in my dinner clothes when I decided I should see what the matter was. I seem to be the strongest of the family, though earlier I could not bear to see that face, that sunken, ghastly face, Ravenwood!

"My father's study room, filled with those nefarious tomes of his that he calls 'treasures of the earth and the unearthly,' was a figure dressed in the costume of a whirling dervish. I could only see his back at the moment but I had never seen a whirling dervish since I had viewed their Sema Ceremony as a child, a ceremony where they all whirl together seeking union with the divine. I never saw a dervish dressed in the color black, but that was what I saw. He had a glinting sharp knife as he turned to look at me. I think he was waiting for me, Ravenwood, to enter the room before he killed my father. As he turned his head toward me, I caught a glimpse of the dervish in black, though I recoiled and moved my glance in any other direction besides the new face, recalling the contortedly evil face of my own father earlier.

"Not looking, I could hear him plunging the knife into my father, and when it was over, when all was silent, I looked up and all that was left was blood and my father missing."

The detective with the changeable gaze had further questions.

"What would you say has really happened, Mr. Cevikbas?"

"We have to find that man masquerading as a whirling dervish. This dervish may be real or may be something my father inadvertently summoned. A demon. A spirit."

"Please describe for me the features of the black-clothed dervish, this man in the deception of the holy Mevlevi Order."

"He had no irises, none at all, just solid black eyes. That is all I saw of his face before I plunged my sight toward the floor."

"Thank you for your time, Mr. Cevikbas."

From the ether, he was expecting to hear his master, the Nameless One, and he did:

"Be on guard, my son, against the wrath of Siva! Come to the truth with Siva's guidance!"

Kelebek continued to sit on the sofa, playing with her jewels and her trinkets. Holding on to them with a grip, she let trickles of tears roll down her face just as her mother let them fall on her own face. The distress of their new circumstances and soon much reduced way of living had taxed her mind as Ravenwood appeared with Ahmet, bringing him back to Inspector Stagg's watch in the palatial room.

Kelebek Cevikbas accompanied Ravenwood to where he was talking with each remaining member of the household privately.

"Ms. Cevikbas, please tell me why you hate your father?"

"Mr. Ravenwood, I hated him because he turned on us. He used to be reliable and dependable, but something changed and he became the complete opposite."

She sat there peering into Ravenwood's multicolored gaze. She continued to play with the tinsel around her neck, her features pretty in the dawning light.

"Can you tell me what happened during last night's dinner with your father?"

"Yes. Yes, Mr. Ravenwood. He arrives after not seeing us for a year. He was absent for a year and off doing who knows what in Istanbul with his book trade. We all thought it odd that he wanted to have dinner with us."

Ravenwood could see that he would have to keep the flow of conversation going with Ms. Cevikbas.

"Please recount all that happened at dinner."

"Well, he was there. He never said a thing, he just sat there, and I, my brother, and my mother could barely look at him. Some physical change had occurred to him and there was something sinister in his face that I had never seen before."

"Can you describe what you saw in his face?"

"That is just it, I did not dare to look. I just couldn't. I saw it from far away as he came through the entrance earlier, just as my mother had, and from that distance knew that something was wrong with his face."

"And so you chose to not look at him because of fear for the rest of the evening?"

"That is it. Yes. Though my brother did look and he ran from the room in horror. I and my mother soon fled. I could feel it was my father, but I could feel a change palpable in the air at the same time. My father was always a generous man before. Now I felt only evil. We ate and drank before we panicked and he went away into his study."

"What did you do after that?"

"I went to my bedroom and had a smoke to calm myself down. I then made sure of my door being as tightly bolted as possible. I was frightened to death, and it came as a huge surprise to me that I was able to fall into a light sleep being as worried as I was."

"And when did you wake up?"

"Ahmet said I woke up around 3 a.m. or so, looking at his clock when I had gathered back into my room."

"So you too got up in the night? Was there a strange sound?"

"Yes, a strange sound, a similar noise that had woken my mother first and then my brother. An animalistic growl is the only way I can describe it. I got up terrified and wanting to investigate, and for some reason I did not contact anyone else in the house to accompany me to see the source of the noise."

"Where was the source of the noise?"

"The source of the noise was my father's study, Mr. Ravenwood. I went there to the door as if in a trance. Something was pulling me toward that door that I knew I shouldn't go into. As I placed my hand to turn the knob, I saw someone there with my father that I had never seen before."

"Describe for me this person."

"Well, he was in a costume of one of the famous whirling dervishes. I'm sure you've seen of them or heard of them, Mr. Ravenwood. They whirl together in dance in their long robes, their clothing under their waists circling and bellowing out. They are of good intent and are good natured followers of the more mystical Sufi branch of Islam."

"Yes, Ms. Cevikbas, I have seen photos and illustrator renderings of the whirling dervishes."

The shy Kelebek Cevikbas was goaded by Ravenwood to continue in the description of the figure and what she saw.

"The whirling person there in the room had the traditional clothing of a dervish, but it was all black, like a night sky, as if someone had killed all the stars and the moon, creating an endless inky night."

"Did you see anything else of note about this person?" Ravenwood asked after a breath of silence from Ms. Cevikbas.

"He had a knife in his hand, a wicked, ungodly knife."

"Did you get to see his facial features?"

"I did not see them, I was too frightened to even look."

"Did you try to leave the room then?"

"I didn't. I knew I had to stay to see something."

"Describe what you saw."

"When I did look up, I saw the dervish plunge the knife into my father's chest many times. My hands flew to my face and I screamed. The next thing I knew, I was in my own bedroom with my mother and my brother there. We all described what we saw but we can't piece together how each of us saw it at different times."

"Do you think you're at all mistaken about the times that you all saw the murder of your father?"

"No, that would be impossible. For in the same room, I would have seen my mother and my brother, but when I went to father's study, it was only me, the dervish, and my father."

"So you surmise that you fainted during your father's murder."

"That can be the only explanation."

"Is there anything else I should know or anything you would like to tell me?"

"Yes, Mr. Ravenwood."

"What would it be?"

Here she muttered profanity about the evening before resuming.

"All of us our innocent. I swear to you that none of us could do such a horrible thing. Though we could practically be on the streets very soon, we are not murderers. I am sure that if you find the dervish, then you will find the killer of my father. My father was mixed up in blasphemous business. He has encountered all sorts of madmen in his occult book negotiations."

"Can you explain to me the Albasti that all of you mentioned when I first arrived here?"

"The Albasti. Yes. The Albasti is a creature from the folklore and legends of my heritage. In Turkic legend, the Albasti is a woman who visits families that have committed crimes or have guilty souls. She tortures them with her visits. The Albasti is similar to the Furies of Greek legend, the ones who hunted down Orestes for committing unpunished crimes. The Albasti also haunts those who are guilty."

"Then you and your mother and brother think the Albasti visited in the night."

"It was my mother's initial thought, that it was the Albasti who has visited us. Therefore one of us four or all of us have a guilty soul that has gone unpunished."

"What do you know of your father's books?"

"I have never touched them. They emanate something I find to be entirely corrupt. Just having them here is sacrilege."

"Is there anything else you wish to tell me, Ms. Cevikbas?"

"I have told you all that I saw. Oh, Mr. Ravenwood, you must help us, you must find the truth of what has happened this evening! I have no confidence in Inspector Stagg, he cannot understand that there is far more to this world than just what we can know with the five senses. I have heard of your renown, Mr. Ravenwood, and it is only you who can help us to make sense of this."

"I will do my best, Ms. Cevikbas. My senses go beyond the normal human ken and are guided by my deep training in the Eastern traditions of life. There is no body here that I can examine, that is fact. All three of you are sure you saw him murdered at separate and distinct times of the evening. All of you seem to have seen the same man, the man in black dervish costume. Could it not be that you were all dreaming?"

"It seemed too real, Mr. Ravenwood. If it was a dream, then why are the bloodstains there? And where is my father? How can all three of us have seen the same dervish?"

"The descriptions of the dervish have all more or less matched from what I have gathered."

"I am as puzzled as you are."

"Siva, the goddess of time and destruction, will reveal in time what is to occur. I can tell you that I see myself in the near future in your father's home city, the city of two identities."

"Istanbul? You see yourself traveling to Istanbul?"

"The city of two identities, half in Asia and half in Europe. Very similar to my own mind, Ms. Cevikbas. I have been schooled in the mysteries of Asia, though my inborn and bred nature is Western. I am of both the East and West and yet I am neither."

"You will find that Istanbul will be the same. The city has one foot in Europe and one foot in Asia. It is the only city in the world situated on two continents."

"My senses are telling me that I myself am in danger by getting involved in this case."

Kelebek Cevikbas could sympathize that Ravenwood felt a sense of peril.

"There are so many possibilities here, Ms. Cevikbas. I want you to know that you and your family will be protected. Be assured that you can stay with your mother and brother in a room I have reserved for guests in my apartment. Please tell this to your brother and mother."

"Thank you, Mr. Ravenwood, thank you," she said as her eyes began to fill.

"Also, Ms. Cevikbas, I want you to bring to me the tea kettle that your father used during dinner."

"The tea kettle?"

"The tea kettle that he used, certainly, Ms. Cevikbas. If you all three feel you are in danger on account of the Albasti, then please all three of you accompany me to my apartment."

Kelebek assented in puzzlement as their exchange concluded.

At the moment, all that Ravenwood could discern was that he was soon to be far away from the Nameless One and in the battle of his life against something previously unknown to him.

"Father? Sire? Have you anything to say?" Ravenwood contacted remotely.

"Beware the perils of Siva, my child! Take heed and know that all is illusion in Maya, this sordid terrestrial earth of ours!"

They were back in the luxurious apartments of Ravenwood, thirty stories above the twinkling luminosities of the city.

"Sterling, can you see to the comfort of these three? They have been through an unbearable situation this evening and I would like them to have some sense of peace so I can get to the truth of this matter."

"Very well, sir," Sterling said in his British pronunciation. "Would you or your company like something to drink as well?"

"I am fine at the moment," answered Ravenwood.

The Cevikbas family immediately went to the room in Ravenwood's penthouse apartment that was offered to them and, wearied with all of what had come to pass for them, they rested immediately.

"Sterling," Ravenwood summoned in a hushed tone as the family was asleep.

"Mr. Ravenwood?" inquired the manservant.

"See that this tea kettle is brought to Dr. Hubermann for analysis. I want to see what the contents contained, if any."

"Indeed, sir," he replied as he took the kettle and proceeded to the phone to call the scientific laboratory.

Ravenwood doffed his Homburg cap and placed his cane elegantly on a table in his study. The office was filled with books, some of them he had written on various topics in Eastern methodology and metaphysics. He loosened his red tie and quieted his mind. He turned on the radio to hear the latest radio serials but actually turned it on as a sort of buffer that eased him into a zone that he visited between reality and meditation.

Deep in a meditative trance, a state that would have taken regular humans weeks to attain with fasting and guided concentration by a teacher, Ravenwood reached this state in a matter of seconds.

As Ravenwood felt himself to attain a sort of clarification of being, a concentration of thought within, he wandered in introspection, further and further away from the jostle of the earthly and everyday level.

Rapidly, he had attained his personal refuge, only to be reached by Eastern procedures. He was at a version of Namtso Lake, a holy lake in sacred Tibet. His version of the lake was a serene emerald in hue, with sands of lavender and a placid mountainous line of cobalt blue. He walked this area often when he needed clarity or needed some personal time in finding the way.

After walking for some while in reflection along the lake, he had sat down in a cross-legged pose under his favorite ashoka tree, also known as the "sorrowless tree" in South Asia and Burma. As the leaves of the ashoka tree seemed to envelop his presence, he closed his shimmering eyes as he had closed them on the earthly level, and here breathed in long and deep, exhaling as deeply, stretching his breaths, elongating his exhales and inhales more and more.

This meditation within a meditation served Ravenwood to attain further insights into the Cevikbas situation. It was here that he knew without searching that something had laced the kettle that Aladogan Cevikbas had served his family during their dinner.

The chemist's report on the kettle that was sent came back fast. Sterling's tall figure entered the study.

"I have come back with the knowledge I was seeking," said Ravenwood after his meditation. "The kettle that you sent for analysis, Sterling, was laced with an herb with three properties."

"I often wonder at how you know things before they happen, as if you had pulled them from the very air. A telephone call, sir."

"I know," Ravenwood replied. He picked up the receiver.

"Mr. Ravenwood, good to hear from you," a mild cadenced voice issued from Ravenwood's receiver as he put it to his ear.

"Hello Dr. Hubermann. What is the name of the herb?"

There was a bit of stunned silence on the phone.

"How did? Oh, it's all right. I know how to work with your sense of forecasting. You seem to know a step ahead or a step beyond all the time, Ravenwood. Well, I'm happy to report to you that the tea kettle delivered this afternoon tested positive for an herb known as a hallucinogen. Its scientific name is *Purpova redolens*, and the particular strain found in the kettle is known to be rather potent stuff."

"Continue, Doctor. What else can you tell me?"

"You may have an encyclopedia handy near you, but I can just tell you. This herb not only induces hallucinations. It is known for its so-called 'magical' properties of protection from evil and inducing purification. The herb is known popularly in the Near East by its folk name, 'Ifrit's plaything.' We'd call it in the West as 'Djinn's plaything.' It is mostly to be found in the Southeast of the country of Turkey and in the Caucasus Mountains."

"How often do hallucinations occur?"

"It's not guaranteed, but hallucinations are likely to occur in most cases if the herb is consumed."

"Are there any other magical correspondences attributed to the herb?"

"Just that, protection from evil and bodily purification. The hallucinations and visions are a byproduct of Djinn's plaything."

Ravenwood thought for a bit and stared at the door leading to the room where the Cevikbas family was recuperating.

"Thank you Doctor for your promptness in tracing the contents of this tea kettle."

"Evidence from a case, no doubt?"

"Yes, Hubermann. Details that I cannot tell at the moment but your findings have certainly cleared up some of the finer nuances of the case."

"Could it be the murder that happened recently? Incredible news on the radio, I heard. How could a man get killed three times?"

"That I cannot say, but I do have some ideas at the moment. Thank you for your time and effort, Dr. Hubermann."

The line clicked as Ravenwood placed the phone on its cradle.

In his study, his colorful eyes wandering the spines of his library, Ravenwood found what he was seeking. In his hands he now held two volumes, *Ottoman and Turkic Folklore* and *Night Creatures of the Caucasus Mountains.* Within both, he went to the entry of Albasti and found alternative spellings of the same creature, including Al Basty and Alkardai. In *Ottoman and Turkic Folklore*, the creature was compared to the deity Tisiphone of Greek legend, the Fury that haunted and punished those who committed murder. The Albasti was also known as the "Red Materfamilias" or the "Red Mother." She hounded the unpunished until they confessed their crimes.

Searching additionally in his archive of books for more information, he looked for entries on the herb "Ifrit's plaything" or "Djinn's plaything." What he read confirmed what Dr. Hubermann had just reported on the telephone. He had also seen a theory that Ifrit's plaything had a legendary relation with the herb moly, the mythical herb that had protected Odysseus on his journey back from the Trojan War in what is now Turkey. This caused him to also think about the lotus-eaters in the *Odyssey* epic, a people that Odysseus encountered during his perilous journey back home, a people who ate the lotus plant, a sedative, as described by the poet Homer.

It was now afternoon, and he visited the troubled family residing with him in the guestroom. They were listening to the radio for the headlines of the day, including the news that Germany had broken the Treaty of Versailles by occupying the Rhineland in Europe and the Prime Minster of Japan being replaced by the extremely militaristic Okada, along with some news from the radio announcer

Ravenwood placed the phone on its cradle.

of the latest developments in the war between Italy and Ethiopia. The station then began its popular quiz show as they moved their attention to Ravenwood.

"The Man with the Zultanite Eyes," articulated Hande Cevikbas in a hushed way, looking at Ravenwood.

The other two nodded in agreement with the name that their mother had given Ravenwood.

"That I am," the detective nodded unpretentiously as he sat before them.

"I have learned more about the 'Red Mother.' Was he visiting your father?" he asked of them.

Ahmet was the one to speak.

"As far as I know, he never mentioned the Red Mother. Did he ever mention this to anyone? Mother? Kelebek?"

"He may have been visited by the Red Mother. That would certainly explain his worn look when he arrived."

"Now that you say so, Mother, yes, that is a distinct possibility," set forth Kelebek.

"Which of you three drank the tea at dinner with him?"

"All three of us."

"Including your father?"

All three of the remaining Cevikbas family said that he didn't drink the tea with them. All three of them looked haunted in the elegant guestroom as Ravenwood spent some time with them before his wanderings through the city in his roadster in order to center his mind. All three of them sought to lessen their fears in their own ways, with the mother pulling out a cigarette, the son pulling out a Turkish cigar, and the shy daughter going from the room to gather her thoughts near the vestibule, taking a stiff drink along with her. Ravenwood enjoyed conversing with the mother and the son as the different scents of the fumes clashed in the air and the lights in the guestroom seemed pleasant.

"Ravenwood, we hope that you will help us. The dervish could be anywhere. We know that he seeks to wipe out this branch of the old Ottoman Empire, our family, for some unknown reason."

The nervous Hande Cevikbas thought of the family lineage, and even though they were an almost trifling branch of the Ottomans she was still compounded with worry. She went to get some vermouth available in the room to attempt to calm her nerves.

"I will let you know that I will do everything that I can to find the slaughterer who has ruined your family. I have brought you here for protection, for your rooms at Hughleigh are not safe. Sterling will see to your needs and concerns. Do not hesitate to call on him for anything you may need at the moment. For now, I would like to take a drive to clear my thoughts."

With this, Ahmet got up to shake hands with Ravenwood. Ahmet's nervous hand was wet with perspiration. The Cevikbas family were grateful for the protection and the shelter provided by the Man with the Zultanite Eyes, the man with the polychromatous gaze eager to take the roadster back to Hughleigh Gardens for another look.

Taking his time as the day slid into night, he brought the supercharged roadster around the crowded city, his mind working on the problems of the Cevikbas survivors, passing in his car the Flatiron Building, Chelsea Market, and Central Park, looking with his mind elsewhere. The winds lashed by his speeding car as he felt his mind starting to penetrate profoundly into the mists that shrouded the unknown fates of the Cevikbas family.

Now at the front entrance of the Hughleigh Garden Towers, he brought his roadster to a halt, parking it along the curb and looking up at where the beleaguered family used to live. All was dark on that floor, as if deserted for months.

He brought himself by the elevator to where he had interrogated the family and to where the irksome Inspector Stagg had tried to trouble him.

The ornate front doors to the elegant apartments were locked fast. Trying with all the surface powers of the East, he found he could not break the lock on the door.

He was about to bring out his Luger to blast open the door, his Western mind dictating, but then decided with his Eastern temperament to reach deeper into his senses.

Ravenwood visualized himself in front of an astral image of the ashoka tree that he visited during his meditations. His hands and sight traveled across from the stalk of the main body of the tree, next running his hands along the other parts of the tree, from the main trunk to the branches, and from the branches to the finer and thinner stems to where the newest buds grew, the burgeons. He went to these new burgeons and here he found the burgeon that he needed to open the lock in front of him without touch.

Instantly the lock to the Cevikbas apartment unlocked itself, and on the other side of the doors he heard a chain rattle to the ground. Softly he opened the doors and entered the darkened chambers.

The expensive rooms filled with costly décor and the rich carpets of Turkish make were all cloaked in obscurity. Ravenwood felt further along the astral ashoka tree and accessed the burgeon of illumination, a branch tender in its delicacy. Working his way through the winding structural pattern of the tree, he located the burgeon he was seeking, and immediately the rooms were flooded with an otherworldly light.

His multihued gaze beheld the rooms of the Cevikbas family and he went right to the room where the collection of books was held.

Here were the bloodstains, now dried and dark and crimson. And here were the books that had fueled the rise of Aladogan Cevikbas. They emanated a strange power from them as Ravenwood had felt earlier.

He touched the stains, and he touched the books. His sight took in everything, inputting the information into his store of memory.

It was here he heard the warning from the ether, conducting itself all the way from the temple in between heaven and earth, the secreted temple of the Nameless One.

"Ravenwood, my son! You are not by yourself in this room!"

Immediately Ravenwood's ethereal hands traveled further along the astral ashoka tree to find the burgeon for concealment. He was about to touch the burgeon to channel its energies but just then he was knocked across the room.

Ravenwood felt himself flying from the brute strength exerted from the figure in the library. He slammed into the wall nearest the door, his head impacting with almost concussive pressure. His body slid to the floor as he felt the consequences of the impact.

Trained as he was in the ways of the East, his body was able to take more than regular human bodies could tolerate. The Nameless One had taught him well how to transcend pain and the corporeal body.

Just then he reached for his Luger and cracked two shots at the figure, but the dervish had whirled, narrowly missing both bullets that hurtled toward his ambusher. The gun smoke had caused a momentary concealing, and Ravenwood now had time to access the burgeon for unseeability.

His astral hand finding the burgeon, Ravenwood now became imperceptible, as if vanished. He then removed his shoes and moved his position away from the assailant.

The dervish was suddenly puzzled and began to search about the air for his target. He could not find where Ravenwood was, and it was at this time that the zultanite-eyed man fired more shots from his Luger.

Again, anticipating the noise from the gunfire attempts, the dervish was able to dance about the pathways of Ravenwood's gun. Ravenwood kept firing until he heard only clicks, his clip empty of bullets.

Having given away his position from the gunshots, the dervish whirled right into Ravenwood, knocking him down into the ground. The knock by the dervish caused Ravenwood to now be seen, his invisibility sacrificed. Blood started to trail from Ravenwood's mouth and nose, the forceful smashing causing his earthly body to feel the harm. He was now visible to his attacker, and once again Ravenwood was hit, this time punched directly in the face. His lips bled, yet he felt no pain as his years of training with the Nameless One showed their benefits.

Ravenwood drew from the martial area of his Eastern disciplines, accomplishing a triangle choke on the target. Ravenwood's muscles brought the brunt of his strength in the move, attempting to incapacitate his opponent.

He then attempted to perform a throw just before his opponent passed out. Ravenwood swung the dervish into position, his breath controlled to time with the throw he had learned from centuries of Eastern defense lore. As Ravenwood yelled, his voice at the top of his lungs, he threw the dervish with an Eastern grapple and release, the dervish's body careening dangerously into the bricked area of the library. The dervish fell to the ground, bricks dislodging and falling along with him.

The figure robed in black twitched on the floor under the fall of bricks for a second, and to Ravenwood's astonished beholding he got up.

Again Ravenwood tried to land a punch, but the dervish revolved out of harm's way, Ravenwood's preternatural strength knocking more bricks to the floor, his fists becoming bloodier.

It was here that he implemented the lightning strike series of punches, a series of blows to the opponent that hit the meridian flow point areas of the human body unknown to Western anatomy yet known and charted by Eastern mystics.

The lightning series of boxes to his adversary had taken him off guard, putting the dervish in a momentary paralysis. Ravenwood continued again with the successful lightning series, doubling his strength as he rained down on the dervish.

While continuing his series of blows, his meditative mind had traveled again along the sorrowless tree, finding the green bud, the burgeon, that accessed unseeability. His ethereal fingers were near, and then had slipped as the dervish had delivered a hard kick to his knee that had jolted his concentration.

At last finding the burgeon on the tree, his being once more started to become invisible, fading from the sight of regular men.

It was then in this mental state that Ravenwood had almost attained indiscernibility that the dervish had returned to his feet and picked Ravenwood up completely with his arms as he was in his state of absorption, his being fading from sight.

Ravenwood's almost incorporeal being was hurtled through the air by the bearish strength of the dervish and crashed beyond and through the brick wall. The wall in the library had toppled, and the bricks along with them, burying

Ravenwood in agony. His senses that had suspended pain had begun to give in.

The dervish had followed his prey beyond the wall and had leapt on the pile of bricks that Ravenwood was confined in. Ravenwood howled in pain, the dervish beginning to perform his whirl that began to pile drive and deliver him into the very insides of the earth. It was now not possible to fully access the burgeon of invisibility.

His mind reeling and not knowing what to do, Ravenwood called upon his father.

For some reason, he found that he was out of hearing range of the Nameless One.

This came as a shock to him as he had never been dissevered from contact with his stepfather.

He called again, reaching out in desperation, his mind widening in its dire wish to contact his mentor for assistance. Again, he could not reach the Nameless One, and Ravenwood's face started to show panic at the fact of incommunicability.

He had one thing left in his repertoire of defenses from the Eastern hemisphere.

He had left the power word for turning his opponent to stone.

The dervish had found Ravenwood in the pile of bricks, his boot set on Ravenwood's forehead and pressing it, about to crush Ravenwood's skull.

With a voice that sounded to be multiple voices of all the tonal ranges, he uttered the ancient Sanskrit power word of the most ancient language of India.

"Pasanasila!" Ravenwood exclaimed, releasing the word just in time.

The dervish's arms flew to his ears as if struck by a barrage of the loudest sounds.

Ravenwood watched the look of astonishment on his inky-eyed face as his whole being started to turn into rock.

There, the dervish was stone, harmless. He had turned his combatant into a statue of granite.

But for how long would the Sanskrit power word bind the dervish was only what Ravenwood could wonder as he dusted himself off. With the great resiliency of his trained physique, he struggled to stand up to see just exactly where he was.

He was on the floor of what looked to be an immense church or a mosque, a holy place, the largest he had ever seen. He knew has was not in his home city. As the statue frozen stood there with the look of shock upon his face, as if carved from stone by a master sculptor, Ravenwood's iridescent gaze surveyed the surroundings.

Ravenwood found himself to be alone, an eerie quietness permeating the place. He saw angels painted in the corners of a wide, vast dome that held fine-looking Islamic calligraphy in circular signs. He saw a mosaic prominently displayed on the focal point of the holy place, and streams of lines suspending from the ceiling, supporting chandeliers that brought a luminosity to where humans could gaze up into the structure and find themselves in a state of awe.

The interior looked familiar to Ravenwood. He knew he was far away from where the Nameless One was, and he had a feeling that he was not even in the Western hemisphere of the world at all.

As he took in more of the features of the place, such as the mihrab marking the direction where devotees could pray towards Mecca, the minbar, a staircase leading up to a minaret where a muezzin would call the faithful to prayer, and the intact mosaics that depicted saints and what looked to be emperors, he knew where he was.

This church, this famous place, changed into a mosque and just last year had become a museum, was the Hagia Sophia of Istanbul.

He was brought here by the dervish, or perhaps it was Ravenwood who had brought the dervish here. Perhaps it was a random occurrence that he was brought to Hagia Sophia.

He had no time to lose as he had to gain the upper hand. His precognitive senses knew that what he encased in stone would soon turn loose again.

Ravenwood sat himself in a seated lotus position, breathing calm, again feeling along the gossamer branches of the sorrowless tree for the replenishment burgeon, the green bud that would restore his being for another round with the dervish. Along the way he had discovered that the open locks burgeon had restored itself, something he felt that he would need in the near future.

Now restored bodily and mentally, his wounds healed, his senses keen and at full capacity, he again tried to call his master. The Nameless One did not respond.

He knew he was in the Hagia Sophia, but was it the earthly Hagia Sophia? There were no people around, an unusual happenstance since this place was now a museum, declared by their leader a year ago. It was also daylight, which indicated that the museum hours were open. He felt warmth surging within him, unusual in a wide and open space. Everything had a dreamlike quality to it. Was this reality? Was this *Maya*?

He knew this to be the most famous structure of Istanbul, the city that straddled both Europe and Asia in the country of Turkey. He knew this was the Hagia Sophia. Ravenwood found himself in bafflement as he pondered how he was transported here, for there was not among his abilities the capacity to travel without physically voyaging the distance. Neither had the Nameless one had this skill. There were a few certain skills that the Nameless One had not taught his young master, only a mere handful, and Ravenwood knew of the existence of these skills which the Nameless One had kept to himself for wise reasons. This skill of moving large distances instantaneously was not among the handful in the Nameless One's keeping.

He looked around and saw the remnants of the brick wall to the other place, Aladogan's profane library. The entrance was still there in midair, and he could see the way back to his own city. The blocks of wall and the dusty mortar pile were still there, but he decided to investigate where he was, if it was reality he was inspecting or something else entirely.

He looked at the statue that he had created and saw that parts of the fabric and flesh were starting to reverse from stone.

He had to arm himself. His Luger was back in the other world, and looking around, he saw an area of the place that contained museum cases.

Wandering the upstairs walkways and galleries, he marveled at the absolute vast beauty of the place. There was no doubt that this enormous architectural wonder was created to reflect the devotions of its creators. And yet, though conquering in its magnificence, there were no people around and everything he saw had a tinge of dream to it, a sense of thistledown, a vapory look. Despite the gauzy aspects that everything he had in sight held, he searched among the museum cases for a weapon to arm himself as the masquerading dervish would soon be back from his statuesque confinement.

Wandering among the artefacts of the centuries, the Roman, the Byzantine, the Ottoman eras of time, he found among the gauze a weapon: a curved sword of the Ottoman Empire, with a placard next to it in both Turkish and English. The English word for it was "kilij," and it was just what he was looking for.

Taking off his impeccably tailored sport coat and winding it around his right fist, he smashed through the museum-quality glass easily and took the kilij into his own hands. The handle had secured his grip by a slight curve, keeping the wielder of the sword's grasp from slipping. The blade as he now saw it within his own hand had curved abruptly from the vertical bottom half, a formidable weapon that was imposing to anyone.

It was here then that he ran to another area with the curved blade, abandoning his sport coat and wearing only his buttoned and impeccable shirt, loosening his tie as he went along.

Not one to hide himself away, the brave Ravenwood went up to the statue as it was returning to corporeality, and put himself in a stance that was ready for the coming onslaught.

His statue self having dissolved, the dervish lunged for Ravenwood. They had gone several rounds as the kilij had always struck air, never hitting the dervish directly. Once, the kilij blade had cut the forearm of the dervish slightly, the red blood trickling onto the ground. The kilij he held in his hand swung again and missed its target, but Ravenwood had positioned himself to bring his other hand up to deliver an attack called the withering palm. He had clasped the correct spot on the shoulder for this defensive attack, and his opponent collapsed to the ground.

The aggressor now in a state of withering agony, he convulsed on the ground.

Ravenwood calmly asked in his voice who he was.

To this, his jaw clenched among the effects of Ravenwood's effective attack, he could not reply.

"Where are we? Is this really Hagia Sophia?"

The writhing figure nodded what looked to be both an affirmative and a negative.

"Then we are neither in nor inside Hagia Sophia?"

"You are here," were his words to Ravenwood.

He brought the kilij close to the dervish's face.

"Tell me who you are, or I will remove those devilish eyes of yours with this curved sword. Tell me!" Ravenwood dealt loudly, his Western nature getting the better of him.

Immediately the dervish grabbed the kilij between his hands, the lethal sharp portion cleverly held away, locking the blade away from Ravenwood and slipping it from his clutch.

Ravenwood retreated from the arena in the direction of Aladogan's library on the other side. The kilij came closer and nearer to him as Ravenwood used every defense known to him to avoid the blade.

It was here again that he was in position and readiness to deliver the withering palm attack again, and just as he was about to, the dervish had whirled him against the ground, his head knocking the stone of the sacred place.

In an instant he was back on his feet and delivered a well-timed uppercut to the dervish's head, knocking him to the ground. The kilij almost fell from his opponent's hands but Ravenwood started to draw himself nearer to the entrance to Aladogan's private room, his infernal room, and as he leapt into the air to lunge back into the room, the kilij was thrown deftly by the dervish in Ravenwood's direct pathway in the air.

He contorted and twisted his body in the air to avoid the lethal blade, and then was able to grasp the blade on the handle while airborne, preventing any injury.

He landed with the kilij in his hands away from his body yet still in his grasp, and found himself on the hallway floor of his own apartment. He stood up and looked closer at the kilij, seeming to have pulled it from a dream. He moved toward his bedroom to the astonished look of Sterling in the hallway.

Sterling had attended to Ravenwood's recuperation from his encounter. Recovering in his sumptuously decorated bedroom, he was able to access the ashoka tree for healing wounds. It was a matter of days till Ravenwood was fully himself again.

Almost unreal but real, the kilij sword was there, tangible, and taken from a museum, decorated with bloodstone and turquoise. Here in his own room far from Istanbul was a genuine curved sword from the times of the Ottoman Empire. In his right hand clutch he held proof that he had visited Hagia Sophia. He wondered if he had visited the real Hagia Sophia or if it was a dream simulation of the actual place.

Throughout his rest, Sterling had assured him that the Cevikbas family was safe and out of danger. Ravenwood did not tell them of his encounter with the dervish that they also had witnessed nor did he tell them about the Ottoman sword from the 19th century that he had pulled from his combat with the dervish.

Privately, he admired the kilij far more than his épée, his Western sharp dueling sword that was concealed in the Tibetan walking cane he usually had about him.

At the same time, he wondered when his next encounter with the dervish would be since he felt that there was to be another one. For their next combat, Ravenwood would come prepared, ready to battle an enemy of the likes he had never been forced to contend with before.

He knew the kilij was not his and belonged to a museum, but still he trained with it, drawing on the swordsmanship skills that he learned from the Khadgavidya school of Indian sword-fighting. The kilij went well with the Khadgavidya method, a method more suited to arched blades than the vertical angle of his épée.

Before going to the *Dispatch* newspaper building, he sought solace and advice from his mentor and stepfather, the Nameless One.

Into the fragrant gloom he stepped. Secluded privately away from the world, here the Occidental patterns of thought and philosophies gave way to the mystic abstractions of the East. Here the anxious rush of the modern world dissipated.

"Hearken, my son! I know what has befallen thee. Know that Siva the destroyer is always with us, building up and bringing down. Only Siva of the blue throat can speak about truth and untruth. It is through the ways of holy India that the soul achieves atman, as a drop of water is returned to the vastest lake."

"Esteemed savant, I have battled with the murderer and brought to the place you have spoken, the place of the East and the West."

His hoary head bowed, his blunted jaw squared, the guardian of Ravenwood remained in stasis within his seated cross-legged position. Since the Nameless One had followed him across oceans to be with him in his home country, Ravenwood had always seen him in this posture, as if the Nameless One would remain seated in this way for eternity.

"Seek answers from the earthen plane, yet know that the Lord of Justice, *Yama*, is imminent! Seeketh answers among the verdure, the pleasantness and light of this earth!"

Ravenwood's eyesight fluctuated blue, gray, and green as he thought about what the Nameless One had instructed.

"What may that mean, venerable seer? Do I visit the newspaper building again?"

"Know that *Yama* is impending, his cup of justice runneth over! Take heed, my son!"

And with that the Nameless One retreated internally, so far internally and ascetically that Ravenwood knew he also had to politely withdraw and to not disturb his stepfather's peace.

Ravenwood searched the newscasts for any mentions of an antique sword taken from the Hagia Sophia in Istanbul. Periodicals from around the globe arrived to his desk daily. The news from the latest days of the *Dispatch* did not mention anything about the Hagia Sophia, only carrying headlines about the advances of Japan into China and more apprises on the situation of a rearmed Germany breaching agreements and threatening. He searched the newspaper clippings that he kept in a file within his desk, a collection of strange items from all around the world that had preternatural interest.

Seeking answers from the earthen realm led to Ravenwood's intuition that he had to visit his trusty friend again at the archives of this newspaper, the *Dispatch*.

Ravenwood had signed in at the office and made it to look as if he was seeking information about something else but was in fact on a venture to look for news of a missing Ottoman sword. Taking his time, he settled into the dusty, bound volumes of back issues, delving into the overflowing envelopes of "the morgue."

He soon found what he was really looking for. There, from a year ago, was news of a smashed museum case in Istanbul in the *Dispatch* of August 8, 1935. The headline proclaimed that an Ottoman sword was stolen from the Hagia Sophia, newly declared a museum, and that no other items of value were taken from the holy place. From the article, Ravenwood read that there was no one inside the whole of Hagia Sophia during the theft and that the proper museum authorities and the international museum community were notified.

He then looked for more news of missing items around the world in the same paper, looking in its archive for 1935, and had found headlines for a set of missing Sèvres porcelain from the Louvre in Paris and a wrought gold bottle from the present day site of Troy in Turkey was also found missing among Troy's valuable collections. The article went on to mention that Troy was an archaeological site where some ancient plants were found and that Troy was also the site that was featured in the *Iliad*, the same city where the famous Trojan Horse was implemented by the Greek army to surprise attack the Trojans in the night.

There were other headlines of missing valuables from private collections and palaces, but Ravenwood could not sense if these were in any way connected at all, if there was indeed a connection existing.

Confounded, he went back to his supercharged roadster built with a racing engine installed and indulged the Western hemisphere of his intellect for a while. He let the analytical faculties of the Western side of his mind possibly find some development in all of this, some tether, some connection, but for the moment, his Western mindset could not compute any linking factors. Still, Ravenwood sped on into the night, the lights of his home city blazing.

Arriving back home, he went to where the Cevikbas family was staying.

They all three of them had an ever present hunted look, as if they were prey. Their facial features all held a certain dread.

Hande Cevikbas, anxiety-ridden, pulled out a Turkish cigarette and soon blue smoke was suspended in the room amongst a feeling of unease.

"Ravenwood!" exclaimed Ahmet, the son. "It has happened. What he had warned has occurred. Here, even in your apartment room, we are not safe. What we feared the most has happened."

"Has the Albasti visited, then?" replied the man with the strange gaze.

"Yes, she has. The Red Mother has visited us!" the nervous Ahmet bellowed.

"Why should she have cause to visit you?" asked Ravenwood. "Is one of you

He looked for news of missing items.

guilty of an unpunished crime?"

"As far as we know, we have not done anything that would rouse the wrath of the Red Mother. She had come in the night, horrifying our dreams. She speaks accusingly at us, but the words are garbled and I cannot hear exactly what she is saying," said Mrs. Cevikbas.

"Ms. Cevikbas, can you hear what the Red Mother is saying?"

"I cannot discern what she is saying, either. I don't know if I am in fact being haunted or if it is a product of the extreme duress we've been under."

"And you, Mr. Cevikbas? Can you hear anything from the Albasti?"

"Nothing whatsoever, Ravenwood. Yet we all three are alarmed and know she is here."

"I will set up vigil. Sterling will be here during the evening hours, and I will have additional help from central headquarters, two of Inspector Stagg's men, come and also keep watch during the day and night."

"We are so blessed to have you on our side, Mr. Ravenwood," said Kelebek.

"Thank you, is all I can say," said the nervous, sweaty son.

"Is there anything that could possibly ward against the Albasti to stop her visit? What is done in your land?"

"In Turkey and the Ottoman Empire," replied a becalmed Mrs. Cevikbas, "we have charms, glass beads that avert the evil eye. They are blue in color and resemble an eye with a lighter blue iris and pupil."

"These have the lore of protecting from evil," added Kelebek. "If you can retrieve these for us from our former home at Hughleigh, we would be most grateful."

Ravenwood was wary of returning to Hughleigh, for there he had encountered the murderer, the man in the guise of a whirling dervish. And yet during this visit he had no time to look for substantial clues. His senses had felt that there were clues he was missing in his search for the truth of the murder of Aladogan Cevikbas. He had been given no time before the attack had happened, and then he was pulled into a dreamlike vision of the most famous architectural building, the icon of Istanbul, the world renowned Hagia Sophia. He still felt that his encounter with the dervish had been part reality and part dream. Yet it had to be reality since he was able to bring back the kilij sword from where he had been.

It made sense to visit again, and this time he would be prepared, knowing what to expect. He would bring the kilij with him, and he would provide more time to access the burgeon of unseeability to conceal himself many moments before even entering the Hughleigh building.

Ravenwood retired to his bedroom to gather his thoughts after he had called the exceedingly skeptical Inspector Stagg to send two of his men to stand guard about the Cevikbas family. He also made a mental note to himself to seek the lawful contents of Aladogan's will to see precisely what the last will and testament of the secret book collector indicated for his beneficiaries, if anything, and just who the beneficiaries were.

There in his luxurious room the Ottoman Era sword from the 19th century stood on the corner of his bedstead. He knew that the kilij was not his and that it should be returned, yet his uncanny senses that somehow he would need it in the near future. He was tempted to give the sword a name because of his fondness for it, but refrained himself from doing do, knowing that the kilij was "borrowed" property.

Training with the kilij for a while after picking it up, he found it much more suitable than his épée. He still reveled in using his épée but found the kilij to be utterly entrancing, as if it had stepped from the pages of the Arabian Nights' Entertainments that he had read as a child in India.

He wielded the kilij in his dominant right hand and the épée in his left hand. The skills of Indian swordsmanship lent themselves well to the dual sword technique. Ravenwood practiced with much adroitness, his skill with these weapons most likely not possessed by any Western person in all of the city.

After some practice with the swords, he then meditated, standing. Ravenwood's training was of such an advanced nature that he was able to meditate while on his feet. Traveling to his version of Lake Namtso, the very name of peacefulness to Ravenwood, he found his favorite tree. All of the burgeons had grown back on the ashoka tree in the ashoka arbor. Encompassing the arbor was an adjoining field of barley and orchards of apricots. He sat beneath his tree for a while, attempting to gather sense, gathering serenity. He could divine no further revelations than what his super-senses had already told him.

Satisfied with his meditations, Ravenwood read for a while from other scholars in Far Eastern matters, those who also gave public talks about their findings as Ravenwood did. He then found himself in an ideal state as he slipped into mortal sleep.

In the center of night, he got up, having suddenly awoken. His hands felt wet with perspiration. There was a faint tinge of haze in the room. He saw the kilij still there, as if shining brightly in the dark. Ravenwood turned on the light on his bed stand and the light softly glowed in the room.

The Cevikbas family was asleep, and he saw that there was a stationed guard there from central headquarters. The cynical Inspector Stagg had complied. Such was the importance of the family that Ravenwood felt that it was not his own personal request that was fulfilled by Stagg but rather the stature of the family that made Stagg consent to have two of his policemen here, one for the day and one at night.

He let his steps bring him to the secluded temple at the corridor in the rear of his apartments, the abode of the Nameless One.

Softly he opened the door and entered the aromatic gloom. Ravenwood saw the father responsible for his second upbringing, an indulgence into the mysteries of eternal India. His hoary headed stepfather, his vision shining, had looked up as Ravenwood entered. As ever, the Nameless One was seated in his cross-legged position, and he radiated timeless and ancient wisdom.

"My son! Soon cometh the culprit!"

"Pardon me, sire?" gasped Ravenwood. He had never seen the Nameless One in a state of agitation. Nothing had ever shaken the Nameless One from his unshakeable calmness. Never before had he seen a sense of alarm on the scale of which he had seen now on his face.

"Behind thee and before thee! Those that know the way know not the way but those that know the way will not say! Wise is the scholar who keeps his knowledge within, for he that knows not appears to the multitudes that he does!

"Behind and before thee!" These statements of the savant were as inscrutable as expected. Yet they seemed more abstract than usual.

"Behind and before thee, reverend sire?"

Ravenwood looked behind him. He saw as if in liquid motion the dervish enter the room, his blade glinting, a serious deadliness in the presentation of the weapon. He watched as the dervish stepped lightly into the sacred space where no one had ever entered besides Ravenwood since he had brought his master to the West three years ago. Seeing someone else enter was a violation of all that Ravenwood held dear to him, his only connection to a sense of family, and to have it disturbed this way rooted him to where he was.

"Ravenwood! My son! Never forget!" screamed the Nameless One as he still sat where he was, inert, as if ready for his fate at the hands of the dervish.

Ravenwood found that he could not move at all, not even to speak the Sanskrit power word to turn everyone within hearing range to stone. The Nameless One would have been impervious to the word. His mouth felt as if it had been sewn shut, and it was himself that he had felt had turned to stone. And yet he was not turned to stone, just rooted and watching as the dervish came closer, the figure that was behind and now before Ravenwood, before the

Nameless One.

The dervish's solid black eyes turned on Ravenwood, and the diabolical features grinned in a profane and offensive way, uttering haughty and blasphemous words that Ravenwood could barely discern.

The knife, the same knife that had killed Aladogan Cevikbas, was now poised above the gentle and delicate heart of the Nameless One. He could not move a muscle and the dagger, still bloodstained, plunged repeatedly into the beating organ of his stepfather.

Scarlet and crimson ran the blood of his master onto the floor, running red on his garments, erupting gruesomely into the sanctified chamber. Ravenwood could not call for help, was shocked as his eyes began to fill, clouding his eyesight.

The Nameless One jolted and did not scream as the stabs hit into his chest. His body crumpled to the floor in a malformed shape. He could hear the evil taunts of the masquerading dervish in black. Ravenwood could not ask who he was, and he kept trying to draw upon the Sanskrit word that he was ready to utter in all vocal ranges, but his mouth was fastened by an unknown force.

The dervish left, diabolically leering before and behind Ravenwood as he exited the room. He replaced the dagger in his belt and Ravenwood watched as he marched inaudibly down the secluded corridor.

As the dervish went out of sight, Ravenwood now felt that motion had returned to him. Instead of charging after the dervish, he went right to where his stepfather was.

The Nameless One's chest mangled, the stepson felt for signs of a pulse. There was none.

Softly he clutched the Indian master to him, the blood soaking his nightclothes.

"No," he muttered as the tears welled up in his polychromatic sight. "No, no, no…" he muttered as the tears coursed down his face. This couldn't be. It was impossible. The Nameless One would have known about his fate and would have warned Ravenwood. Ravenwood also would have had a sense of this death beforehand. He would have then prevented it.

His regularly stolid and strong nature gave way to the gloom that recurrently permeated the room.

He cradled his father and rocked him as if he was trying to induce a sort of sleep in the hapless body.

His head lifted to the sky, Ravenwood now let out a scream that could shake all the glass in the world. His grief shook him as his body wracked with sobs.

Having had his hour of mourning, the usually composed Ravenwood had felt bitter defeat at the hands of the charlatan dervish. He lay the Nameless One in a respectful pose, the way that he would wish to be put to rest. His spiritual father's eyes now shut forever, Ravenwood wiped his tears away after allowing himself a brief indulgence in grief. He then had no time to indulge in his sense of grief and to pull himself together to find the culprit and bring him to justice once and for all.

The now fatherless Ravenwood was made twice fatherless now by the plague killing his biological American father years ago and the death of his stepfather at the hands of the dervish. His source of security that had trained him and made him the man he was today was dead. Two dead fathers for Ravenwood. It was too much to bear for regular men, but Ravenwood let his training from his stepfather take hold of his mind. He knew from the teachings of the Nameless One that everything in the physical world was ephemeral, that the timeless wisdom of India constantly reinforced that all things were impermanent, as a castle built on sand. Still, his Western mind rebelled at the thought that all things were impermanent, according to the wisdom of the Indian philosophers. It was to Ravenwood's Western mind that he felt he had to not let this death go unpunished. For once, he let his Western half take charge of his being, the impatience and the call to duty pulling him in the direction of where the dervish went.

His face showing his sorrow, he tried to put on his usual face of bravery. He went forward to arm himself with the weapons found in his bedroom.

Wisely, the Eastern half of him tactically and defensively sought the renewed burgeon for unseeability. The murderer was in the shadowy unknowns of his apartment here, and he did not want to be ensnared as he was during their previous fight in Hughleigh and then in a real or unreal Hagia Sophia in Istanbul.

The Nameless One's son reached the meditative version of his hands, the ethereal hands, to find the burgeon on his ashoka tree that granted invisibility. Touching the knots of the tree and the whorls of wood, he guided to where the burgeon was to be found, on a branch that was as intricately placed as expected for such a capability. It took minutes rather than seconds to find the burgeon, and at last he found it, this time successfully touching it without being attacked in the midst of his meditative search.

Gradually Ravenwood's whole physical being became invisible.

Drawing on all of his training in moving without being seen, he removed anything on his person that would make noise. Having done this, he crept stealthily into the corridor that led into the rest of his place, and the household was still asleep. The Cevikbas family, the only three left, were safe in their chamber guarded by the policeman, who could not see or hear as Ravenwood passed right near him on his way to check on Sterling. Sterling was undisturbed and sleeping in his room. Passing now into his bedroom, Ravenwood could find no trace of the dervish. His senses told him that the dervish may be hiding in anticipation for Ravenwood. It was then that Ravenwood realized that he could not get his weapons, the kilij, the épée, his Luger, for the dervish knew that retrieving these weapons would be his next move. The stepson wondered now how to retrieve them without falling into another trap set by his opponent.

Even if there were other weapons in his apartment, Ravenwood knew these also would be possible ambush points for the dervish to take advantage of. There were no other weapons he could use, so he chanced to not take any of them and lie in wait. There was the possibility of going to the kitchen to grab a butcher knife, but this was not what Ravenwood wanted to take a chance on. The formidability of the kilij sword, his épée, and his Luger were what the dervish would possibly be staking out his position for, there in the jagged shadows, his night-raiment camouflaging naturally with the darkness to attain his own competing form of hiddenness.

Ravenwood had his own fists and training to rely on, and his hands were weapons. The kilij, if not retrieved by him, would then go to the dervish, along with the épée and the Luger. And then Ravenwood would be at a considerable disadvantage.

His wits being both of East and West, and yet wholly neither, his train of thought clashed until he decided to take a chance and go for the deadliest weapon of the three: the kilij. The Luger his opponent had easily dodged before, and the épée he had not had a chance to use in combat with the pretender dervish. The kilij also lent itself to Khadgavidya, the Indian sword fighting system, better than the épée.

It was then that after double-checking to see that everyone was unharmed in his apartment, Ravenwood soundlessly went for the kilij in his bedroom. He felt he had to take the risk or lose the chance.

The moonlight provided enough illumination to see the kilij where he had left it, bolstered against the corner of his bedstead as if it was an enchanted sword from the myths of the Near East.

He tread silently, closer and nearer to the right-handed kilij. There was no warning of danger from the Nameless One. The Nameless One was forever silent, and the stepson felt the painful realization of this as he did not hear anything, any advice, whether enigmatic or clear, from his ancient father.

Inaudibly and with the most trained patience did he inch closer to the Ottoman sword, moving with surgical precision, his senses expanding as he stretched his hearing to detect if the dervish was there in the room with him, waiting.

He held his breath and his right hand reached for the handle. As his fingers closed on it, a crackling shot rang out from Ravenwood's own Luger, grazing him in the neck.

Ravenwood reeled back, still on his feet, his invisibility away, as he lunged from more shots from his own Luger. Rolling like a ball to the floor, he was able to escape the following shots ringing from the gun. It was when he retreated to behind a full-length mirror that a bullet crashed through, shattering the glass and scratching Ravenwood's cheek.

Another bullet followed and the kilij leapt into deed. Ravenwood brought the kilij sword and with the flat side had swatted a bullet away from its course towards the middle of his forehead as if it was a mere fly.

Two more bullets fired again, towards other vulnerable areas, as Ravenwood deflected them with the flat of the kilij, swiping the bullet that went for his heart and then striking with the kilij again the bullet that targeted an area of his brain, the bullet diverted again from harming him.

He felt himself more vigorous than ever, and the heat of battle and the anger of being twice orphaned had propelled him to indulge his more reckless Western nature. He lunged closer with the blade toward the dervish now that the chambers of the semi-automatic pistol were empty. The dervish threw the empty gun at Ravenwood, which again Ravenwood deflected with the kilij as he launched in midair and bellowed out a warlike yell from the core of his very being.

The blade had again hit the masquerading dervish, deep enough that blood started to flow scarlet, yet not decisive enough to lay his assailant to the ground.

It was here that the dervish held the flat of the kilij between his two hands. With Ravenwood's right hand still firmly gripping the sword, he found that he couldn't move it from his opponent's grasp. The curved sword was held fast in the viselike grasp of the ink-eyed man who leered at him and taunted him.

Ravenwood's Western half in total control, something he had not experienced since before he had met the Nameless One, he neglected to call upon the power word to turn his opponent to stone. He could have drawn from the burgeons of the ashoka tree that granted him various uncanny abilities, he could have used the powers that the Nameless One had taught him. Instead, his fuming and appalled Occidental side had completely dominated his movements and choices.

Seeing that Ravenwood was at a standstill, he lifted Ravenwood above his head by using his grip on the kilij. To Ravenwood's astonishment, he had held the kilij so firmly that the dervish was able to lift the kilij and him into the area above. Ravenwood did not at all want to release his own firm grip on the kilij, for that would be giving his enemy the Ottoman sword and its benefit in the combat. Knowing this, the dervish attempted a total bodily throw of Ravenwood, and he effectively accomplished this as Ravenwood still had the kilij in his hands.

Flying in a twisting, coiling fashion in the air from the sheer strength of the throw, he crashed through his bedroom wall, rending it down as he crossed his arms before him to shield his face from the collision.

Again the dervish had efficaciously thrown Ravenwood through a barrier, a barrier not made of bricks this time as the barrier was at their previous match in the Hughleigh Towers. The dust and materials that comprised Ravenwood's bedroom wall rained softly on him as he immediately got up, breathing, panting, his face showing tears, trickles of lifeblood, and perspiration.

He got up and didn't recognize where he was. It did not look to be anywhere he had ever been before. Again he had the feeling that he had been transported elsewhere without the regular physical means of travel. He knew he had no time to look around before the dervish breached the uncanny gateway between his apartment and an unidentified someplace which Ravenwood could only see peripherally as he focused his concentration on the coming onslaught.

His wounds still bleeding from the graze of gunshots, he again could not hear the voice of the Nameless One, who would have told him in panic to release the Western half of his mind and access the Eastern thoughts that the stepfather had cultivated in his own stepson. He would have told him to advance his hands to the ashoka tree to have a possibility to defend himself, but this was advice that was locked beyond the walls of death.

Taking his offensive stance with the kilij at the ready, the dervish approached closer. As the dervish lunged for him, he brought the curved sword down on his adversary, who deftly sidestepped the attempted blow. This was what Ravenwood wanted, and with his left arm, he delivered with all of his remaining strength a well-placed blow to the underside of the dervish's chin.

This had taken the attacker unawares, and he reeled back in a momentary stun. Taking advantage of this, Ravenwood buried the sword deep into the left shoulder of the dervish. His opponent howled in pain. He then next moved with the blade to cut off both of the dervishes legs at the area of his knees, but the dervish had started to whirl in time. Ravenwood had narrowly missed but had drawn blood from him.

"Who are you?" the stepson had suddenly asked, gathering his breath.

"Do not you know?" answered the dervish, in agony. "I am the killer of Aladogan Cevikbas."

"What are you?" answered back Ravenwood.

"That is for you to find out, Ravenwood," was the reply, and the stepson of the East felt fully unnerved at the dervish saying his name.

He....didn't recognize where he was.

"It does not matter what manner of monster you may be, this will be the last stand between us!" screamed Ravenwood, his normally calm voice wiled away. "Only one of us is leaving wherever we may be. One or the both of us is going to be dead here, do you hear me? Either one of us or the both of us!"

With this, he charged full on with all of his might, the kilij sword flashing without the training he drew from the East.

Easily the dervish spun aside, Ravenwood's blade cutting only air.

It was here that the sly hands of the sham dervish were able to take the kilij out of Ravenwood's right hand clutch.

With the curved sword that Ravenwood had just held, he slashed right into Ravenwood's side.

Blood welled forth as, crushed, he fell to the floor. Ravenwood lay still, marked for death. It was his turn to lose, for he had won the first meeting with the killer.

There on the ground he could only hear the jeering and evil mocking of the dervish, the sacrilegious phrases spewing in a stream of invective that Ravenwood, in blinding pain, could still hear. Ravenwood had never felt such physical pain.

He could no longer make out what the blasphemous voice had said, such were the depths of agony that Ravenwood found himself in.

The dervish swiveled closer, victory ringing throughout him, intent on delivering the coup de grace that would shut the multicolored eyes, completing the extermination of both the master and his son.

Ravenwood's blood was pouring on the floor, the puddle expanding in a mock sea of defeat, heartbreak, and trauma. He was inert in his paralyzing pain, the deep laceration to his side overtaking him.

Closer the dervish came, the kilij hanging above him as he now knelt directly above a hapless Ravenwood.

In the throes of suffering, his right hand started to grasp. There was nothing in his right hand. He had expected the kilij to be there, but he had only felt the shock of air.

It was here that his senses started to connect and repair themselves. There in the deepest throes of pain, which was meditative in its own dazedness, the stream of thoughts and philosophies of the Far East reset themselves into his mind as the clashing Western thoughts receded into the background. It was the meditative state of deepest pain, what some of the ancient mystics and ascetics from the East had inflicted upon themselves, sometimes with extreme hunger, to achieve a rarefied kind of meditation that allowed Ravenwood access to his inner wisdom and power again.

He could now hear the dervish and he could now see the kilij ready to strike him down just as his master was stricken and silenced to death.

"Do you have any last words, Ravenwood?" he asked, his face contorted into the most loathsome and despicable of expressions.

"Yes, I do."

And here he summoned all the vocal ranges in the human scales and said the word he needed to say.

"Pasanasila!" Ravenwood sung into the air, and the dervish started to turn into the most welcome of statues made of stone.

Back on the other side of the curtain, as Ravenwood was exploring just where he was, the Cevikbas family was asleep. Kelebek had just woken in the night, her lovely face showing uneasiness. They had not heard anything at all during Ravenwood's second duel with the dervish, and a large stiff clothed policeman had safeguarded their doorway all night. Kelebek felt more protected from the dervish and also the Albasti that was disturbing what was left of her family. The Albasti, the Red Mother, visited Kelebek in her dreams. Dressed all in flowing rubicund garments that spectrally confirmed how she had pictured the Red Mother as a young woman, in Kelebek's nightmare the Red Mother looked similar to the illustrations in books her father thought "safe" for living room consumption. The Red Mother had spoken only the word for "guilty" in Turkish again and again.

Her mother and brother in Ravenwood's guestroom with her were away in a troubled sleep. She could hear them both emitting horrid sounds as if being stalked in their nightmares by the Mother in Red. Her brother was especially tossing and turning at the torments of the Red Mother.

Here Kelebek muttered some coarse language to herself and crossed over to a table that ran alongside one of the elegant walls of Ravenwood's guestroom, a table holding various liqueurs and other strong drinks. She poured herself some green chartreuse and sat on one of the well-designed sofas in the room, her willowy hand resting on the plush fabric as she sipped on her crystal glass and watched the last of the Cevikbas branch of the once mighty Ottoman Empire, the Turkish Empire that ruled the Near East for centuries. Her features now held a tough look of defiance mixed with concern.

She let the chartreuse course through her, its effects relaxing her and putting up a sedative barrier from the harsh circumstances facing the family. Her father was dead, killed by the dervish in black. The three of them were being disturbed by the Albasti, who only sought those guilty of unchastised crimes. Her father's body was missing but the bloodstains were still there on the floor of his evil study. All of these thoughts were massaged away for a bit as the slight inebriation took hold of her.

From her cigarette case, she retrieved one of the Turkish cigarettes she was fond of. The effects of the chartreuse combined with a cigarette would do her well with regard to her nerves, Kelebek thought. As the blue smoke ringed around the room, she thought and thought, her intellect becalmed yet still ruminating on what could possibly be happening.

After some while in a pensive mode, she shakily stood from the sofa and moved to open a window slightly so as to let out some of the cobalt blue haze she was generating. She did not want this to bother her family. She walked carefully but tipsily and opened a window slightly ajar without waking her mother and brother.

There she sat looking at a gibbous moon, glowing, the moonlight spilling into the room, decking everything with a sheen of silver. It made the whole room fairylike as a midsummer daydream and it was soothing to Kelebek.

Her thoughts going this way and that, she mused upon happy thoughts and both sad thoughts. She thought of Ravenwood and what his chances were of rescuing them and finding the murderer. Somehow she felt confident in the detective with the unorthodox faculties of mind. She herself was much in touch with Eastern ways of thinking, her father having propagating it calculatingly into the family. She thought about how she would love to just run away from it all and start somewhere else with a new name, a new way of life, in a place more peaceful than the jostle and push of this city her father made her and her brother grow up in, thinking that it would make them happy. Perhaps she would find contentment with a new life in the country of Morocco, in a small village near the purple Atlas Mountains. Maybe she'd be happier with a quieter life in the medinas of the smaller towns in French Morocco. She would learn the French language and the Berber languages common there, and get away from such a troubled family.

As she dreamed of these hypothetical plans of hers, she realized that wherever she went in the world, there would be advantages and disadvantages. There was no place in this world that was completely without disadvantages. To balance the good, there always had to be its direct opposite for it to exist. But still, the trade-off, she felt, was worth it.

In the collective mists of the chartreuse and the tobacco, she heard the incessant traffic of the city thirty floors below the penthouse. Her mind ventured from here to there on the world, searching for a place, a fabled place where she could find absolute satisfaction. She wondered if such a place existed and here she gave a mocking, petulant jeer.

As she took another sip from her crystal glass, a sudden thought had returned to her, something that startled her back to cold sobriety immediately.

That night, that fateful night, she realized that she had seen the murder of her father not just once, but twice.

Yes. She remembered now. It was obscured before in her shyness and alarm that night, but now she knew that she had seen the dervish stab her father to death two distinct and separate times in the evening.

Only one of the killings she could establish a time without doubt. That was at 3:11 a.m. as she was returned to her bedroom by her mother and brother who had found her unconscious as she witnessed her father again being murdered by the dervish.

The previous time she saw her father being killed by the same dervish that same night was a time she could not establish. Yet she knew that she had seen him murdered once earlier, and then again the same murder happening later, all in the same night. Both of these identical events took place after midnight, that she knew with conviction.

Did her mother and brother also see the dervish kill her father more than once in the night?

Kelebek, startlements intersecting on her face, decided to keep this a secret and only tell Ravenwood.

It was time that she returned to bed to gain a restful night's sleep. The protection from evil charms were still in Hughleigh and Ravenwood was unable to bring them here. Nevertheless, she still felt secure in having Inspector Stagg's policeman vigilant and taking watch. If she was to encounter the Red Mother in her sleep, then so be it, she reasoned with herself. When next she saw him, the man she properly addressed as Mr. Ravenwood, then she would tell him privately that she remembered, that she recalled clearly that she saw her father murdered not once, but twice.

Outside the door, the policeman sent from central headquarters by Inspector Stagg was worried for the family. There was no doubt that they were a prominent family, prestigious, and able to make their way in a high class area of Manhattan. He was used to guarding such families who lived in ivory towers and privately he felt jealous. He felt as if he was a secret service agent put there to guard a foreign head of state's family.

His badge name, Herman, had shone in the fully lit penthouse apartment so he could see everywhere and not have anyone or anything creep up unbeknownst to him and catch him off guard. Officer Thomas Herman had his gun at the ready, his bulk and musculature intimidating. He stood there on constant vigil until ready to be relieved in the morning by another of Stagg's uniforms.

Officer Herman wondered how it was that such an eminent family who had looked to have almost everything be in such a situation. Unlike his boss, Officer Herman was no skeptic. He believed in the occult of the East and had been witness to some uncanny moments in his own life. He remembered as a boy his uncle who had committed his own death by hanging, an uncle whose death could have been prevented had they known that he was going through some turbulence in his financial life. The crash of 1929 had so affected his sensitive uncle that he had hung himself in his own garage, sending shockwaves to all of his family who always considered him a strong man of upstanding character.

It was about two weeks later that Herman saw his uncle in his living room. There was a large upholstered seat there, and in the darkness of the room, it looked to be a ceremonial chair in a way. He thought he saw his own father sitting there in the shadows, which was unusual since his father never used the chair. He started to call his father's name into the dark, asking what his father was doing there sitting all alone in the night. He kept calling to his father but was too frightened to enter the darkened room. The figure in the chair never budged. Yet Thomas kept calling, asking, and then pleading with his father to come up from the chair.

In this uncertainty of fear, he had suddenly heard his father speak on the phone in the kitchen, his real father. However, the figure seated there remained stock still. It was then that Thomas had fled from the room in pure terror, his skin crawling and his adolescent eyes weeping of fright. He fled into his father's arms and knew the man in the chair was none other than his uncle who had died two weeks earlier.

The memory to this day still sent him a cascade of shivers.

He had had further brushes with the spectral and the spiritual so he had to keep all of this to himself when the gravelly opinions of Inspector Stagg constantly scolded the "hocus" that was involved in Ravenwood's investigations. Stagg had no trust at all in Ravenwood.

There was some reason why he, Officer Herman, was posted here to protect the Cevikbas family and his department knew that it wasn't on account of Ravenwood's personal request that he send a uniform to protect the family.

Officer Herman did feel a tinge of envy as he saw the brilliantly arrayed Kelebek Cevikbas in her expensive Turkish jewelry. He saw the bespoke suit that fitted Ravenwood perfectly, the most perfect suit he had seen, and felt green with covetousness.

He was here not to indulge in his natural feelings, but for some other purpose yet to be revealed to him and his friends in the department. When he left headquarters, there was something in the conduct of Inspector Stagg that was hiding something.

Here he took out a pack of cigarettes, something to while away the hours, and felt amused when he heard his girlfriend calling them "coffin nails" as they were known colloquially. A coffin nail is just what he needed at this time as he waited till dawn.

Ravenwood knew that the turning to stone of the dervish would not last. Now that his Eastern knowledge had flooded back to him, he was grateful for the deep level of pain that only the most rarefied ancient mystics sought to reach. The meditative result caused his trained mind to be available. Even so, that excruciating level of pain was something that he would not want to feel again.

The kilij was also bound in stone as was the rest of the dervish. As for himself, Ravenwood's clothes were shredded and his chest partially exposed by the gashes of the kilij that the dervish had.

It was now that he felt along the ashoka tree for the replenishment burgeon. He found it instantly and his bodily wounds began to heal quickly. It was mere minutes before he could bring himself up from the ground.

He had to look for weapons, just as he did before in the Hagia Sophia of Istanbul when he broke the museum glass there to get the Ottoman sword.

Looking around, he recognized on the instant that he was India. It had to be India, he had grown up there, and he had trained there with the Nameless One. The familiar styles of architecture and bas-relief work stood out in sandstone and granite.

He knew where he now was to be a Hindustani healing temple. The atmosphere was as dreamlike and gauzy as his first travel with the dervish. Reverently, the Brahmins started to file in, priests of the topmost caste of India, and just as suddenly were they shaken when they saw the stone statue with a threatening sword there in their sanctified place of worship. The Brahmin priesthood that had entered the temple after Ravenwood's fierce combat had looked quizzically at the shattered wall that led to Ravenwood's bedroom.

Ravenwood then touched the burgeon of unseeability and then he became imperceptible to the Brahmin throng.

Again, he knew it was a matter of moments before the stone statue would become flesh again. Ravenwood had to look for a weapon.

In the temple, he had found no weapons, but he had found a Sanskrit calendar that he could read well. He read that the year was 1935, a year from his current situation in 1936 in New York.

Invisibly roaming around the healing temple as softly as he could manage, Ravenwood saw an area that was sealed from prying eyes. The doors were shut with prepared bolts, and Ravenwood did not attempt to open these with physical force. Noticing that it was the only area that was locked away from the rest of the complex, his astral fingers felt along the sorrowless tree, seeking the burgeon for unlocking.

His hand feeling around for the exact burgeon he needed, he had found it on a particular bough after navigating some leaves and knots of the tree.

The lock in front of Ravenwood had given way, and he entered the now unsealed room, closing the door behind him.

Inside this healing temple's room were scrolls upon scrolls, the room watertight and airtight to preserve these treasures. Ravenwood perused some and recognized familiar scrolls that he had read in Sanskrit as an adolescent training with the Nameless One: the *Atharva Veda*, the Vedic scripture on medicine, magic, and sorcery. Most of the *Atharva Veda* was known to Ravenwood already since he had a copy in his book collection. There was the famous *Charaka Samhita*, another text on Hindu medicine. Ravenwood also possessed a copy of this and had devoured it till memorization. There were more scrolls, all on the subject of the healing arts, and some scrolls unknown to him.

Coming across this vast healing temple in India made him wonder if somehow he had subconsciously willed himself here to find some healing secrets for the Nameless One. In this sacral temple dedicated to restoration and recovery, the mysteries of the human body were mapped, detailed, and answered. Maybe it was Ravenwood's doing this time that brought him and the dervish to this repository of healing in India in the year 1935, a year before the present.

And here now was the *Kurma Purana*, though when Ravenwood opened it, it looked different. It was in flowing Sanskrit, which he could read easily. However, there was something more to it. The *Kurma Purana*, which he had seen often, detailed how to create gem elixirs for healing. In ancient Indian lore, there were seven principle gemstones that were said to match the seven cosmic rays, the light rays that make up the universe. The *Kurma Purana* said that the seven planets known to the ancients were condensations of these seven rays of light, which match exactly the seven colors of the seven major chakras of the human body. Chakras were major healing points on the body and if they were blocked or stagnant this caused pain and disease. The text then goes on to describe the Seven-Gem Elixir and the Nine-Gem Elixir, with the Seven-Gem Elixir using emerald, diamond, ruby, moonstone, sapphire, cat's eye, and pearl. The Nine-Gem Elixir uses coral and onyx in addition to what is used in the Seven-Gem Elixir. These gems were put in water and soaked for seven days and nights as the gems released their recuperative powers into the water naturally. The elixir drops were then administered to the patient for healing.

This was something new to Ravenwood's eyes. Here, never seen or heard of before in Ravenwood's years of training or even hinted at in the Nameless One's vast storehouse of centuries-long learning was a Twelve-Gem Elixir. In beautiful Sanskrit writing, Ravenwood read on in suspense as to what the Twelve-Gem Elixir was supposed to do. By adding three gems to the Nine-Gem Elixir, these being the tiger eye, opal, and the extremely rare alexandrite found in Andhra Pradesh in India, the Twelve-Gem Elixir was supposed to heal all manner of wounds, snake bites, poisonings, and even, to Ravenwood's utter amazement, to bring back the body from death.

Seeing this, a startled Ravenwood kept on reading this version of the *Kurma Purana*. He could possibly bring back his stepfather, the Nameless One. He could possibly bring back his father and mother that were killed due to plague when he was a child. All sorts of possibilities opened in the mind of Ravenwood.

Knowing that his time was limited and that the dervish was most likely going to be full flesh soon, he tucked the secret version of the *Kurma Purana* that held the instructions for the Twelve-Gem Elixir into the waistband of his pants. He was now ready to return back to the present and to his apartment before the entrance sealed and the kilij whipped toward him again in the uncased hand of the dervish.

The Brahmins were expectantly there and Ravenwood, almost visible, gave a Hindu greeting, the namaskar, in which Ravenwood brought his palms together before his chest and bowed. The Brahmins were not fooled since they did see the Twelve-Gem Elixir scroll from their sealed room with him. They were also alarmed at his bloodstained nightclothes.

In the background he saw his opponent mostly made full flesh again and on seeing this, Ravenwood touched the unseeability burgeon on the sorrowless tree. Instantly he was made imperceptible again to the exclamation of the Brahmins.

Quickly he moved toward the still-open entrance to his bedroom and as he walked through, the entrance closed behind him. He was safe from the menaces of his torturer, the spinning figure clad in black.

Ravenwood, with the secret *Kurma Purana* that held the possible solution to bringing back his loved ones from death, felt contentment suddenly. It was as if these "journeys" a year back and oceans away were a controllable phenomenon where a possible greater control could be had if he experienced more of them.

Back in the present, Ravenwood looked around and immediately went to rest after placing the *Kurma Purana* he had obtained from the healing temple in a hidden place. Only the alexandrite gemstone would be a burden to find since it was one of the rarest gems in India. He would have to make another "journey" without physical transport if he wanted to revive the Nameless One.

Sterling had tidied up the startlingly untidy bedroom, having only seen Ravenwood's bedchamber always neat and impeccable. Sterling informed him that the Cevikbas family were at breakfast and that he had several phone calls to follow up on, including a call from the attorney for the estate that handled Aladogan's last will and testament.

On learning this, Ravenwood decided to pass breakfast and head to his study where his phone was located. He gave a nod to the uniformed policeman at the doorway to the dining room and saw that his badge name proclaimed him Officer Herman.

Gently Ravenwood picked up the receiver. Ravenwood already knew the contents of the will before the attorney was about to speak it. He just wanted his thoughts confirmed for he still felt bewildered about some finer points in the case.

"Ravenwood, we have the details of the last will and testament of Aladogan Cevikbas," said the drawling voice on the line.

"Please tell me what you have found," he answered, already knowing most of the contents of the will, his senses already having picked up most of it beforehand.

"The will divides up his savings equally among his family members, a modest sum. I and my firm found that this will was not going to make any of the remaining Cevikbas family rich. As you already know, the Cevikbas family were down to their last chips financially. This will is not going to help them at all in that regard."

Having his thoughts confirmed, Ravenwood thanked the attorney on the line.

He then wanted to visit the *Dispatch* to see if there were reports from a year ago in the archives about an Indian healing temple having a treasure taken. He confirmed this too and found that the year of the article was 1935, one year ago from the present. Ravenwood knew that when the Brahmins described the suspect that had taken the treasure, they had described him accurately.

Taking the supercharged roadster further along the city that he so loved, he breathed in the air and drew in long breaths, expanding the length and breadth of each inhale and exhale. Driving through Times Square in the daytime was always a pleasure he indulged in, its bustling crowdedness overwhelming for the casual visitor to the city but for a person of Ravenwood's Eastern temperament was something that could be delighted in without causing pressure.

Visiting the American Museum of Natural History in the Upper West Side of the island, he talked with his contacts on the staff there to see if they had an alexandrite gemstone in their collections. They had searched and said that they did not have any alexandrite on the premises. This did not deter Ravenwood as he had felt that he would have to make a "journey" again somehow, risking the dervish breathing down his neck, to find the alexandrite gem. Gladly, at his penthouse apartment, he had the other eleven gems ready.

It was all up to him if he wanted to resurrect the Nameless One. Maybe it was better that the Nameless One had passed to another reincarnation, or perhaps he needed the Nameless One more than ever, and would always need a father throughout his entire life. The stepson's forehead creased, his luminescent eyes changed in their colors as they lamented again at the death of his holy stepfather. He tried not to think about being orphaned twice as he stepped on the roadster's gas pedal with a renewed sense of determination to get his revenge on the dervish and to bring him to the altar of justice.

It was then that he heard the voice of his father, disembodied, coming from where Ravenwood always had heard him.

"Ravenwood, my very own son, child of my heart! Do not let the illusions of Maya break you! Doomed is he that letteth delusion overcome him. He that seeketh me will find me where I am always to be found!"

Arriving to the floor of his penthouse in Sussex Towers, he immediately went to the back corridor that led to where the Nameless One's temple between heaven and earth was secluded away from the constraints of everyday life.

Stepping into the fragrant gloom, Ravenwood saw his father, the Nameless One, alive and sitting where he had always sat.

"It cannot be! Are you alive, wise One? What have I seen? Is this an illusion?"

He inched forward to the hoary headed savant, and touched his forehead lightly. The Nameless One was tangible and was not of air.

There he was, the Nameless One alive after all.

This had puzzled Ravenwood even more. Now there was no need to retrieve the alexandrite gem from Andhra Pradesh, if this truly was real and not just a vision.

"My son, I know that you are perplexed. Take this as you will. Believe that you see me or do not believe that you see me. You are soon to come upon the truth."

Not wanting to admit to anything since he was unsure if the appearance of his father in front of him was real or a misconception, he wanted to tell him that he felt that he was arriving soon to the unraveling of the circumstances surrounding the remaining members of the Cevikbas family. If he admitted this to the illusion before him if illusion it was, then he could possibly be admitting to his opponent that he was getting closer on his trail. Ravenwood could not take anything for granted.

Even so, he had heard the Nameless One's voice while driving through the city, the way that he had always heard the Nameless One when he was away from his apartment. He had heard the Nameless One's voice countless times, and all were heard in the same exact way as he had heard this afternoon after his visit to the museum to look for alexandrite.

"Ravenwood, you are not alone! I will advise thee as you arrive to the hidden truth. Turning back the wheel of twelvemonth is what you have been doing. Though you turn the wheel, as you go back, you cannot hear me. As you travel away, also I cannot be heard. Know then, my son, that I will guide you and warn you when appropriate. But know this, that the kilij sword closes upon you! Beware of this, Ravenwood!"

Ravenwood, his eyes filling and not knowing what was real, returned solemnly back to his study after this and placed his head on his desk. He knew he could not discuss the case with what he didn't know was his father or not.

After a while in some thought, his sense told him that he had to visit the chemist, Dr. Hubermann. He knew ahead of time that Dr. Hubermann had information that would help the case just as the burgeon on the sorrowless tree could open all the locks that Ravenwood faced.

Having groomed his appearance in the mirror, making sure his tie and custom-made suit fit perfectly on him, he was about to grab his Homburg, cane, and his reloaded Luger when he ran into Kelebek Cevikbas.

She had a strained look on her, the frequent hunted look that the family had.

"Can I be of help, Ms. Cevikbas?" offered a surprised Ravenwood.

"Mr. Ravenwood, something has just been reminded and I need to tell you in privacy," she said, barely audible.

She looked around to make sure that she was out of earshot from anyone else in the apartment.

As noiselessly as possible, Ravenwood guided Ms. Cevikbas back to his study. He made sure that he and Ms. Cevikbas were alone and in full privacy.

"Mr. Ravenwood, I saw the murder of my father twice. Not once, but twice!"

"Please tell me how you know this, Ms. Cevikbas," urged an intrigued Ravenwood.

"I had risen in the middle of night. I knew that I had remembered something important, as it was there in my grasp, almost there, and then progressively mine. I came to the full realization. My father was murdered twice before my eyes, both times by the sham dervish."

Here she let loose some invective and profanity about the dervish pretender.

"Only one of the murders was the real murder. I don't have the time of the first murder, but the second murder I know to have happened at the time I had said before, at 3:11 a.m. I cannot discover when the first murder of my father took place."

His gaze shifted from gray to green to blue as he pondered this new piece of information. He searched his mind on where it fit in, and it occurred to him where he could possibly put it.

"Thank you for your recollection, Ms. Cevikbas. I will now bring you to the guestroom where your mother and brother are. Please keep safe and know that you and family are being guarded at all hours."

"The Red Mother is torturing us, Mr. Ravenwood. I do not think any policeman can withstand the torments of the Albasti if she is seeking a reckoning for a crime."

With this, Ravenwood brought her back to the guestroom and thanked Ms. Cevikbas again, this time silently. Hande Cevikbas and Ahmet Cevikbas were there and all three of them looked the picture of quarry in headlights. Again, that sweaty handshake by Ahmet and a nod of reassurance from the mother. Again she called him the Man with the Zultanite Eyes and tried her best to smile.

Privately, in his roadster, he thought about a person witnessing the murder of her father twice in the same night. He also thought about four distinct times that the father was witnessed murdered in the night. Four murders now of the same man, Aladogan Cevikbas. Four murders to sort through. A body to find, Aladogan's body. A dervish to capture. A vengeful spirit to defend a family from. His own missing stepfather or his own present stepfather. There was so much on Ravenwood's mind that all he could do was drive and drive into the night, into the city, onto Brooklyn Bridge and back to the island again. The city blazoned, a panorama radiant and proclaiming proudly its world city status. He could only look at it abstractly as his mind worked on all he had seen and experienced in this case.

“Thank you for your recollection, Ms Cevikbas.”

His forward senses knew he had to visit the chemist soon. There was something there that his advance cognition knew was vital to the mystery. He knew it had to do with the lotus-eaters from the *Odyssey*, for some peculiar reason.

Night had fallen, and Officer Thomas Herman settled into his watch after relieving the day shift guardsman. Inspector Stagg still would not say why the Cevikbas family were of the highest priority. Thomas Herman was one of the best guardsmen in the ranks of policemen at central headquarters, having guarded heads of state and visiting dignitaries without mishap.

Just who or what Officer Herman was to guard against was not told by Stagg and his department. There were whispers of the Albasti spirit, an entity similar to the Furies of Greek myth that avenged unpunished mortal crimes. He fully believed in Ravenwood's uncanny abilities, unlike Inspector Stagg. Thomas Herman held that science could not explain everything and there were miracles and occurrences where the laws of science were limited and inapplicable.

He was instructed to keep total watch, meaning that he was not to be distracted in any way. He was only allowed to bring himself and no other objects such as a newspaper that would divert him from his job of protection.

One of his further instructions were to not let any of the Cevikbas family leave their guestroom without Stagg's permission. If any of the three wanted to leave Ravenwood's guestroom, Officer Herman would have to phone Inspector Stagg for his consent. So far only one of the three had done this, and this person had bribed the Officer to keep it hush. The money was a considerable sum, and the envious Officer who wanted the good things in life for him and his girlfriend, accepted the bribe. The officer felt that if Stagg was going to be secretive about the whole affair, then he was entitled to his share of secrecy. Besides, the whole watch seemed safe, and if this family member was in any sudden danger, he would immediately be at this person's side for protection.

This Cevikbas was only away for five minutes and returned to the guestroom, therefore Thomas felt that no harm was done. Possibly this member of the last of the Cevikbas family had to retrieve something from another room in the penthouse.

This happened recently, and the whole apartment was undisturbed, save for sounds of sleeping people, which was usual.

So far he had not seen the Albasti, also known as the Red Mother, appear before him. He had not seen any would-be assassin or assassins targeting the

Cevikbas family.

He settled in again for a long night, expecting to see the sun rise and the Cevikbases still intact. That family kept secrets, this he knew.

It was a late night visit to the chemist, late night being 8 p.m. to Dr. Hubermann. Hubermann expected Ravenwood at just so this time at eight o'clock, sharp and punctual. One of Dr. Hubermann's largest pet peeves was anyone being late. He detested anyone being late for his appointments, which he thought ruined everyone's schedule.

Ravenwood appeared before the hour of eight, his appearance impeccable as always.

"Good evening, Dr. Hubermann," he greeted as he doffed his cap and perched his Tibetan cane on the upholstered chair in front of Hubermann's desk. Ranged round the room were shelves of scientific and chemical apparatuses, along with pharmacopoeias and books of herbalism.

"Dr. Hubermann, can you tell me again the properties of the Ifrit's plaything herb that you found in the teakettle during the last dinner Aladogan Cevikbas had with his family?"

The chemist answered immediately.

"Ifrit's plaything, also known to us here in the West as 'Djinn's plaything,' has the properties of protection from evil, inducing hallucinations, and purification. Ifrit's plaything was administered to everyone who had partaken of the tea at the dinner table that night."

"Which was probable. Yes, it was probable that all three of them had taken the tea. What do you surmise, Dr. Hubermann?" Ravenwood wanted to see what Hubermann's guesswork was.

"Well, the absent father returns all of a sudden after being away for so long from his family here in New York. From the properties of Ifrit's plaything, it is my scientist's opinion that he administered this herb with the intent to protect his family. One of the properties of Ifrit's plaything in addition to purification and the potential for hallucination is protection from evil. There was something evil that Aladogan was protecting the family from."

Ravenwood's shimmery eyesight signaled Dr. Hubermann to continue, for he looked to have more to say.

"It is documented in the scientific literature that Ifrit's plaything is most used for its protection from evil property. The other properties of physical purification, that is, purification of the body and not the purification of the spirit of the person, and the potential for hallucination are not mentioned as frequently as its use for its powerful protection from evil capability."

"And this is documented among the historic Ottoman Empire, the Turkish Empire that lasted for centuries."

"Yes, indeed, Ravenwood. The Turkish Empire has written that the use of Ifrit's plaything was most frequently for the protection from evil that it provides."

Ravenwood thought about what Hubermann had said to him.

He pulled a handkerchief from the front pocket of his jacket.

"Here is a handkerchief that may have something or nothing at all. Can you subject it to your examination tonight? How long will it take for results of your tests?"

Dr. Hubermann looked at the handkerchief with interest. He knew it was part of Ravenwood's case and straightway he found a plastic bag for it to be placed in by Ravenwood.

"If you can wait about an hour, I can subject it to my experiments to see if it tests positive for any substance of chemical value."

"I can wait, Doctor. How obliged I am to you."

Ravenwood waited, hearing the voice of the Nameless One and not knowing if he was really hearing his stepfather or otherwise. He could not be sure that it was the Nameless One. Just as the dervish was, it could be a pretender.

The Eastern patience that he had within him clashed with his impatient Western half. He was very eager to see what the handkerchief contained. He could not help watching as the chemist put it under his microscopes, had applied stains of agents on it, and had looked at it with his scientific scrutiny.

"Well, I'll be," he whispered to himself, although Ravenwood could hear him. "I'll be a mother's gunsel. If it isn't the *Ziziphus lotus!*"

The chemist had motioned Ravenwood to sit back at the desk so he could convey the results of the tests.

"The handkerchief contains remnants of the *Ziziphus lotus* plant, the same plant that was used by the lotus-eaters in Homer's epic adventure known as the *Odyssey*. Odysseus, the hero of the tale, was journeying his way home after the war in Troy in present day Turkey. After the Trojan Horse defeat of the city, he journeyed with his crew on a water voyage back home to Ithaca in Greece. Along the way he encountered many monsters and creatures of fable, including the lotus-eaters.

"Odysseus and his crew landed on the island of the lotus-eaters, a people who consumed the *Ziziphus lotus* plant for their food. The *Ziziphus lotus* plant, according to the epic poem, released these lotus-eaters from the cares of the world. Odysseus himself was so afraid that he would lose his crew to the dangers of the lotus that he literally forced his men back to the ship and away from the island."

"What are the real life properties of *Ziziphus lotus* then? Speaking of modern day uses."

"Today it is used for just that, as a sedative. As in regard to other properties of the *Ziziphus lotus*, there are none besides that. It is just a deep tranquilizing herb."

"Is there anything else I should know about, Dr. Hubermann?"

"That's just it. There are no occult or metaphysical properties of this lotus. It only possesses a tranquilizing effect."

"And you are sure that this is the plant that you speak of?"

"Yes, I vouchsafe it is."

Ravenwood retrieved his handkerchief within the bag and preserved it as evidence for the future. His forward senses knew it would be of use in court.

"As always, thank you for your time and effort, Dr. Hubermann. I will show myself to the door."

Ravenwood nodded in gratitude to the chemist. As he walked to the door, he felt that the events surrounding the Cevikbas family were becoming focused and sharper, his mind connecting the dots and the sequence of events. He was glad to have visited the chemist's office.

Having driven more into the night, in confidence about his thoughts, Ravenwood sunk into the attractions of having clearer roads in the city at this time. He did not return to the penthouse at Sussex until around 1 a.m.

When he returned, he was surprised to see all the lights on in the penthouse. Even more startling was seeing Inspector Stagg, a look of revulsion on his face.

Sterling was standing motionless as he looked at the body. Both he and Stagg were looking at the body, the huge, muscular body that had suffocated.

On the floor with his gun clutched in his hand in a grip of death was Officer Thomas Herman. Around his neck was a red sash, obviously the weapon used to kill the officer. The sash was as red as could be, and Sterling mouthed silently the words "the Red Mother."

For once in his life, Inspector Stagg was not his skeptical self. He did bully Ravenwood with his disbeliefs of all things mystical.

The family was in the guestroom, all three of them frightened.

"The Red Mother was here," cried Hande Cevikbas. The other two were speechless and distressed from gripping fear.

The body was properly prepared for examination as to cause of death, but Ravenwood already knew that Officer Herman was asphyxiated.

A new group of guards was brought to protect the Cevikbas family in Ravenwood's guestroom. Instead of just one guard, there were now eight guards stationed in his penthouse.

He unrolled the scroll on his desk, the *Kurma Purana* that he had brought with him from a year ago in the colorful temple of healing in India. Here in this secreted version of the *Kurma Purana*, an underground and unsurfaced *Kurma Purana* that only those Brahmins knew of, was an unfathomable secret. The existence of this version was only known to Ravenwood and those Brahmin priests that he had seen at the temple. Here in this elegantly written Sanskrit scroll was the method to bring back Aladogan Cevikbas and Officer Thomas Herman if he should need it. There was so much magical command contained in this scroll that he chanced to find in the Hindustani healing temple.

And yet he knew that he did not need to bring back Aladogan Cevikbas or Officer Thomas Herman to get to the center of the maze. He felt that he sufficiently connected the main points of the case and knew mostly what had actually happened. There were still parts of the entire picture that boggled his mind but he knew that these would be resolved in time. He felt that he needed to visit Istanbul to finalize the details from people who knew Aladogan firsthand, and Ravenwood had booked a flight to physically visit the storied city, the city the French conqueror Napoleon once deemed the capital of the world.

The first thing Ravenwood did as he arrived to the penthouse in Sussex after a weeklong visit by real air flight to Istanbul, after being briefed by Sterling that all was as he had left it a week ago, was saunter past the crowd of guards and the Cevikbases to get to the Nameless One's room.

There in the fragrant gloom was the stepfather, his true stepfather, and Ravenwood's coruscating eyesight welled slightly in seeing him again, for now he knew that this truly was his stepfather, the venerable oracle that guided him and brought him wisdom, protection, and peace. He no longer was suspicious that the "resurrected" Nameless One was a pretender.

"Sire! I am back from the city of the West and East! I know all that has happened surrounding the Cevikbas family!"

The hoary-headed mystic, whose shining eyes delighted in his stepson recognizing him again, turned up his sight on Ravenwood.

"My child, I am light of heart now that you have found the truth! Siva, the

Lord of Energy and Time, has made it so. Be blessed knowing that the light shineth on what was formerly abundances of shadow.

"Go forth, my son, and illume these occurrences."

With this, the Nameless One retreated to his deep meditative state as Ravenwood nodded and brought his palms together before his chest and bowed to his mystic father. He looked at the *yantra* next to his stepfather and at once felt his senses expanding, heightening his awareness.

He closed the door to the secluded place, a world away from the panic and hectic flow of the world without. He had the solution prepared and was now about to bring all interested parties together to explain.

Ravenwood gathered the three remaining members of the Cevikbas branch of the Ottoman Empire and Inspector Stagg into his study as evening proceeded. Ravenwood brought in all eight of the policemen that were brought to protect the Cevikbas matriarch and her son and daughter. The family were seated in posh chairs while everyone else stood.

Ravenwood began right away:

"To begin with, let me state the facts of the case.

"There were three murders initially reported of the same man, Aladogan Cevikbas, on the night in question. The first murder was witnessed by Hande Cevikbas at 12:15 a.m., fifteen minutes after midnight. The second murder of the same man was witnessed by Ahmet Cevikbas a while after, at 1:42 a.m. The third murder of the same man was witnessed by Kelebek Cevikbas in the night at 3:11 a.m.

"Hande Cevikbas claims that her husband was neglectful in my private interview with her that night. In fact, all three of you claimed to have hated him for not being present and not for providing for you. I have just returned from visiting his book market in Istanbul and talked with those who knew him at his own market. I had to verify two things: that he was a good man, and that he was a victim of a wasting disease. These things were confirmed. He was suffering from a private disease and did not wish to let his family know. That is why he has not been present for many years, and possibly why his fortune had run out on him. This disease caused a distortion of his face, a hideous symptom. He sought the cure to his disease in Istanbul and felt it would be found there, not here in New York. He felt that by staying in Istanbul he would be healed.

"In the course of his investigations and close study of the occult, he felt that neglecting his family as he did was a crime. It was so tough on all of you that all three of you hated him. As Aladogan started to give in to his disease, he felt that the Albasti, the Red Mother who avenged unpunished crimes, was after him. He became so paranoid and so protective that he would visit here for one last time.

"That night, at dinner, he administered the Ifrit's plaything herb into all of your tea. All of you had taken this tea. This tea has the properties of protection from evil, creating hallucinations, and purification. It was one of these properties that your father wanted to take effect. He wanted the protection from evil property to protect all three of you from the Albasti. You see, your father visited you with good intentions in mind.

"I had the tea kettle checked by the chemist I know, Dr. Hubermann, and he confirmed the traces of Ifrit's plaything. It is mostly used for protection from evil, but again, the other effects of it include hallucinations and purification of the physical body.

"It was shortly after this time that I had my first encounter with the masquerading whirling dervish, the one all three of you claimed to have murdered your father.

"I was transported to the Hagia Sophia of Istanbul, but it was a year ago in time. I had traveled a year back into the past and had traveled oceans without physically moving my body. I was able to bring back a priceless treasure, an Ottoman Empire sword of the 19th century called a "kilij." This treasure was brought by me to this present time, and I had kept it safe in my room here in these apartments.

"All through that time with the first encounter I had with the dervish there in the Hagia Sophia of a year ago, I had never physically left the apartment here. The whole time I was in my bedroom in what seemed to be a natural state of sleep, but in fact I had somehow found a way to travel a year back into the past and to travel as far away as Istanbul without physically moving. As proof of the "journey," I had a kilij sword from one of the museum cases. This "journey" I experienced is also proven real by the articles I found in the *Dispatch* archives of a year ago that reported a kilij sword missing from the museum cases after the glass had been smashed in.

"This first encounter I had no control over, and it brought me to a random place. My mind must have jumped to the iconic Hagia Sophia in Istanbul because I had been hearing of Istanbul all night during my interrogations with the three of you.

"The second encounter I had I felt I had more control of. This time I knew that I needed to be somewhere to find something.

"I had hallucinated that my stepfather, the Nameless One, was murdered here in the apartment, murdered by the whirling dervish just as you three had

...visiting his book market in Istanbul...

witnessed the murder of your father by the same whirling dervish.

"This was a hallucination, as all three of you hallucinated the death of your father, Aladogan Cevikbas."

The mother, the son, and the daughter all reacted differently to this. The mother protested, the son stood up in defiance, and the daughter turned away her gaze.

"In despair and shock, after seeing my father 'killed' by the dervish, the same culprit that 'murdered' your Aladogan, I became unseeable to protect myself. I then went to see if the dervish would find the kilij I had from my first 'journey' to Istanbul, and then we had our second combat.

"This time I had more control. My mind subconsciously picked the place of where I would go. It picked a Hindu holy temple of healing. My thoughts had picked this temple consciously, subconsciously, or a combination of both because I needed to bring back my stepfather from death. That was my reaction at the time and it was an immediate reaction.

"Through this method, I was able to find just what I needed, and I found the cure that would 'resurrect' my stepfather."

Here Ravenwood proceeded to unlock a drawer in his desk. He brought out an antique scroll that looked to be from a faraway place.

"This is physical evidence and proof of my second journey from the past, twelve months ago, of my visit to the Hindustani healing temple. This scroll, the *Kurma Purana*, contains the secret to an elixir that can resurrect those that have gone beyond.

"This is absolute power, and a secret of great magnitude. I now had the power to bring back Aladogan, Officer Herman, and even my own mother and father. I also had the power to bring back the Nameless One.

"But this secret is so closely guarded by the priests of the temple that I had obtained it from. It is so guarded and bolted away that to let it loose on the world would change everything. If there were no consequences to death, if suddenly all the dead could be brought back, this secret would open up all sorts of new challenges and would also challenge the faith of many. Therefore, this healing secret was closely guarded for centuries until I journeyed in and brought it back with me."

He locked the scroll back into his desk and had two policemen guard his desk. Hande was permitted to light a cigarette, and Inspector Stagg joined her in creating a blue-tinged climate. Ahmet had rubbed his left shoulder as if it pained him and Kelebek was in enthrallment with Ravenwood's explanations.

"Technically, a third journey could have been possible, but I was sure that the whirling dervish would follow me and this time, kill me. I was lucky he didn't the first two times. There were things I needed to confirm before I could put all the pieces together, and I had to seek information from those who worked for your father in his occult book market and those who continually work for him.

"Your father was a good man. He was devout, worshipful, and did not want to cut you off. He wanted to protect you from the Albasti that he felt was haunting him for neglecting the three of you.

"There is a power that he is unaware of that he keeps in his library at Hughleigh Towers, the library that holds the most precious of the arcane books of sorcery that he has gathered in his lifetime. This powerful secret is the ability to travel back in time one year to any place of the person's choosing. There were side effects, such as hallucinating murders of those close to you, but the trade-off more than made up for seeing murder.

"This person or persons had discovered this secret power that allowed a travel back of twelve months to a place of his or her own choosing. At first the power was scary in that it first could not be controlled. It would bring the person to a place that was foremost on the person's mind, or foremost on the subconscious of the person's mind. This was how I traveled to Istanbul the first time. Using this power, this undiscovered secret found in Aladogan's library, I subconsciously traveled to the renowned Hagia Sophia of Istanbul since I had been thinking about Istanbul and was facing the murder of a prominent member of a near royal Turkish family.

"Someone had to induce this power within me. I was given no training in this power to travel without moving and to travel a whole calendric year back. During each use of this power, I was able to bring back treasures that were closely guarded, and even a piece of information that could tip the balance of spirituality and rend the concept of death and life forever.

"Yet each time I traveled with this new power, I had to have been exposed to a substance that would allow me to do this. I only traveled twice with this power that was put upon me, and each time I was attacked by the murderous dervish.

"Why would someone or persons unknown want to induce this power on me without my consent? Why would someone want to give the power to me without my permission?"

The crowd was silent and seemed to be as if in the very midst of an ensorcelled telling. They wanted to hear more from Ravenwood.

"The only reason this newfound power was put on me was to murder me and get away with it."

At this, there was a collective intake of breath, with a look of dawning light in some of the uniformed policemen.

"During the both times of my journey, the dervish was there, ready to kill me. I had thankfully defended myself after nearly getting killed both times. To do this, the dervish must also have traveled with me and to have induced this state on himself or herself.

"The hallucination of my stepfather was due to the same exact effects of the Ifrit's plaything. Yet I did not drink any tea that evening. I confirmed with the chemist I know, Dr. Hubermann, that Ifrit's plaything only has the properties of protection from evil, hallucination, and purification. Ifrit's plaything, also called Djinn's plaything here in the West, did not have the power on its own to grant the power to travel twelve months back in time and to transport to anywhere in the world.

"The dervish must have been acquainted with this power for some time, for this person was so experienced in it by now that he or she could find where I was twelve months ago and attack with the hope of killing me. You see, my entering the picture of this whole circumstance was not planned. I, the occult detective, who is renowned in the occult book field, who has written monographs and whole books on the subjects of ancient and metaphysical Far Eastern philosophies, posed a danger to the uncovering of the truth, and therefore I had to be killed.

"Though, let me say again that I did not take any tea during the evening I saw my father being 'killed.' I did not drink anything that evening besides water.

"The Ifrit's plaything had to be brought into my system another way. There were other ways of bringing a substance such as an herb into someone's system without them knowing it. It could be brought in by a sneeze to the eyes. This did not happen to me. It could be sprayed into my nose. This was not done. The herb, Ifrit's plaything, could be put into me by injection. I was not injected with anything that evening.

"So, no tea, no injections, no sprays into the nose, ear, or eye. Nothing was placed under my tongue or between my gums and cheek.

"Yet one of you three brought the herb into my system in a casual way. Still, I wondered why. What was the reason for someone wanting me to hallucinate the murder of the Nameless One? What was the motive for me witnessing that?

"There was no other motive besides wanting the herb present in my system, and I had thought for either a protection from evil effect, a purification of the physical body effect, or to witness the murderous dervish.

"And now we come to the murder of Officer Thomas Herman, the night guard on duty protecting the Cevikbas family. He was killed here in the present by a red sash, strangled to death. Why would someone want to kill the guard that was protecting them from the Albasti and other threats perceivable and unperceivable?

"Inspector Stagg here reported to me that he had found a sizable amount of cash in the apartment shared by Officer Herman and his girlfriend. This cash was probably given to him in bribery for his silence for something. Later on, the murderer regretted what they did and became paranoid, deciding that Officer Herman had too much information to give away.

"Officer Herman was killed because he was bribed to allow a member of the Cevikbas family here out of the guestroom without phoning Inspector Stagg. This knowledge proved to be too threatening to that member of the Cevikbas family, so they decided to kill him and make it look that the Albasti was to blame.

"There was and never has been an Albasti, or Red Mother. The Red Mother was just a decoy from the real happenings of this case."

Inspector Stagg, the skeptic, seemed vindicated in this at least. The three of the Cevikbas family all held inscrutable faces, waiting for Ravenwood to continue.

"Yet Inspector Stagg was guarding this family with a secret service level of protection. I knew they were mildly royal and were a far-flung branch of the Ottomans. Was it because of their near royal status that they were protected?

"No, it wasn't because of their near royalty that the three remaining Cevikbases were given such strong protection. I filed this in my mind as something very noteworthy to the case.

"So now, the kilij that I brought from the Hagia Sophia of a year ago is missing. I know it is in this apartment. Whomever has the kilij is also the same person who stalked me during my travels to Istanbul and the Hindu healing temple."

The three of them still remained there with faces that gave nothing away. They neither looked nervous or wary.

"I would like all of you to remain here as one of the officers searches the guestroom for the kilij."

The Ottoman sword was soon found, having been secreted in the mattress of the bed of the son, Ahmet.

There were gasps in the crowd as all eyes turned on Ahmet, the son and last male of the Cevikbas family.

Ravenwood was given the sword and he held it in his right hand.

"I noticed this evening during my explanations that Mr. Cevikbas here has been rubbing his left shoulder in winces of pain. This is because I had wounded him deeply in his left shoulder with this kilij during my journey to the Indian temple."

The guilty Ahmet did not peep a word as he stopped rubbing his left shoulder. Ahmet was the whirling dervish in disguise, who had so mastered the art of nonphysical travel to a place twelve months into the past.

"Ahmet had to kill me because this was not a part of the plan. He and one other member of the Cevikbases here had to get rid of me in order to keep the secret of nonphysical travel to the past of a year ago safe in their hands."

Ravenwood, his polychromatous gaze shifting with the tranquility of his Eastern training and the competitiveness of his Western mind, held the kilij sword a bit loftier into the air in a sort of victorious stance.

"I noticed that Mr. Cevikbas's palm was very sweaty as I shook hands with him before the first nonphysical travel. I filed this in my brain as a piece of information that could come handy later on.

"I then wiped my perspiration with my handkerchief after my second nonphysical travel when I went to India to retrieve the scroll you just saw.

"I brought this handkerchief to Dr. Hubermann for analysis. He concluded that it was the same herb eaten by the lotus-eaters in Homer's the *Odyssey.* It was the herb *Ziziphus lotus.* We both confirmed the microscopic structure of the herb in his office. This herb, the *Ziziphus lotus*, only has the property to bring tranquility to the taker. It has no power of nonphysical travel to a place of a twelve-month period into the past.

"So, the person had to introduce the *Ziziphus lotus* into my system for some reason, and I knew it was not for its sedative and tranquilizing properties. I have been a tranquil person since my training in the ways of the Far East. But if not for its sedative effects, then why would Ahmet bring the *Ziziphus lotus* into my system?"

Again, the eyes of the room turned to Ahmet, the guilty Ahmet, expecting him to rationalize himself.

He said not a word.

"It was only later as I mused about the case, looking it this way and that, that the combination of the Ifrit's plaything herb with the *Ziziphus lotus* herb caused the person to travel back into the past twelve months to a place of their choosing. *It was the interaction of the two herbs that causes this power.*"

Everyone expressed their look of awe at Ravenwood.

"Of course!" exclaimed one of the police officers, a russet-haired man who was the most attuned to Ravenwood's solutions.

"Yes, the interaction of the two herbs is the secret that causes nonphysical travel to the past of twelve months. This is the secret that was guarded so jealously and secretively by Ahmet and one of the two lady members of the family here.

"So now we know that Ahmet brought the *Ziziphus lotus* herb into my system by applying it onto my skin. I absorbed it topically. There were traces of it as I wiped what I thought was sweat into my handkerchief after the second travel to India where I nearly was killed by Ahmet, the fraudulent dervish here.

"Ahmet had applied the *Ziziphus lotus* while I was sleeping to my hands, one of the areas of the body where skin is the thinnest, after he had bribed Officer Herman and entered my room.

"But then how was the Ifrit's plaything brought into me? Once more, I had not taken any tea or done anything I thought to have brought it into me physically.

"The way Ifrit's plaything entered my system, an herb that interacts and combines with *Ziziphus lotus* to cause this power, was breathing it in.

"I breathed in the Ifrit's plaything through the cigarette smoke of Hande Cevikbas herself."

At this, she stopped her cigarette and crushed it with the heel of her boot on the floor.

She showed no resistance.

"You are right, as ever, Man with Zultanite Eyes."

"You and your son Ahmet discovered the secret of nonphysical travel into the past for one calendrical year. You had to keep it a secret because it was something that could possibly bring you all out of the coming poverty you were facing. You both found this secret in Aladogan's library.

"The real power of this secret is obtaining secrets. Infiltrating behind enemy lines. Finding inside information that could be used to tip the balance of power on a worldwide scale.

"The kilij sword was a hint at the real power of the secret of the two-herb interaction. It was on finding the scroll in the Hindu healing temple that I then eventually pieced together the enormous power of what you both had found in Aladogan's library. This secret I have now of resurrection will be kept a secret as I will return the scroll to the temple whose location only I know of, as I will return this kilij to the Hagia Sophia."

He placed the kilij in the safekeeping of one of the uniformed guards by his desk. Ravenwood also instructed a further search of the guestroom, which turned up more of Hande's cigarettes and a small vial of *Ziziphus* herb in the pockets of Ahmet's clothing.

"Please enter these as evidence, Inspector Stagg."

Stagg remained quiet, surprisingly so, at the confirmation of a supernatural way to travel to places of a year ago, all without moving.

"A power like this could cause anyone to travel anywhere into the past of twelve months to infiltrate enemy lines. Germany, for example, could travel to the past of twelve months here to obtain secret American plans and schematics for weaponry. Italy could do the same, and so could Japan. Whomever was the highest bidder could win any war in this way. This is why this secret has to be kept in the dark."

He let those following let this information sink in and its implications and applications to warfare thought upon.

"The secret service level of protection was not to protect the Cevikbas family," continued Ravenwood. "It was to protect them from getting out of custody and selling their secret to the highest bidder."

Inspector Stagg's gruff voice gave a confirming sound. Here he began to explain his reason for secrecy.

"I was instructed by the U.S. Government after Aladogan's murder," spoke Inspector Stagg, "that there was something that had to be protected tactically and militarily, and that I had to keep the whole matter hush, even from my own department. I had to keep it under wraps from Officer Thomas Herman, who was killed because Ahmet had bribed him so he could get out of the guestroom without a phone call to me."

"Yes, Inspector Stagg," replied Ravenwood. "The application by Ahmet of the *Ziziphus lotus* to my skin took only a few minutes, perhaps five minutes, and he went back to the guestroom with only Officer Thomas Herman knowing. Ahmet then applied the two-herb interaction to himself in the guestroom to locate me in my nonphysical travel and try to murder me again as the pretend dervish.

"Later on, Hande and Ahmet, mother and son, had strangled the huge officer with a red sash with their combined strength. They wanted it to look as if the Red Mother was responsible. This was done while Kelebek, innocent Kelebek, was asleep."

Kelebek played with her jewelry after she moved her chair some inches apart from her mother and brother.

"Kelebek was never a part of the plan. They had to trick Kelebek into witnessing the murder of their father.

"To protect the secret, they had to kill the mostly absent father because they knew that if he had ever gotten hold of the two-herb combination secret, then the riches and wealth it would bring to them would be out of their hands forever. They never knew that the reason why the caring Aladogan was gone for most of the time was because of his terminal disease that he didn't want to trouble his family with. It mattered not in the end, since he was killed at the hands of his own wife and son.

"The earlier incidents of the 12:15 a.m. and 1:42 a.m. murder were indeed witnessed by the mother and son respectively, but they were hallucinations by the Ifrit's plaything that they had taken in tea given by Aladogan Cevikbas during dinner. Or perhaps they were both so already used to the hallucinations brought by Ifrit's plaything that they made up their testimony of seeing Aladogan's murder that night. Ahmet and Hande had experienced these type of Ifrit's plaything hallucinations before since they had tested the Ifrit's plaything and *Ziziphus lotus* interaction secret on themselves already.

"Now was their chance to have a witness from their own family and to do away with Aladogan Cevikbas to keep what they discovered in his occult library a secret.

"Kelebek later recalled and told me that she had seen her father murdered not once, but twice in the evening. She was so shocked at the occurrences during my first interview with her that she had not recalled this until later.

"The first murder she saw was a hallucination brought on by the Ifrit's plaything she took at tea during dinner, served by her father for the purposes of protecting his family from evil. It is pure coincidence that he used Ifrit's plaything, the other partner in the two-herb interaction secret.

"Son and mother then set up the real murder of Aladogan Cevikbas. Kelebek was awakened by a strange sound in the night made by them and walked to the library, and what she saw was not hallucination. There she saw her brother in a whirling dervish costume kill their father with repeated stabs to the chest while her mother watched from behind, waiting for her to swoon. Once Aladogan was killed and Kelebek had fainted, they brought Kelebek to her bedroom and hoped that when she regained consciousness that she would confuse the two murders she had seen of her father to be one murder.

"That is the explanation behind the three reports of murder of the same man in the evening. Yet the real murder was only witnessed by Ms. Kelebek Cevikbas here."

Ms. Kelebek's tears welled as she stared into the betrayers' faces, her own mother and her brother.

"All of this, for money?" was all Kelebek whispered.

"Don't you know, child," answered back Hande, her mother, "that there will soon be a war in Europe and Asia. Just look at the news. Germany has taken back the Rhineland and Japan is menacing the East. If we sold our two-herb interaction secret to the highest bidder in this game of world domination, then our troubles of being on the street would be over. We would live in wealth and luxury again and never have to worry."

"Did you really think it would come to that?" retorted an offended Kelebek. "We would not be on the street. We would have been kept in the hands of the government here."

Hande had more to say, turning to Ravenwood.

"I congratulate you, Man with the Zultanite Eyes. You have uncovered me and my son. But what of the secret now? Everyone here knows it, including you, Inspector Stagg, and all of the numerous officers here of the police."

"It will all be kept a secret," replied Ravenwood. "In fact, these are not members of Inspector Stagg's police headquarters. After the murder of Officer Thomas Herman, the guards stationed here in this apartment have all been government agents. They are all secret service members of the U.S. government who will keep this two-herb interaction a secret indefinitely."

"Such a secret, if given in the wrong hands, such as Italy, Japan, Germany, or any of the agitating powers, could tilt the balance in the upcoming war," said Inspector Stagg. "This secret will be kept safe by Ravenwood, the government, and all three of you here. Mrs. Cevikbas and Mr. Cevikbas will be kept in custody indefinitely for murder and to keep their secret secure. Ms. Cevikbas, though entirely innocent of the matter, will work with us in the upcoming war in our intelligence agencies. We will beseech her to do so for it is much better than us keeping her under lock and key to keep the secret from falling into German or Japanese hands. This will serve to bring a better legacy to the Cevikbas line."

"Do you agree to work with us, Ms. Cevikbas?" asked one of the secret service officers.

A higher duty, a calling, was roused in Kelebek Cevikbas. A sense of clearing the Cevikbas name and being a key ally in the war to come on the side of the U.S. would be a destiny that she found compelling.

"Yes, I will work for my country and will do my work in all fidelity for the upcoming war to make sure that good will prevail. Just as my father was a good person, I am also willing to demonstrate principle and integrity."

She stood up from her chair and went to the side of the secret service members and away from the side of her mother and brother.

"I have only one question," replied a normally cynical Inspector Stagg, who knew what the stakes were this time. "Where is the body of Aladogan Cevikbas?"

"I traveled with it and hid it in Istanbul of a year ago," responded Ahmet. "I will show you where it is."

"And how did U.S. Intelligence know about the secret that my son and I discovered?" enquired Hande.

"Our operations have our ways," said one of the secret service members.

Ravenwood watched as the mother and son were led away from the apartments, and Kelebek stayed behind and chatted with her new colleagues.

Inspector Stagg told Ravenwood that he still believed in rational explanations for such things as nonphysical travel, but he wisely chose to keep these matters to himself, knowing how sensitive the information was that was to be guarded. Instead of pestering Ravenwood, he offered to give

Ravenwood some commendation from his department, some medal for valor in the landscape of looming war.

Ravenwood thought about the honor, but mostly thought about how his life had returned back to the way it should be, the comfortable way of life with his stepfather and his meditations and books. He would never use the herbal secret again, in reverence to his country. His iridescent eyes shining, he thought he would visit the archives of the *Dispatch* again for some amusement after the case. The supercharged roadster brought him there full throttle as he took in the evening air of his city, gratified, with a smile overflowing on his face.

THE END

A DEVIL BY ANY OTHER NAME

by Michael F. Housel

"We're at absolute wit's end," the middle-aged woman in high-tiered, auburn hair and shiny-black mink spewed at Chief Inspector Horatio Stagg. "That pompous, petulant fiend has mesmerized her. We've been left with no practical means to severe the spell. Someone of authority must intervene—someone like you, Inspector Stagg."

Stagg tossed a roasted peanut into his mouth, rolled it about his tongue and coughed. The damn woman got on his last nerve. He thumped his chest and cleared his throat. "Seems your daughter needs a specialized sort of help, Mrs. Cherub."

"And you, my dear sir, are the latest in that ongoing line, which I do hope has now come to an end. We went so far as to hire a hypnotist, I'll have you know, but even he failed to break what this monster implanted."

"Hypnotist? Sounds gimmicky. Maybe you should pursue a referred psychologist." Stagg reached into the bowl and shot another nut past his teeth, chewed fast and swallowed, hoping the flavor might overrule the woman's unpalatable obstinacy. "I hear some are quite skilled at what they do."

"The hypnotist was referred by a psychologist, and the psychologist referred by a social worker who, in turn, our general practitioner recommended. Can you appreciate our exasperation, Chief Inspector?"

"So, if these highbrows were unable to assist, Mrs. Cherub, what would you have me do? I realize your desperation, but you said your daughter is twenty-one. That means she can make her own decisions, rub elbows with whomever she wishes. That also means she can reject her family, sad though that may sound. If this fellow—this eccentric, for a lack of a better term—is causing no adversity beyond your daughter distancing herself from you, there's no crime committed."

"But a crime has been committed, Inspector. The man has stripped our dear daughter of her free will."

Stagg groaned. "As I said, I'd like to help, but unless you can show me something substantial, that this, uh, Mortimer Pringle has done something truly egregious that can justify an arrest or head to a court of law, my hands are tied." He smiled, hoping to take the edge off. "Maybe look at it this way. This Pringle may be no Little Lord Fauntleroy, but perhaps if you gave him a chance, you'd come to appreciate him. Ask him to dinner, find out how much he earns with the Svengali gig and decide from there if he's right or wrong for you daughter. Who knows? You might find he's not quite the ne'er-do-well you presume him to be."

Mrs. Cherub quavered. "How dare you, Inspector Stagg. For one, what would the neighbors say if he were to pay us a call, with the way he dresses and all? He never sheds that ridiculous satyr suit—goes so far as to wear it in public, don't you know? And of all conspicuous places, Gwendoline arranged for us to meet him in the park not long ago, though it was obvious the cretin was pulling the strings, if only to add insult to injury."

Stagg glanced at the publicity photos on his desk and focused on the one to his far left: a man sporting a skull cap, horns, pointy beard, with arms folded over his robed chest like some high, dark chieftain.

"The satyr looks more like a standard, Trick or Treat devil to me. Shoot, one of my men wore pretty much the same get-up at the precinct's masquerade ball last season."

Mrs. Cherub groaned. "Mr. Pringle has upgraded his semblance since then. It's more extravagant now, more, well, unsettling. If you took the time to scrutinize the photographs, you'd see how he's progressed—indeed, an incontestable demon at this point."

"Ah, devil, demon, satyr, it's all the same, nothing more than old, carny hijinks. Listen, these magic-show goofs always make the rounds. They recruit pretty girls as a distraction. It's par for the course. They all do it, from top-drawer performers like Harry Blackstone, right down to the seedy, midway hacks. At worse, the lower-echelon ones are just two-bit swindlers. Nothing to get unhinged about."

"There's nothing two-bit in the way this man has swindled Gwendoline's cognition. In fact, he's swindling my entire family of its sanity. You can't possibly know the pressure he's put us under. Alfie—my poor husband— is beside himself—can't concentrate at work and paces all hours of the night. Our dear son is no better. He believes his sister is to become the veritable Bride of Satan."

"All right, Mrs. Cherub, I get the gravity of the situation. Perhaps investigative delving is warranted." He locked his fingers and with authoritative tonality, continued, "There's a special agent, an acquaintance who I've enlisted for, uh, some of our unique cases."

Mrs. Cherub arched her eyebrow. "Agent, you say?"

Stagg smirked. "Ravenwood ring a bell?"

"Ravenwood?" The glint in her eye hinted recognition. "My heavens, you don't mean that occult detective from the papers?"

"The one and only. Many do place stock in him."

Mrs. Cherub glared. "And do you, Inspector? Some of your early quotes, as I recall, imply a lack of faith. In fact, now that I think of it, your relationship seems more derived from a Hildegard Withers/Oscar Piper routine than one of earnest mutuality."

Stagg certainly did not consider Ravenwood a charlatan, though he doubted the man possessed genuine, mystical attributes. He perceived Ravenwood more a crème de la crème magician. Whatever his aptitude or label, the "occultist" could decipher clues better than any gumshoe. In this regard, Stagg presumed Ravenwood could sniff out any balderdash practitioner, for it did take one to know one.

"Withers and Piper, you say? A swell comparison, Mrs. Cherub, but I assure you, despite whatever insinuations you may have culled, I've utmost confidence in Ravenwood. Indeed, he's considered good—real good—at what he does and for good reason."

Mrs. Cherub nibbled a nail, though the sway of her hips implied acceptance. "I can't help but be wary, Inspector, and yet."

Stagg shrugged. "Really, at this point, what do you have to lose, ma'am? This could be the alternate avenue you been seeking."

Mrs. Cherub tapped her foot, pretending to ruminate upon the matter. "Oh, very well. So, when might I meet your clairvoyant confidant?"

Stagg snatched another peanut, tossed it toward his mouth, only to have it bounce off his bottom lip. He watched it hit the floor and sighed. "Tell you what, Mrs. Cherub. I'll escort you to his residence right here and now. He lives at the luxurious Sussex Towers, a meager hop and skip from this very locale."

A solemn aura occupied the Nameless One's chamber: no candle light or fragrant flow.

"You feel it," the Nameless One whispered, his thin, loin-clothed frame looking rubbery and slumped at the chamber's center. "You sense a pressing solidity, of a concern that could be too hard to budge."

"Yes, sire," Ravenwood replied, "all too well. The cause?"

"There are times when things are not as spiritual as one might wish. Sometimes, reality can become an all-consuming thrust, as was the case when that ferocious feline nearly took my life those many years ago—and would have, if not for your courageous father. Oh, yes, the blood and bone of reality can shackle all perception, leaving only fear and doubt in its wake. You recognize this, do you not, my son?"

Ravenwood nodded.

"Excellent. You are in tune."

A knock echoed from the living room. Ravenwood heard his valet, Sterling, hasten to it, eliciting his brisk, British accent, "Coming, coming."

"Stagg," Ravenwood deduced.

"Yes," the guru purred, "and he is with someone in need."

"Someone weighed by reality."

The Nameless One grinned. "A reality wrapped in fantasy, perhaps the worst kind."

Without further ado, Ravenwood exited the chamber, just as Sterling was about alert his master of the visitors, but then the manservant paused, watching his employer stride past him.

Stagg's smugness was palatable, but there was a spark of carefree confidence behind it. His companion, however, projected urgency through her taut gaze.

"Ah, Chief Inspector Horatio," Ravenwood acknowledged with exaggerated glee and shook his hand. "How nice of you to call." He gestured at the two, his scrutiny settling on the woman. "And who is your charming companion?"

"You're the one with the insight, Ravenwood," Stagg snapped with a wink. "You tell us."

"You well know that even I can't absorb all that's hurled at me. I'd end up in an asylum otherwise." Ravenwood gave the lady a bow and in so doing, crept closer to her essence. "Hmmm. I sense you have a problem, one stored beneath this your angelic aura—and a name that matches that aura. Please do share it, Mrs. Cherub."

"Gertrude. Cherub," she added, her gaze meeting his, as she clumped her pocketbook's long loops with unconscious vigor, impressed that he had discerned her name. All the same, she was most pleased to see him. Ravenwood knew this beyond any doubt, and yet she harbored a hesitation within her tension, something that tainted the surface cause of the call.

She cracked a smile, noticing how his eyes had dipped from blue to gray.

Stagg cleared his throat. "Uh, Mrs. Cherub claims some fellow has been influencing her daughter in an adverse way. He's one of those carny, sleight-of-hand types and—"

"And naturally, Inspector," Ravenwood interjected, "you believe that since I possess the same sleight-of-hand ilk, I might offer some insight as to his methodology." Ravenwood tapped the woman's pocketbook. "May I have a look, Mrs. Cherub? You have photographs, I believe. If I could touch them, scan them, I might gain a deeper vantage into the circumstance."

"Oh—oh, yes," she trilled, further flattered by his intuition, watching his eyes then shift to an earnest brown. She removed the photos. "Here you are.

The culprit uses these to peddle his propaganda. He's responsible for my dear Gwendoline's muddled mind." She shivered. "Such an obnoxious man—if he can be called a man. The shyster goes by the name—"

"Mortimer Pringle." Ravenwood stated. "His name is on the lower border of each photograph, along with a fanciful proclamation." He flipped through the set of images and with mocking intonation read, "The Great Mortimer Pringle, Practitioner of Devilish Delights and All Things Real and Ethereal: Embodiment of Man, God and Devil, Necromancer of the Naked Truth."

"Blasphemous—and as such, arrogant." Mrs. Cherub's contemptuous aura made Ravenwood wince.

"I won't argue that, Mrs. Cherub. His pomposity bleeds through in spades." Ravenwood fanned the photos between his index finger and thumb, making them aligned. "However, is it simple ballyhoo or something of dark consequence?"

Ravenwood knew the answer, of course. Pringle's appearance went beyond mere masquerading. For one, his look had evolved, commencing with an effective, but amateurish, facial build-up, but over time, the details blended more so into his skin, in a way that may have made even the late, great Lon Chaney envious.

"He's definitely grown adept at his craft. In the initial image, the horns are smooth, small, nondescript, strapped by a band along the hairline. There's also a gleam about the bases...spirit gum, I presume. These traces are far less visible in the progressing photos, while in the final entry, the protuberances are curled, implying that they may have sprouted from his skull. The bases are heavily fringed—putty, I would surmise, but then again..."

"What's the big deal?" Stagg asked. "Make-up is make-up. He's a skilled phony. No revelation there."

Ravenwood focused on Mrs. Cherub, whose nervousness had grown more acute, leading him to question her sincerity. "Mr. Pringle gave these photos to your daughter?"

Mrs. Cherub shrugged. "I suppose it was his strange way to impress her, perhaps."

"Well, by sharing his progression, he also shares his deceit. He's just a man in disguise. That could imply honesty."

"Ridiculous," Mrs. Cherub snorted. "There's nothing honest about Mortimer Pringle."

Ravenwood glanced once more at the last image. "You're likely correct, Mrs. Cherub, but it's a matter of how far our charlatan wishes to extend the charade. Run-of-the-mill photographs can only exude so much. Still, I can infer that Mr. Pringle does take pride in his appearance: for all intents and purposes, as good a transformation from 'man, god, devil' as one might find."

Ravenwood shifted the photos atop one another and returned them to her.

"So, you agree," Mrs. Cherub pressured, "that his intent is devious, perhaps criminal? Please understand, he has left Gwendoline as starry-eyed as a ghost. She speaks mechanically, if she speaks at all, and the words never seem to be her own. She's more a puppet, a doll than a living entity."

Ravenwood's orbs rolled to an inquisitive hazel. "He may, indeed, be slipping her subliminal signals to harness her behavior. However, his profession does require a certain degree of charisma, albeit a unique sort in this instance. It could be that the young lady is no-more-or-less awestruck to a fault. At this point, I can only speculate. Nevertheless, if he is toying with your daughter's mind, then that does make the situation troubling and therefore, criminal."

"I trust you will tend to this for me—for Gwendoline and my family," Mrs. Cherub implored, "hopefully halt it before it worsens, if it can possibly grow any worse."

Ravenwood offered his consent with a fluid bow.

"You will be well compensated, naturally," Mrs. Cherub assured him.

"In this instance, my lady, the simple chance to investigate the particular dynamics will suffice." He turned to Stagg. "To get a firm handle on Pringle, I must meet him, of course, and to have one of authority in my presence would prove beneficial."

"I'll be right at your side," Stagg confirmed. "Mrs. Cherub mentioned that Pringle is performing tomorrow night at the Wilkes Theatre. Maybe you can drill him before the show."

"Or after," Ravenwood suggested. "It would be better if I observed the entirety of his act before interrogation."

Mrs. Cherub looked pleased. "Gwen will be involved in the production, abetting Pringle's shenanigans. She phoned us to confirm, mechanically, that is."

"Very well. I'll tend to the tickets." Ravenwood's pupils brewed an encouraging emerald. "The Wilkes Theatre is smaller than most school auditoriums and by tradition, modestly lit. There will be little more than a minor glare from the stage's standpoint. I'd imagine that Pringle and any of his cohorts would as such spot you without much trouble. Your daughter's reaction to your presence, if any, would prove edifying. It might, that is, relay the degree of her mentor's influence."

Mrs. Cherub smirked. "I must say, I do like where this is going, Mr. Ravenwood."

"As do I, Mrs. Cherub." Ravenwood looked to Sterling. "Would you be so kind to call the Wilkes to verify the showtime? I'd like us to get there early, if only so that I may scan the atmosphere, but by no means should we arrive too early. A casual semblance would prove a wise stratagem. Oh, and by the way, Mrs. Cherub, I take it that your daughter has joined Pringle on stage prior to this, that this is not her first venue with him."

"I believe it was only once prior, at an engagement somewhere in Pennsylvania. She claimed it was for a charitable cause, though I much doubt it."

"Do you recall the establishment's name?"

"I'm afraid not, Mr. Ravenwood. However, I believe she mentioned Phoenixville in her robotic reply."

At a small, adjacent table, Sterling readied for the table phone.

"Did you get that, Sterling—Phoenixville, Pennsylvania."

"Yes, sir. I'll see what information I can gather after I call."

Ravenwood gave Stagg a shrewd sideways glance. "Ah, the initial phase is in motion. A good feeling, wouldn't you say, Inspector?"

"Sure," Stagg concurred, though was perturbed that Ravenwood had paved the basics before he could. "Of course, nothing counts until we conduct a proper inquiry. So, you're confident you can crack this nut, eh, Ravenwood?"

The mystic looked to Mrs. Cherub and answered. "I most certainly do. In little time, we'll have Mrs. Cherub's conundrum tucked and settled."

No sooner had Stagg and Mrs. Cherub departed, Ravenwood returned to the Nameless One's chamber.

"And so, your assessment, sire?"

"The situation feels pedestrian on the surface and yet, something profound stirs below."

"It rests not so much in the man's disguise, but his motive."

"Yes," the Nameless One murmured. "Per his charade, he harbors foolishness, and in foolishness, there is always danger."

"Mrs. Cherub has good reason to fear, then."

"She does, but as you have stated, the conundrum will be remedied, though it may take more time than you suspect."

"No matter. This isn't the first time we've wrestled a devil. For certain, Pringle's true cause, whatever it may be, shall be exposed, as will Mrs. Cherub's."

"Ah, the famous occult magician," Alfie Cherub chirped, his thick, white moustache flapping. He had been waiting for Ravenwood with his wife and pudgy, teenage son. They were garbed with prim and proper rigidity, anxious and eager. "I'm glad to meet you, sir. Gertrude is impressed to no ends, though I doubt hocus-pocus is the antidote. By the way, I do fancy your walking stick—goes well with your occupation, but the Stetson, not so much. A top hat would be better suited. Still, I appreciate whatever psychological means you can employ to solve our problem." Mr. Cherub extended his hand. "You obviously know what tricks work better than I."

"Good gracious," Mrs. Cherub exclaimed. "He's not a magician, Alfie. I've told you how many times already?"

Ravenwood gripped the man's hand and shook. "It's all right. Many believe that my techniques are propelled by common, stage trickery. No offense taken."

"Who you kidding?" said Stagg, sneaking up from behind, tipping his hat, while pushing his other arm past Ravenwood's, so that Mr. Cherub could seize it. "Trust me, sir, humbuggery has its place, but good old-fashioned police work is what solves matters in the end, whether on my end or Ravenwood's."

"And so, you're the precinct detective," Mr. Cherub acknowledged, "that chief inspector whose name populates the papers—Horatio Stagg. I do appreciate your participation. It does lend tonight's strategy validity." He gave Ravenwood a sorrowful glance. "My apologies. It's just that—"

"He understands," Mrs. Cherub seethed with a roll of her eyes. "Really, how many times, Alfie? How many?"

Mr. Cherub cracked a grin and pointed to the flaxen-haired youngster at his side. "This is our son, Alfred. We call him Junior. I'll have you gentlemen know, he's a real, cynical chip off the ol' block." Mr. Cherub gave his son a proud pat on the head.

The young man blushed and offered his hand to Ravenwood and Stagg, who reciprocated.

"These formalities are holding us up," Mrs. Cherub huffed. "A dozen people have entered. Why must we dawdle? I, for one, am most anxious to get the proceedings underway."

Ravenwood tucked his stick under his arm, pulled out his wallet and yanked some bills. "Of course, we should head in, and you're all covered. The ticket desk is straight ahead, right beyond the front doors."

As they proceeded into a dowdy alcove, a couple of crinkled burlesque posters beamed from the far wall. Beneath them was a small desk with a large white bowl atop it, next to which stood a ghoulish-looking vendor, his hair parted in eerie precision, wearing a long, dark-blue robe with white, crescent-moons upon it.

"Get a load of that goon," Stagg said from the side of his mouth.

Ravenwood grinned and approached the dreary figure, with the Cherubs following. The man exuded a judgmental glare, his focus on Junior.

"Five, please," Ravenwood requested, snapping his bills.

"No set fee or stubs," the ghoulish man grumbled, pointing to the bowl, his gaze still glued to the boy. "We accept donations—whatever one wishes, before or after the presentation." He cleared his throat. "However, we do not encourage children to attend our events. Mr. Pringle's content is mature and often intense. This is referenced in our advertisements, if one cares to discern the fine print, though word of mouth is our biggest advocacy." The man cracked a smile. "Mr. Pringle's reputation does tend to make the rounds."

"Come on," Stagg chortled. "It can't be any worse than those slapdash striptease acts they perform here. I mean, the boy isn't a baby. I'm sure he can handle a little spook show."

The man looked about, regarding those who milled in the sidelines, some of whom were dressed in sinister fashion as himself, while the majority of folks were just curious patrons, who eyed the large "Man, God and Devil" canvas that was propped on a flimsy, rear easel. "I'll require Mr. Pringle's approval. Please, if you'd excuse me." The man headed toward a side door and paused to glance back at Ravenwood. "If anyone should inquire, I'd appreciate you explaining our donation policy."

"I'd be happy to oblige," Ravenwood consented, though he had no intention of doing so.

Junior tugged as this father's sleeve. "I'm not afraid. Like the inspector says, I can handle a spook show." He swallowed hard. "Really, I can."

"Perhaps, this wasn't such a wise choice, after all," Mr. Cherub remarked, squinting at Ravenwood. "It might be better if you and Inspector Stagg tend to it from here." He grabbed Junior's arm and motioned to his wife.

"Wait a moment," Mrs. Cherub scolded. "Mr. Ravenwood has gone out of his way to assist us, and we shall see his plan through, no matter the unpleasantness." She then whispered to Ravenwood, "You don't think it will be too debaucherous for the boy, do you?"

Stagg gave Ravenwood an inquisitive glance.

"All will be fine," Ravenwood assured,

The ghoulish gent returned. "Mr. Pringle does not object to the young man's presence, leaving it to his guardians' discretion. He takes no responsibility, however, for any adverse outcome."

Mr. Cherub twisted his mustache and looked to his wife. "I still think this will prove awkward, considering his sister's involvement, but if Junior feels up to it."

"Sister?" the ghoulish man inquired.

"Yes," Ravenwood explained, "we're not here so much to see Mr. Pringle perform, but rather the lovely Miss Gwendoline. I've been led to believe that she's one of Mr. Pringle's assistants and open to having her family attend the presentation."

The man raised a finger and started again for the door, but Ravenwood tapped his shoulder with his stick, and when the man turned, Ravenwood rolled its tip with quick, hypnotic flair. "Is there a problem, sir? Surely, something as subsidiary as a family's attendance would not alter Mr. Pringle's decision, would it?"

"I appreciate your eagerness," the ghoulish man replied with a wince, his eyes widening as the tip slowed to a stop, "But I still believe it would be better to—"

"Let us enter." Ravenwood lowered his stick and tossed his bills into the bowl. His eyes locked upon the man's, changing their hue several times over.

The man nodded and stepped to the side.

"Thank you, sir. We appreciate your compliance." Ravenwood motioned Stagg and the Cherubs to the auditorium doors.

They squinted as they entered the chaired expanse, for the lighting was low, as were the patches of curtain that adorned not only the stage, but portions of wall.

Stagg twirled his hand. "Your pick, Ravenwood."

Ravenwood pointed his stick to the middle row. "There we go, not too far in, not too far out, just within casual view."

Stagg wasted no time in swaggering to his seat, though the Cherubs lingered, anticipating Ravenwood's genial lead.

"I know this may be difficult, perhaps even embarrassing," Ravenwood told them as he led the way, "but you must trust the process, see it through. There's no doubt something odd about this set-up, beyond its dubitable, charitable con, something deeper, darker. I know you sense it as well, but we will stir the pot, rattle the chains to get what we want."

"Be assured, we're in league with you," said Mrs. Cherub, glancing back at her husband and son, who reciprocated their conviction with firm nods. "Do what is necessary, Mr. Ravenwood. It's for Gwen's sake—for all of our sakes. We will be just fine."

They proceeded to their seats, Ravenwood positioning himself next to Stagg, placing his hat on his lap, his stick between his knees. The Cherubs took theirs opposite the former, with Junior snug between them. They had an excellent view of the stage and would not be missed by anyone from that standpoint, no matter the glare, which then emitted a slight strobing effect.

Ravenwood discerned that the pulsation stemming from the stage's inner edge, which was hooked by a subtle string of cupped bulbs, not part of the typical furnishing. He glanced behind and spotted larger, shadowed variants latched along the back wall, fronted by cold, protruding lenses, not yet activated.

Stagg rubbed his eyes, "I'm getting a damn headache." He nudged Ravenwood. "Why test the damn lights now? Damn amateurish, if you ask me."

"Couldn't agree with you more, Inspector. However, I'd hesitate to call Pringle an amateur. I can only presume the lightshow is a hypnotic prelude, a means to wedge us into the necessary mindset."

"Hypnotic prelude?" Mrs. Cherub interjected. "I don't like the sound of that."

"Nor do I," Ravenwood replied with a wry grin, "but for better or worse that's my assessment. I don't suppose we need worry much. I've witnessed similar techniques: a common enough way to transmit underlying messages at séances and the like. The process is designed to make spectators more inclined to believe in the shenanigans that unfold. Of course, nothing that Mr. Pringle administers will unhinge us. After all, we're immune to any such nonsense, aren't we?"

The Cherubs smiled, while Stagg mumbled and again rubbed his eyes.

Meanwhile, more people flowed in, and soon an impatient hush fell. A thin, spectacled man in a disheveled suit then clicked his way from the left, holding a violin. He centered himself before the front row. A beam descended upon him. He cleared his throat, positioned the violin against his neck and began to play, accompanied by a sudden spurt of fanning, multicolored rays.

His notes were discordant though purposeful in orchestration, swaying with each synchronized beam.

Bits of coded messages floated among the rays, which Ravenwood discerned with deft clarity, while he realized others could only digest such on an unconscious level. Within the intersecting light, such brazen words as REGRET, BETRAYAL, DESPAIR and DOOM flashed, along with sweeping billows of INDULGE, REBEL, REJECT.

As the lightshow lengthened, the stage's faded curtains parted, jerking along with several yanks, though the lack of fluidity seemed to mesh with the violinist's ensuing plucks and squeals.

For a moment, the stage remained dim, with little more than a hint of throwback light, which upon occasion kissed the tip of a chair, its arched wicker strands flanked by a flicker of crimson and the flanking crest of an apparent, high collar and lo and behold, a foreboding figure seated, rigid but projecting an omniscient glint.

The beams then highlighted five Roman pillars. The violinist elevated his notes as a simulated smoke spread, revealing the hazy hint of a young female before each pillar: hair tiered upward, barefoot, their curves swathed in makeshift gowns twirled of gauze, their porcelain skin bleeding through the fabric with libidinous command.

A ribald guffaw rose from the man in the chair, drowning the violist's chords. Through the drawled laugh, the man's enveloping arrogance proved so fulsome that Ravenwood may have grown nauseous from it, if not for his ability to block the offensive charge. Alas, his swift shielding also blunted his means to consume the extent of the man's aura, and auras were so essential to ascertain an opponent.

As the man's guffaw petered to a snorting snicker, Ravenwood noticed the audience had become enthralled by his presence, their shoulders swaying to the music.

Stagg managed to shake his off and elbowed Ravenwood. "So, that's him—Pringle, right?"

Ravenwood winced at the obviousness. "I'd place a hardy bet on it."

"Heck, I'm beginning to understand Mrs. Cherub's concern."

Ravenwood found the remark amusing, despite his rising agitation. He realized that Pringle's unblinking bevy was anchored in a collective stupor. Now, which of these ladies was Gwendoline? Mrs. Cherub had not said whether she was a blonde, brunette or redhead. Ravenwood settled back, folded his fingers and focused.

The violinist elicited a sharp, final reverberation and then clicked from sight. This left their sinister host to stand, his horned crown and crimson cloak better illuminated as the light curled up from the audience and settled on the stage.

Gasps and nervous snickers ensued, as the light expanded, making the women more visible.

Ravenwood's eyes fell upon the forefront lady: a blonde, indeed. She remained rigid, yet due to Ravenwood's mental draw, he managed to jostle her stare. He then nurtured her attention enough to harbor a brush of trust and with this—and the assistance of his soothing, gray eyes—influenced her to engage her family.

"Oh, Gwen," Mrs. Cherub muttered, catching her daughter's shifting orbs, while unconsciously attempting to block Junior's view. "Poor, poor, foolish girl."

The young woman gave her mother a meticulous scan, before moving on to her father, who quaked at her scrutiny, and from there, she settled on her brother, who stiffened with curious, though dumbfounded unease.

Once more, Stagg elbowed Ravenwood. "Say—I bet that's her, the daughter." He then gave the young woman a salacious once-over. "Real cutie."

The women were all, in truth, worthy of Stagg's categorization. Ravenwood not only wondered how deep Pringle's influence was over them, but how he had initiated it. He refocused on Gwendoline in hopes of finding the answer, but the demon disrupted the intent.

"Ladies and gentlemen," he boomed in a voice that was smooth yet piercing, "you are about to witness an allegorical tale, one of the end of days." The lights coddled Pringle, revealing the spiraling heft of his horns, his protruding brow, which appeared at once primitive and profound. "And I request that you not dismiss what you see as mere Vaudevillian tease." He raised his long-nailed index finger like a dagger. "Contained within this presentation is a prophetic warning, to which you must take heed." His nostrils flared as his mustache and goatee shifted from side to side. "Understand, my friends, we are doomed—each and every one of us in this chamber and even those beyond." He spread his crimson cloak, revealing a blood-red tuxedo and matching bow tie. "The fate that awaits us—that awaits these alluring, young women stationed before you—will be more cataclysmic than any you could imagine or fear."

Gwendoline remained stiff, her stare again stationed straight ahead. Even so, Ravenwood could sense a trace of tenderness behind her cold glint, as well as in the eyes of the other ladies. He scrutinized this strange common denominator with each florid roll of Pringle's silver tongue and exaggerated gesture. Indeed, they believed in this man but what was the incentive or advantage? To one who relished independence, such resignation seemed alien to Ravenwood.

"I will tell you this, my good people," Pringle continued, raising his finger ever higher. "These women embody the purest components of sin. However, it is not sin in the righteous way that most would presume. It is rather a rejection of life's entrapments, of marriage, children and dull abodes. And so I ask, why do so many embrace the ordinary? These women could have fulfillment, if they wished. Perhaps it's not too late. They now stand disrobed for all the world to see. An honorable start, I say, but how far would their inhibitions go? How far might they shed their shame?" He glanced at the Cherubs and with a Cheshire Cat grin, pointed to Junior. "Will they consent to die in order to live?"

"Crackpot," Stagg snorted. However, contrary to his expressed disdain, he seemed to be enjoying the gaudy display.

"Crackpot is right," Mr. Cherub snorted back, "and a most unsavory one, at that." He glanced at his son and then at Ravenwood, stating, "Perhaps, sir, now would be a good time to act."

The lights ebbed inward, outward, and within each interlocking beam, Ravenwood sensed something strange forming. He had to unravel it.

Mrs. Cherub supported her husband's suggestion. "Perhaps Alfie is right, Mr. Ravenwood. This seems as good a time as any."

...the demon disrupted the intent.

Junior tugged his father's hand. "I don't wanna see Gwen this way. I don't like it at all. I wanna leave. I wanna—"

The collective beams formed a frame of snaring slants, which rolled farther out, creating a translucent, splashing shore and bumpy beach, which circled Pringle and his harem.

Gasps ascended. Mrs. Cherub grabbed her husband's hand, forcing her fingers between his.

Ravenwood felt every trace of the audience's enveloping awe, but despite, or maybe because of it, indifference tapped him. The latter seemed to emanate from Pringle's women, in particular Gwendoline, but then Ravenwood deduced that she and the others were only abiding by Pringle's direction, who performed as both conduit and catalyst for this play.

The limpid waves splashed higher, insinuating the advent of a storm, devouring the simulated sand and circling the women's feet in a whirl of impetuous figure eights.

The lower fringe of Pringle's cape danced with the moist flow: a purposeful, hypnotic pendulum as it were, designed to deepen the ensuing trance. However, Ravenwood was impervious to this dark draw, recognizing the expansive parlor-room trickery, which he knew spewed from a concealed projector.

"Life," Pringle bellowed, flinging his arms about like a preacher, "will devour you if you are not careful. It moves fast, when you move slowly, and much will you miss if you dare to blink." He turned to Gwendoline with a pitying pout. "These fair maidens were once consumed by stationary misconception and let their demons peck at their vim, leaving them as statues, oblivious to the world's gifts."

The stormy display altered, the water forming into a transparent foam and rock, and through the layering details, other formations formed: five in all, ranging from twelve to fifteen feet in height, writhing toward the women like Willis O'Brien animations, their long necks and ferocious faces poised at their potential prey.

"What the—?" Stagg blurted.

Ravenwood mopped up the mechanized projection, most curious to see what it might reveal.

Hints of the creatures' green and brown skin seeped through the warbling projection, revealing wee, clawed arms and hefty legs: dinosaurs for certain, though a makeshift variant that may have sprung from Hell. As they continued to slink, their whipping, spiked tails came into view, as well as the redoubtable nails of their feet.

One swung its leathery neck toward Gwendoline, unhinging its colossal mouth with slow menace, revealing the gamut of its slimy, serrated teeth.

Shrieks cascaded, but no sooner subsided to a tremulous hush. With the exception of the wary Ravenwood, all were transfixed. He gazed in defiance at the display, his eyes mirroring its fluctuating rays.

Pringle, meanwhile, pranced through incorporeal foundation, granting the replicated reptiles smoother advance.

"Do you see?" he cried, twirling his wrists, "Do you see how the allegorical calamity crashes down, with age-old jaws unhinging, antiquated fangs gleaming? Trust me, dear ladies and gentlemen, nothing is ever quite as it seems, no matter how many times we are told that it is. Look closer. Look deeper. See the utter horror—the veritable madness that thrives and dominates every speck of the natural beauty. See what happens when one shuns the world's gifts in favor of restrictions—a game that's been played since the beginning of time, and yet time after time, we continue to grasp it, pretending it's the only path we are allowed to travel. Why, oh why?"

What happened next broke with thunder-clapping rapidity, as each monster sprung upon its sacrificial lady, However, Gwendoline was the one to sharpen within the violent swoop, wiggling upward inside the beast's pellucid belly. The same went for the other women and their devourers. This surreal sight prompted Pringle to resume his vigorous guffaw, causing Junior to shake and sniffle.

And then in a flash, the prehistoric nightmare ceased, the crossing rays summoning a new display. Each lady remained in place, resuming rigid stances, as the ground sprouted ghostly-white walls adorned and flanked by (of all strange, mundane things) hooked frying pans, sinks and stoves.

Gwendoline's face contorted with panic, cueing her companions to follow suit.

Among their house-bound prisons, the women's frames looked starker than before, their skin so sheer that their skeletons dominated. Within their dainty rib cages, their ruddy hearts pumped with visible thrust.

FIGHT BACK, BREAK FREE seeped through the subliminal glow. LIVE TO DIE, DIE TO LIVE.

Ravenwood blocked the messages, concentrating on the bevy's parabolic emptiness, knowing full well that though the audience did the same; its members lacked his intuitive objectivity.

"Poor, poor Gwen," Mrs. Cherub groaned, tears trickling. "Poor, poor me."

Bleary-faced, suited men then formed from whirlwinds of smoke, appearing on seated, outlined chairs, leafing through glassy newspapers. Countertops mounted round them with utensils as nondescript children silently wailed in high chairs, only to disappear, so that adolescent versions could appear, shaking their fists with self-entitled insistence.

The ladies frowned in sullen defeat, their skeletons and beating hearts fading, as their fair flesh returned to prominence.

Gwendoline's eyes rolled toward the audience, touching her mother's, her father's, her brother's, slipping past Stagg's, and then settling once more upon Ravenwood, who felt the surge of her searing contempt, albeit manipulated by her clever captor.

Pringle tottered at the far left, one eye aimed at the occult detective, knowing who he was and daring to test him.

Pringle felt Ravenwood's penetrating spirit and flicked his tongue at it, while flailing his arms in such a way as to turn the intangible expanse into a wall of impetuous fog.

The women retook their positions at the pillars, though now with expressions calm and clear.

Pringle slid toward center stage as the fog fell, taking a pensive breath before uttering, "Why this strange pageantry, you ask? Well, it's to teach you a lesson: a pensive prompt to open your bloodshot eyes, to wrack your trembling souls enough to see circumstances for the drab, muddling anomaly you have forged and now must purge."

The women bowed their heads in eerie unison, draped by shadows, as only one stream of light remained, singling out Gwendoline.

"The final passages of this fragile, fickle world are ticking, my frustrated friends," Pringle sermonized. "Why not purge your old demons and seize some joy—some lust, some hate, some raucous passion—while there's still the chance? Life, while it dares to prevail is but a whimper that few ever caress. Think of it. Today might be the last you will suckle the air, the last you ever walk, talk, sing or dance."

"A horrid prospect," the numbed Mrs. Cherub remarked.

"One perhaps too true," the equally numb Mr. Cherub added.

Ravenwood's heart sank. He wished to smack their cheeks, insist that they break from their hypnotic vim.

The women took a few steps forward and with feigned smiles, curtsied, while Gwendoline maintained her illuminated ground, glancing at her parents and brother, giving them a wee, mocking wave. Her gaze slid once more to Ravenwood, her glint seeming to say, "*It appears I've gotten one up on you*," but Ravenwood knew from whom the smugness emanated and from it, received an additional, albeit ambiguous message, which came with an upward twist of Pringle's fingers—tossing words like DESOLATION, HUNGER and FUTILITY off his shimmering nails—hitting like a hammer to Ravenwood's brow, burning through his skull.

Ravenwood blinked fast to shake the rooting sensation. Whatever the trick's effect, it had departed no sooner than it had entered, or had it?

Applause filled the theater.

"One crazy presentation," Stagg declared. "Wonder how the flimflammer does it." The detective pushed back his hat, scratched his brow, as a thick haze left his eyes. "Say, you sure better drill that son of a gun. Who knows, Ravenwood? You might even learn a new thing or two."

Ravenwood grinned, ignoring the jab, for he was glad that Stagg had snapped from his trance, but what of the Cherubs?

Ravenwood glanced at their stony scowls. For all they knew or cared, he could have been nonexistent.

As Gwendoline and the ladies glided from view to each side of the stage, the lights continued to dim. Ravenwood watched Pringle exit with a flap of his cape. The curtains closed with a slow, ominous drag, followed by a brush of dense darkness, before the lights flashed back on, settling on a flat illumination.

Mrs. Cherub's began to sob.

Junior whined, "I wanna go. I wanna."

"It's all right," Ravenwood informed the lad, loud enough for all to hear, many of whom began to rise. "It was only a show. We wished to be scared, and that's the cause to which we donated. We certainly got our money's worth, I'd say."

"Sure did," said Stagg. "It was a hoot." He winked at Junior. "Nothin' to fret over, son." He then whispered to Ravenwood, "I do hope that's the extent of it."

Mrs. Cherub overhead the remark and ceased her sobbing, "He's a bully," she sputtered, "and his show—if you wish to dignify it as such—nothing short of profane. So, what do either of you plan to do about it? Surely, there's no need for an interrogation. I suspect an immediate arrest would be in order."

The audience moved from the aisles with dazed, bleary expressions. When a few pushed past the Cherubs, the couple gave stuffy snorts.

"Well, we, uh," Stagg stammered.

"We do intend to settle the matter," Ravenwood interjected, popping his hat upon his head and giving his stick a determined tick, more concerned in keeping the clan calm than reaffirming trust.

"Oh, this was a terrible idea," Mrs. Cherub fumed. "You saw how Gwendoline was dressed—or rather undressed." Her husband braced her shoulder and handed her his hanky. "It was nothing short of decadent." She dabbed her eyes with aggrandized fervor. "And poor Junior—I do hope the bizarre display hasn't left an indelible mark on him." She brushed his brow. "He's at such an impressionable age—puberty, you know."

"I wanna go, Mother. I wanna—"

Ravenwood winced. "It was my hope to assess your daughter's behavior, and that I've accomplished. I am sorry if the display unsettled you and your family, but it's clear that Pringle holds an uncommon hold over Gwendoline, as well as the other young women. I'd like to probe the precise hows and whys, if not the ulterior motive of his presentation. That, by itself, would speak volumes, for I dare say, I suspect his showmanship is designed for more than financial gain."

Mrs. Cherub was about to protest, but instead found the mettle to take a deep breath. "Very well, Mr. Ravenwood. And how might this probe be conducted? Is this perhaps the *inquiry* you've referenced?"

"One and the same, Mrs. Cherub." Ravenwood's eyes turned a crafty green as he pointed his stick toward the stage. "Only one modification. We'll all be present when I chat."

"All of us? You mean Junior, as well. Do tell." She turned to her spouse. "Oh, please chime in, Alfie. This is not the time for restraint."

Much to her dismay, Mr. Cherub had flowed into the crowd, wallet poised as the ghoulish gent neared with bowl hoisted.

"Alfie! What in the world—?"

The ghoulish gent grinned as Mr. Cherub deposited his bills.

"Alfie!"

Mr. Cherub turned and waved. "Oh, sorry, dear. Felt compelled to make a wee donation."

"Donation? For heaven's sakes, Alfie, are you out of your mind?"

Stagg shook his head as Mr. Cherub strutted back. "Look at him," the inspector whispered. "All glassy-eyed. Bet he doesn't even realize he handed over his cash. Mind control for sure. Glad the two of us were strong enough to thwart it, Ravenwood." The inspector watched as several others layered the bowl. "Crafty stunt—real crafty."

Ravenwood appreciated Stagg's assessment. The effects of Pringle's lightshow had a deeper effect than he would have presumed. "Let's head backstage, shall we?"

"Yes, let's," Mr. Cherub agreed, his demeanor once more turning terse. "I, for one, would like to give that con man a piece of my mind." He raised a fist and shook it, much to the others' chagrin. "Maybe a tad more than that, if given the chance."

"I respect your vigor, Mr. Cherub," Ravenwood replied, "but please allow me to take the lead. I'll know what to say, what to ask."

"That's why we enlisted you," Mrs. Cherub inserted, "but I must warn you, Mr. Ravenwood. If anything goes awry—if Gwendoline continues under this madman's spell for any further, extended time—I will report this entire account to the papers, bring it to the radio stations, if need be. Not only will

Pringle be exposed as a charlatan, but you and Inspector Stagg. I'm truly that adamant, truly that desperate."

"Fair enough," Ravenwood accepted, but as much as he wished to dismiss the feeling, sensed the worst.

"Impressive visuals," Ravenwood remarked, with a firm tap of his stick. "The projections, for a lack of a better term, were the best I've ever seen and unnerving enough without reverting to Grand Guignol May I ask, from what manufacturer did you procure your system?"

"I relish the compliment, sir, but a performer worth his salt never reveals his secrets. Nevertheless, it is a veritable joy to meet you, Mr. Ravenwood." Pringle sat before a mirrored bureau, though it was devoid of make-up supplies or removers. He seemed content to remain as he was, admiring his reflection whenever he could. "I am aware of how renowned you are within the paranormal circles: the premiere psychic of your day, some would say." His goatish face scrunched. "Please indulge me if you would, Ravenwood. Were you ever challenged by the great Harry Houdini? He sought out those of your prominence, if only for the sake of exposing their trickery."

"Mr. Weiss never had cause to investigate me, let alone doubt my integrity."

"I see." Pringle shrugged. "So kind of him to let you be."

An uncomfortable pause followed, wherein the Cherubs and Stagg fidgeted, eyes rolling here and there, trusting Ravenwood might get to the point. Their agitation, however, was not due so much to the duo's contention, but rather Gwendoline, a most distracting mannequin who stood at Pringle's side.

"It also could be," Ravenwood rationalized, "the Great Houdini bypassed me because I dared not take advantage of people for monetary gain, whether through visual manipulation or hypnotic trance. I possess enough funds so as not to take advantage of others and need no elaborate mechanisms to compensate for a lack of innate ability." Ravenwood's eyes glazed to an icy blue. "Now perhaps, Mr. Pringle, you would indulge me. Were you, by chance, ever challenged by the tenacious Mr. Weiss?"

Pringle twirled the point of his beard. "I should think you'd know the answer to that. Houdini also saw fit to let me be, though his untimely death may be the true cause behind the matter. You see, I came into prominence much later. Prior to my ascent, I was not what one might call high on the performance food chain. My obligation to educate people is more or less current."

Gwendoline sighed.

"What is it, dear?" Mrs. Cherub reached out. "Are you all right? You look flushed, drawn." Mrs. Cherub smiled to distract from her developing tears. "You don't have to participate in this man's farce. You needn't be part of this obscene troupe. You deserve much better than that. Please, Gwen, won't you come home with us? We do miss you so."

Ravenwood could have gone without the sentimentality. However, with no other choice at hand, he made the best of the situation by suckling the young woman's listless aura.

Pringle clicked his nails. "Come now, answer your dear mother. She only wants what's best for you."

Pringle's tone was mocking but in such a way as to imply a long-established familiarity with the woman, and perhaps that was just what the two held. It was hard to say at this point. Mrs. Cherub was too anguished for Ravenwood to read, and Pringle's mental shield far too strong to penetrate.

Gwendoline released another sigh, though this one smooth, if not orgasmic, as if to say she was, indeed, more than fine. She then swiveled her frame toward her mother and as if by stilted rote explained, "I am at home, Mother. I'm doing what I wish to do, among the company I prefer." Her lips curled into a forced smile. "I believe in Mortimer's intent. I believe what he believes." She looked to her father and brother. "I do not mean to cause offense or sorrow, but I would be appreciative if you would let me be."

Again, Mrs. Cherub reached out to her, but Gwendoline resumed her unblinking mode.

"You don't mean that, dear." Mrs. Cherub regarded Ravenwood and wrenched her fingers for help. "Oh, Mr. Ravenwood, please."

Ravenwood took her hand, pulled her close and whispered, "It's unwise to force the matter. For now, let it be."

"Yes, but."

Pringle beamed. "Ah, then, it's settled. There's nothing more that can—or should—be said or done." He squinted at Mr. Cherub. "Unless another donation should come."

"Watch your step, wisenheimer," Stagg barked.

"And you watch yours," Pringle retorted, springing up, his cape snapping like a whip. "Need I remind you, you're an officer of the law? You should, therefore, respect your limits, as well the rights of hard-working citizens."

"No reason for anyone to get riled," Mr. Cherub said, rubbing his fingers, though unsure why. "All's fine." He glanced at his son and smiled. "We're all fine, aren't we, Junior?"

"Yes, Father," the flushed-faced boy squeaked, giving his sister another uneasy glance. "Just fine."

Ravenwood moved toward Pringle, his thrust formidable enough to make the ersatz Pan skid into his chair.

"Indeed, watch your step there, Pringle." Ravenwood restrained a laugh.

With a snort, Pringle resumed his lofty pose and looked into Ravenwood's blurring gaze. "From green to blue to brown and blue again—a most intriguing stunt. Special lenses? Where were they fashioned? Hollywood? Ah, no matter. Considering your crafty novelty, you might wish to join my tour, though I'd likely relegated you to the sideshow sidelines, a precursor to my grander sleight of hand."

"I'll pass, Pringle. I'd rather not waste virtuous mesmerism on injurious folly,"

"Folly?" Pringle scoffed. "What I preach is anything but. It's the gospel truth, by my sole standards. For one, I do believe the world as we know it will end, just as will our lives someday. Neither you nor I can stop that, and so why not seize the day?"

"Of course, an end will come, Mr. Pringle, but peddling suggestive fear so that people may act on reckless impulse is just plain impolite, not to mention unethical. Surely, you could make an honest dollar if you put your mind to it, but then honesty doesn't appear your forte. Nonetheless, if you're more inclined to play carnival geek, then so be it."

Pringle grimaced. "I'm far from a carnival geek. I am as genuine as you, my judgmental friend—genuine, through and through. And as for your highbrow degradation…"

"Yes?"

Pringle turned with nose in the air. "I only hope you'll depart with my message ingrained." He swayed back toward Gwendoline. "Perhaps, after a time, my words will even resonate with increased depth." He wagged his finger at Stagg and then at the Cherubs. "That goes for the rest of you, as well." He lowered his hand and bowed. "You'll all be the better for it." Then with great vim, he pecked Gwendoline's cheek. "At least dear Gwendoline knows. She has seen the cold, hard light, as it were."

Mrs. Cherub grabbed Ravenwood's arm and squeezed, but despite the pinch, he remained as insouciant as Pringle.

"If you say so," Ravenwood concluded. "In any event, our time here is through."

Stagg looked alarmed, for he had presumed the exchange had been leading up to something more substantial, but the ambiguous hue of Ravenwood's eyes insinuated something all together.

"Through?" Mrs. Cherub muttered.

Ravenwood directed her hand into her husband's and to the couple whispered, "Wait outside with Junior. Inspector Stagg and I will meet up with you shortly."

Mr. Cherub cleared his throat, seemingly offended. He pulled his wife close, maneuvering her and Junior to the door. The boy gave his stiffened sister one last glimpse, with sorrow overflowing.

"So," purred Pringle, "since you can't figure me out, you don't wish them to know." He looked at Stagg. "This policeman won't be of any help, either, you know. He's as much a novice as you are—two frauds for the price of one." Pringle folded his arms and looked upward. "Anyway, blabber and blurt all you wish. It'll get you nowhere."

"Perhaps," Ravenwood consented, "but still, if you wouldn't mind."

Pringle raised an eyebrow, as Ravenwood pulled a small, silver camera from his jacket pocket.

Pringle sniggered. "You wish to take my picture. Dear, sir, I have plenty of photographs to share for the mere asking. I use them for publicity, as you rightly know."

"Yes, I'm aware of that." Ravenwood poised the camera before his face, "but those are staged to your specifications. I wish something spontaneous and therefore more sincere. This wee camera doesn't miss a trick. Please, if you'd just move a tad to the left."

Pringle shook his head. "Very well."

Ravenwood clicked. "And now, a bit to the right."

Pringle's expression soured, but again he obliged.

Ravenwood clicked. "Turn around, please. I'd like a shot of you from the rear."

Pringled turned on his heels, his cape swirling with superfluous flair.

Ravenwood again clicked, but in the process also captured a few shots of Gwendoline.

Pringle turned and yawned. "Would you like close-ups, as well?"

"That won't be necessary, Mr. Pringle. I do believe I have enough."

"I see—only full-figure photos your keen inspection. That camera—a unique sort, I take it."

"It was constructed for me by the renowned Harold Edgerton: the most recent model in a series of such. Quite handy for any investigative cause." Ravenwood smiled. "You see, I'm not afraid to share my secrets and do consider myself quite a deft performer, even so."

Pringle sneered. "So, then, your device captures spirits and other ethereal phenomenon? Not so surprising. It would go with your trade, but still a useless means to demean me. However, I'll give you this: You are, indeed, in league with the Great Houdini, with that nagging urge to besmirch that which you don't understand."

"Thank you."

Stagg found the melee engaging and wished it would go on, but Ravenwood had gained all he wished.

"Come, Horatio." Ravenwood tucked the camera into his pocket and motioned his companion toward the door. "Thank you, Mr. Pringle. It was quite edifying meeting you, and I do believe I also speak on behalf of Inspector Stagg."

Pringle shrugged and with a lustful gleam, wrapped his arm around Gwendoline's waist and placed his cheek to hers as the two exited.

"Really, that's it?" Stagg admonished, as Ravenwood ushered them onward. "Hell, I thought you were just warming up." The Cherubs stood a few feet away, looking anxious. Stagg lowered his voice. "I mean, you had him cornered." He gestured to Ravenwood's pocket. "And what's the deal with that camera? Like Pringle said, he's got plenty of pictures to go round."

"The camera is, in fact, a special one, Horatio. Trust me on that. It seizes more than most would suspect." He smiled as the two approached the Cherubs. "So, how are you fine folks holding up?"

Mrs. Cherub's impatience was apparent as she tapped her foot. "We would be doing better if you gained something of value, Mr. Ravenwood." She squinted at Stagg. "Such as a means toward an arrest."

"We're getting there," Stagg blurted, his tone forced and creaky. "These things do take time, after all. Right, Ravenwood?"

"Yes, Inspector."

The beleaguered Cherubs appeared unconvinced.

"I appreciate your apprehension," Ravenwood expressed. "Inspector Stagg is correct, however. As the saying goes, Rome was not built in a day. Mr. Pringle will not be torn down in one, either. We do need more time, and granted that time, we'll do right by you. Gwendoline will be extracted from this mad magician's grasp, and in the process we will uncloak his self-serving scheme." He glanced at Stagg. "We stake our reputations on it."

Stagg grunted halfheartedly.

The Cherubs nodded and flustered, sauntered away.

"We'll be in touch," Stagg told them, "one way or the other," but whispered to Ravenwood, "You better have a solid plan up your sleeve to crush this crackpot before he gains any more gumption. He's got another show scheduled tomorrow night. I hate to see good people scammed, the Cherubs or otherwise, so it's best we fix the situation sooner than later."

"I will, Horatio." Ravenwood's eyes spiraled to a dubious black. "I have this under control."

Did he, really? Ravenwood could not shake the unnerving sense of blandness that had begun to intrude his cognition. It was the sort of stark, pragmatic thing that only mundane reality could instill and therefore, far removed from his natural state. He could only hope that with some hearty attentiveness, he might get back on mystical track and then squash the bastard's subliminal discord decisively.

Ravenwood was unable to sleep and so decided to develop his film. It was as good a time as any to scrutinize its details, but the results in one sense left him unimpressed; in another way, they jarred him to the point of vexation.

When his lack of assuredness peaked, he slipped into the Nameless One's chamber.

"I must speak to you, sire."

"I thought as much." The Nameless One now floated with legs crossed in a wave of fresh candlelight, his frame tipped in such a way that conveyed not only intuition, but empathy. "You have something to show me."

"I do, sire."

"And you are hoping that I might ascertain something you cannot."

Ravenwood fanned the photos before the guru. "I am. I had hoped to find a trace of astral angst, a smear of ethereal aspiration, unshakable evidence that this man is in league with some great, netherworld evil. However, what I captured is something different."

The Nameless One glanced at the imagery but choose to analyze his disciple's expression. "Yes, my son?"

"It's something rudimentary, no different than the publicity stills he peddles. There's a bluntness within them, something that I believe he implanted in my head via rapid suggestion, a means to break my confidence."

"Go on."

"I can subdue the command, now that I've identified it. In a way, though, I'm grateful for it. It's helped me recognize the same bluntness in the photographs. Pringle may hold a flamboyant facade, but his perspective is fueled by pure narcissism. And as for the young lady, her recorded aura isn't much different. She's an inconsequential link to his banal core."

The Nameless One smiled. "It then appears this man practices what he preaches. He is no more than a skillful manipulator. Is that so unusual among the swami imposters?"

"No, sire." Ravenwood's gray pupils dilated. "But this goes beyond that." He flipped through the photos, focusing on the unflinching flair of their subjects' positions. Ravenwood wondered why he had not discerned the secular-based staunchness sooner, as well as the evil that bordered it. "What I have here—

what I met in that dressing room—is unpretentious and in the strangest way, empty in heart and wide-range passion, even if adorned by the panache of horns and a cape. This man believes in neither God nor Satan. He's determined that any ethereal variant is fake. The benefit of his view is illogical, and yet he wears it in pride."

"Can you be so certain? Can even your specialized photographs reveal such absolutes?"

"They match my gut feeling and therefore my perception. I'm not mistaken about this, sire. This charlatan isn't a charlatan in the traditional sense. He's made himself a veritable monster, all through the sheer power of raw, temporal thought. His plans are not steered toward typical glory, but something more hardened, something more personal."

The Nameless One tipped a tad, his aura bright and pleased. "So, this man is a player of a unique sort, looking to test the waters from a non-transcendental vantage. Without religion, without sorcery or spiritual conviction, he has only fleshly delights to define him. Unfortunately, there is power in that stance, especially when forced upon others. If you fail to crush his philosophical expansion, the consequences could be dire, perhaps fatal. That is the size of it, is it not, my son?"

Ravenwood nodded.

"I do not believe this mystery is impossible to solve. It only needs a few informative shoves. In any event, you can—and will—peel away your opponent's psychological skin."

Ravenwood tucked the photos under his arm and turned. "Thank you, sire. As always, your guidance is most appreciated."

"A courteous librarian allowed me to borrow this," Sterling stated, positioning himself next to the renewed Ravenwood, who sat in a firm chair of his contemplative study. "It's from an entertainment section, regarding a particular Phoenixville theater."

Ravenwood's eyes gleamed hazel as he took the sheet.

"The Burlesque Inn's stage was sparse," he read aloud, "lit in a multi-tinted way, with cheap columns and an arched wicker chair. The so-called play was foolish and preachy, like some fire-and-brimstone sermon one does not wish to sit through on any given Sunday. The five women on stage wore little and for the most part, did little. Our poor man's pipe-less Pan informed the audience that these stagnant souls were due for the first in a string of weird outcomes, which featured projected, splashing waves and ghostly saurians.

"Can you be so certain?"

The culminating warning implied that we must avert the contrivances of humdrum life." Ravenwood lowered the page and shrugged. "Precisely what we witnessed. No huge revelation there, Sterling. It merely confirms a pattern."

"So sorry, sir. I did my best. Perhaps, this Pringle wishes no more than to sprinkle his unorthodox sermon about like Johnny Appleseed, to ensure his act catches on for fame and fortune's sake."

"If he were some run-of-the-mill performer, I'd agree, but fame, fortune and the cash that follows are but fringe benefits to him. No, this character is motivated by an intrinsic, ardent cause. The Nameless One concurs."

"As he would," Sterling chided with a sardonic smack of his lips. "So, it comes back to a possible challenge. It's not that far-fetched. Why else would Pringle stumble into Ravenwood's backyard? You are known in most eccentric circles and would be an ideal opponent to prove one's superiority, rather like seeking out the great Wild Bill for a name-making showdown."

"Maybe, but then there's the girl. Her presence isn't coincidental or inconsequential."

"There's always a girl. They come. They go. Pringle may be a ladies' man. That's often the case with these showbiz sorts."

"Pringle wouldn't be guaranteed that I'd get involved because of a girl. Mrs. Cherub is likely the greater draw." He folded his fingers, looking pleased. "Yes, this lies more with her, and her daughter is but a connecting component, a foil for some cutting cause."

"You might like to know, sir, that in addition to locating the Phoenixville article, I took time to comb the social sections of our local papers. The Cherubs are major contributors to the Catholic Diocese. This struck me as odd, since they're not Catholic. Their children have never attended a single, parochial institution. Still, to the greater point, they are seeming do-gooders, but ones who chose to stay within the altruistic margins. Per my lifelong observations into such practices, many well-to-do are incessant interlopers when it comes to any financed flaunt, ballyhooing their presence to ensure their money is well spent, but more so to receive those compulsory pats on the back. The Cherubs don't fit the pattern, though there's nothing necessarily wrong with that, and still."

"Who can say why people do what they do, Sterling? Anyway, Pringle wouldn't care about the Diocese or its contributors." Ravenwood took a deep breath and massaged his brow. "Or would he?"

"He does dress like a devil. Perhaps he's adverse to virtuous pursuits as a general rule of thumb. There's also that staunch, secular slant you referenced. At any rate, I'll return the article to the library. Do you require any further research?"

"Uh, no need, Sterling. I believe there's only one, immediate path for this investigation. I must speak to Mrs. Cherub. I sensed something amiss with her on our initial meeting. As much as she wishes my help—and Stagg's, she fears we might uncover an underlying catalyst and wants matters settled without her secret revealed: in other words, her cake and eat it, too." He rubbed his palms, his eyes beaming a sprightly azure. "Well, now—a next, essential step has formed, hasn't it?" He sprung up, grabbed his jacket, Stetson and walking stick. "If you'd excuse me, Sterling, I have another inquiry to conduct."

"Why, Mr. Ravenwood, what brings you here at this early hour?" Mrs. Cherub tightened her feathery robe as she peered from the crack of the door. Her hair was disheveled, and she wore no make-up. "Do you have an update on Pringle, perhaps?"

"Alas, I don't, but I do require more information from you. I trust you'll help." Ravenwood tapped his stick to punctuate the urgency. "May I please come in?"

"Yes, yes, of course, please make yourself at home, Mr. Ravenwood." She moved to the side. "Normally, the maid would answer, but I gave her the day off. Alfie is at work and Junior at school." She shut the door. "Neither one slept very well last night. You know, Alfie doesn't recall having made that donation. He denies it, in fact." She patted her hair in an attempt to look more presentable. "If I didn't know any better, I'd say he's in the throes of a hangover." She giggled, but then sensed Ravenwood's urgency. "There's something wrong. I can tell."

Ravenwood scanned the posh surroundings: the oversized couch, robust chairs, ornate sculptures and fine, framed artwork. "That should go without saying, Mrs. Cherub."

"Please, do call me Gertrude." She began to step away. "Let me just head to the kitchen. I'll get coffee. We can discuss whatever you wish."

"Kind of you to offer, Gertrude, but I must decline. I'm edgy as it is."

"Then what is it? What brings you here and why do you look so grim? Is Mortimer Pringle to be let off the hook? If so, I must protest with every fiber of my—"

"As I said, I need information." Ravenwood's eyes fanned a fiery orange, "Information that you've thus far concealed."

Mrs. Cherub trembled, wondering how he might know, though in a way, not at all surprised, considering his honed intuition.

"That's right, Gertrude. There's more to this matter than you've let on. I don't wish to play games. If you want my help, you'll do us both a favor by fessing up."

"I don't appreciate your tone," she bristled. "Perhaps you should return later, when Alfie is home." She pointed to the door. "Now, please—"

Ravenwood turned. "Very well, but do consider me off the case, and though I shouldn't speak for Inspector Stagg, I believe he'd likely redirect his attention to other concerns, as well."

As Ravenwood moved toward the door, Mrs. Cherub implored, "Wait one moment."

Ravenwood paused.

"Perhaps I was a tad hasty, perhaps a bit confused and scared. This has been a most traumatic time for me and my family, as you know. They say your instincts are genuine, that it's more than just investigative know-how. I can tell that you're sincere. It does show in your eyes, in their varying shades."

Ravenwood swiveled and bowed. "So, you'll talk to me? You'll tell me the truth?"

She nodded. "Yes, Mr. Ravenwood. I will. I'll tell you everything."

He allowed her to get dressed and apply some make-up. If she felt more comfortable in his presence dolled up, she might be more receptive to his questions.

They sat across from each other, she snuggled within her plush chair, he on the edge of his, hands folded, his hat placed on his walking stick, which he had propped at the chair's side.

"This feels like a confessional, Mr. Ravenwood, or maybe like I have the Sword of Damocles dangling over my head."

"You needn't feel that way. I want you to be at ease. Talk to me as you would an old friend, and remember, I'm here to help." His eyes transmitted an amiable, steady brown. "Now, your connection to Pringle—it has roots beneath these recent circumstances with Gwendoline."

Mrs. Cherub threw back her head and sighed. "Yes, I regret to say so."

"Elaborate, please."

"It may seem that I've known Mortimer Pringle within a recent stretch, but I've known him since he was a mere boy."

"I suspected as much," Ravenwood murmured, though dismayed he had not confirmed the fact in advance. "I couldn't break the code, not while emotions were running as high as they were in his dressing room, and on an emotional level, you've proven quite scattered, to say the least—not the easiest to read, that is."

She nodded, not holding it at all against him, and continued. “Mortimer was the nephew of a priest who held sermons at Holy Mary’s Church. However, Alfie and I have held no substantial ties with the establishment other than its related, social functions. We became friends with the young Father Franklin and affiliated with those within his prestigious circle. That included Mortimer, albeit indirectly.” She laughed in a self-mocking way. “The boy visited his uncle to an absurd extent. Father Franklin was like a surrogate guardian to him, since the boy’s parents were avid travelers, who found their child a hindrance, in particular Franklin’s brother, who was said to have syndicate ties, among other questionable links. At any rate, those within Father Franklin’s realm had become a makeshift family in their own right, without the pretentious, religious baggage to weigh them down, either. Alfie and I fit in nicely, respectful to the religious symbols and customs as most God-fearing people would be, though by no means fanatical.”

“Father Franklin evidently did not practice what he preached.”

“I suppose that’s the way with many clergymen, once the pomp is rubbed away. They’re no different than any of us with their donnish quirks. At the outset, what did we care if he seemed off-kilter?”

“Off-kilter in what way?”

“He held a blatant eye for the fairer sex, and he preferred his females young—far too young.” She frowned in disgust. “After a time, the rumors found their way to the upper crust. That’s where the money rests, along with the obvious, political swing.” She fought her tears. “We had to ask questions, intervene. It was our duty, and yet it was hard to swallow the truth. We otherwise liked this man, and as my misfortune had it, so did Gwendoline. Alfie and I presumed she was visiting the abbey to see Mortimer. He was older than she was, but they were within the same age range. There was no reason to suspect, no reason to think the worst, even when I did catch the dashing Father Franklin pinching Gwen or stroking her hair. I presumed the affection was innocent, but sometimes we see only what we wish to see.”

“When did you realize the affection had become more than incidental?”

“Gwendoline’s despondency brought it to light. She would lock herself in her room. We’d hear her crying. We thought she might be having trouble in school or perhaps had a rift with Mortimer, since she stopped going to the abbey. We asked if the two were at odds, but she was defensive of Mortimer and to a convincing degree. It had to be another matter that was troubling her. When the rumors reached their summit, I had to accept the dismal possibility that Father Franklin might figure into it.” Mrs. Cherub paused and exhaled before resuming. “Gwendoline did finally confess to me that he had been affectionate with her—forced petting, embracing and the like. That was bad enough and all

I needed or cared to hear. I dared not tell Alfie at first, so instead went to our prestigious peers, those select few I felt I could confide in."

Ravenwood felt her mournful flow and deduced, "It was then that you decided to usher Father Franklin out of town. He didn't put up much of a fight, I sense, after you confronted him with the accusation."

"An insightful inference, Mr. Ravenwood. Yes, that's how it went, but there was also a condition made."

Ravenwood smirked, further assessing the progression. "He would give up his position—no longer perform as a priest, no matter where he roamed, and with that, he would curb his urges and deeds."

She bit her lip, knowing how foolish it sounded.

"He promised you that he would keep his word, but even so, why would you think him trustworthy? He could still prey on girls. You must have realized that, of course. You could have reported it to Stagg—to the police in general. Better that than letting it ride as you did."

"I wished the situation to fade. I didn't want Gwen to go through any more than she had. The sordid affair could have entered the papers, become the unending talk of the town."

"I see. And where did it leave Mortimer?"

"We presumed his parents would finally live up to their responsibility, tend to the boy as they should have from the start."

"Much to anticipate, considering their evident behavior." Ravenwood's eyes blackened. "Nevertheless, the boy appears to have found his way."

"To say the least." She squirmed and wrung her wrists. "And you're right. His parents did not want anything to do with him. He moved from relative to relative. He was quite quarrelsome with most, we were told. He missed his uncle. The separation made him vindictive." She shook her head. "Over time, we did lose touch with him. Our concern faded, though Gwen—dear Gwen—would occasionally inquire about him. There was still a fondness there, regardless of his uncle."

"There was a point when Gwen and Mortimer contacted the other."

"He wrote her. She wrote back. I read his letters. She didn't hide them. I inferred that Father Franklin had distanced himself from Mortimer. I believed he was abiding by his promise. Unfortunately, there was a much deeper cause behind it." She shot Ravenwood a daring glance. "Can you guess?"

"He died." Ravenwood's eyes turned a chilled lime, as his intuition peaked. "Suicide. Mortimer had a difficult time dealing with it. His resentment grew greater as a result."

"In his correspondences, he minimized it to Gwen, focusing rather on his academic achievements. His disgruntled relatives had placed him on the college-preparatory track: expensive but strict, both in daily habit and scholarly doctrine. They believed that if he were to pursue secular studies, it might break a link to his hypocritical past."

"But it only strengthened it." Ravenwood recalled Pringle's unshakable girth. "I'm beginning to understand."

"Are you, Mr. Ravenwood? Mortimer Pringle is a complicated individual, more than I would have ever suspected. When he wrote Gwen, I was definitely displeased, but I never thought she'd rekindle a serious interest in him. By association, Mortimer was for all intents, a stained figure. Still, she eventually found cause to sneak away to see him. She even phoned us after the fact, rubbing it in to upset us, though there was that strange, cold tone. Naturally, Alfie and I forbade the relationship from developing any further, but she continued to stay with him, calling on occasion to share the details, including those of Mortimer's conniving occupation. When she did return home for a spell, it seemed more a matter of her testing us—or perhaps Mortimer doing so through his indirect influence. She was generally cruel, but mostly despondent, slipping into trances. We sought help for her, but nothing worked, not even the hypnotist we hired. He said that her numbness was too entrenched to break, that it might even grow even deeper given time. I decided then to employ an investigative approach with Inspector Stagg, assuming he would reach out to you. A combination of your insight combined with police techniques might rattle Mortimer's chains, if only enough so that he would reconsider his vengeful path."

"Our trickster is a manipulator of the highest order and won't be easily dissuaded, as evidenced by your daughter's sorrowful state. As it stands, I fear Gwendoline is but one step in his grand scope of his revenge. He's tasted its sweetness and now desires more through cat-and-mouse ploys."

"You don't think he'll take up residence here, do you?"

"Why not? I say he'll first mount clout within the community as a novelty act and from there renew his roots and mingle among your upper crust—with your trophy daughter at his side, when he's not employing the others." Ravenwood regretted his words, but it was hard to curb his disdain. After all, the poor, impulsive woman had dug a most imposing hole. "How does that strike you, Gertrude?"

Mrs. Cherub glowered. "You well know how. And so I ask, now that you have the unsavory scoop, how shall you proceed?"

Ravenwood's eyes sparked a cunning cerulean. "The same way I did by visiting you, through additional questioning." He grabbed his walking stick and hat. "The situation may appear dire, but its underlying quintessence is growing more distinct: a step in the right direction."

Mrs. Cherub rose. "I like the sound of that. I wish to assist."

Ravenwood shook his head. "Sorry, but you've done enough damage. If I'm to succeed, you must keep your distance." He bolted for the door, his zeal growing. "It'll all be for the best, my dear Gertrude. In the end, you'll see, and no doubt, with a substantial lesson learned."

Ravenwood's conviction dug ever deeper, so that the sunlight became like a metaphoric curtain about to part, his eyes stinging the whole while, his brain burning at each prodding thought. As his pace quickened, he felt the trees stiffen, the ground harden, and as he did whenever weighed by a great quandary, he envisioned the Nameless One and heard his voice.

"So, Pringle wants to punish the lady and maybe not just her, but the whole family through a vast, lascivious mislead.

"So it appears." Ravenwood's heels clicked hard as he turned the bend, the Wilkes coming into view. "It's not surprising, really. Bad begets bad."

"Is that not the way of evil? Its urge to trick and twist is like a disease, unending."

"That's why I must bring Pringle down as soon as possible." Ravenwood approached the theater and pressed his palms—his mind—upon its doors, forcing them open. He slipped in, his hearing sharpening. Voices beckoned, and he followed.

"Good luck, my son. Stay strong in your conviction, for as the magnanimous Shiva knows, your adversary will do the same."

"A six-week run, you say?" the tall, goateed man in shabby suit ruminated, "And I'll get a substantial percent of the donations, ticket sales or whatever we should arrange? I like that. I like that a lot, Mr. Pringle. I must declare, we haven't booked anyone of such ambition at the Wilkes, in well, too many years to remember. Are you anticipating the same high-class draw tonight?"

"Absolutely." Pringle was still garbed as he was the night before and exuded the same hateful haughtiness. As Ravenwood paused at the hall's end, Pringle turned enough to grant him a deploring glance. "Through word of mouth, we'll pack the house every night. The golden opportunity is right at your fingertips, Mr. Staint, if you're game."

As the tall man writhed in thought, he turned a tad and noticed Ravenwood. "Hey—you. How'd you get in here? We're closed." The man placed the edge of his hand against his brow and squinted. "Wait—say, aren't you Ravenwood. Yeah, sure, that's who you are. You were here last night." He looked at Pringle.

"So, you two pals?"

"A lovely prospect," Pringle purred, "but I'm certain our distinguished guest would object."

Ravenwood found Pringle's smugness fulsome, and Staint's eagerness just as foul. He cleared his throat and tapped his stick. "I'd like a word with you, Pringle."

"By all means." Pringle wiggled his fingers, the light glistening off his nails. "Come forth, good man."

"We converse in private, Pringle—just you and me."

"Oh, I get it. You don't wish to be shown up again. I must confess, I am rather disappointed. I'd have thought you to possess more fortitude than that."

"Hold on," Staint protested. "Are we finalizing this deal or not?"

"Construct a contract," Pringle directed. "I'm sure one of your burlesque queens can apply the secretarial skills. The document need not be typed, just legible."

"Sure, Mr. Pringle, you got it." Staint turned. "It won't take long, and I trust your meeting with Mr. Mystic there won't either."

"It should be swift, Mr. Staint, unless Mr. Ravenwood succumbs to his penchant for verbosity."

Ravenwood ignored the remark, and Staint departed with a confounded shake of his head.

"People do seem to pass through this area more than not, Ravenwood. Why don't we head to the dressing room? As you experienced, its sparse confines are ideally suited for humble dispute."

Ravenwood conjured a steadfast coolness. "Fine with me, Pringle."

The satyr snapped his cape and with an anxious snicker, led the way.

The room was lit more dimly than the night before, with a gas lamp flickering on the desk. Pringle sat and gazed at his radiant reflection. "I daresay, I am a handsome devil."

"You're a man garbed as a devil," Ravenwood reminded him, "but then, based on one's actions, a devil by any other name would still be a devil, I presume." He smirked at his cleverness. "Please pardon the Shakespearian contortion."

Pringle gazed deeper into his reflection, his expression defensive and defiant. "So you did talk to her—got all the nitty-gritty. In that case, you do know how devilish I am. I've certainly had just cause to adorn this dandy set of horns." He rolled his head, pulling Ravenwood into view. "Consider the many devilish delights I've thus far initiated even beyond my appearance. I trust I'll accomplish many more given time. I like to think of the world as my oyster. Why not swallow every bit of it? Besides, there are many to pluck to abet my selfish crusade. I even planted a little notion in your head in hopes you'd succumb to the bait." He scoped Ravenwood's eyes and sighed. "Ah, I see it's been cleared. No matter. The odds favored you'd shrug it off no sooner than it had fermented. Anyway, just wished to test you, as you're now testing me."

"Why not drop the tit for tat? Quit while you're ahead. You've more than rubbed your success in Gertrude Cherub's face. End of story, I should think."

Pringle rapped his jaw. "Tell me, Ravenwood, is it really that wrong to prolong punishment? You've no idea the pain I've endured. I still ruminate upon it day in, day out. I only ask for an even exchange as compensation: that proverbial eye for an eye, though maybe with a few fringe benefits to go along."

"I've also lost loved ones, Pringle. Who hasn't? I know you mourn your uncle's death and that you wish to avenge him, but there comes a point when one must let go. That goes as well for those young women you've harnessed. You can keep your basic gimmick for entertainment sake. Keep raking in the donations as it were to sustain your troupe. It would be a respectable enough form of chiseling as it stands, in proper tune with P.T. Barnum's legacy, with all the associated winks and nudges to match. Yes, a reasonable compromise, all in all, I say."

"Oh, what do you know of showmanship? Hell, what do you know of my uncle?" Pringle raised a fist, as if he might spring up and strike Ravenwood, but then dropped his hand. His tone grew more contemplative. "What do you know of the anguish that poor man endured? He didn't deserve to be alienated, to have his passions defiled and ripped to shreds. What gave that brassy woman and her censorious compatriots the right? And what gives you the right to question me, now? Eh, Ravenwood? What makes you so superior?"

"Mrs. Cherub said your uncle was a violator of children. Gwendoline Cherub was one of those children. You're harming her all over again, albeit in your own sick way. Admit it."

"I admit nothing, sir, though I will agree that my uncle was not a perfect man. He used the priesthood as a means to an end, but how is that wrong? No matter what people say, they want to stroke their urges, though few possess the courage to do so. At least my uncle had that courage."

"There's nothing courageous about molesting children. On those grounds alone, Mrs. Cherub was right to stop your uncle, even if her methodology proved flawed."

Pringle shrugged, again admiring his reflection as he stroked the cusp of one of his horns. "Your eyes are red, Ravenwood—a deep, dark red—like blood. Have I struck a chord? If so, I'm pleased and say so without a speck of apology. My uncle wished to live life to the fullest and encouraged others to do the same. His habits were anything but evil and completely sincere. I have always respected his honesty, and I have long aspired to recreate his tradition and perhaps even take it to a higher level. Unlike my uncle, paranoia won't get the best of me. I would never resign my life with a bullet to my brain in some dank hotel room. I'm more inclined to fight—and triumph—no matter the odds."

"You can rationalize all you want. I'm not buying any of it. You've no right to enslave those women. You've made them bleary-eyed puppets. Your uncle likely did the same to his victims, forcing his will upon them until they were stripped of their own."

"I'll have you know, Gwendoline accused my uncle, not because she was adverse to his advances, but because she was misled to think his behavior—and hers—wrong. She did, in fact, enjoy his interaction, or else would have rejected it any time she desired. She eagerly chose otherwise. She told me so when we reunited. She said she made a terrible mistake by singling him out and wished to make amends for it, though neither for my uncle's sake or mine. She wished to make amends for herself. Now, based on our present arrangement, I take care of her, placate her. She's content with that. Even you, with your alleged cognizance, cannot discern the delicacy of such an exceptional bond. Gwendoline Cherub succumbed to me by inherent desire. Not you nor the Cherubs have the right to take that away."

"I beg to differ, and because of that, I intend to free her. You're going to leave this town—leave it without her. Take the rest of your mind-numbed entourage if you wish, but Gwen—and the other women you've twisted—will remain. Understood?"

"And what will you do if I refuse? Will you sic Inspector Stagg on me? Better yet, perhaps you'll challenge me to a bout of sorcery, but of course, there is no such thing as sorcery, so what's the use?" Pringle formed a mocking pout. "Please why not make it easy? Let me be to do as I see fit. I would hate to have to, well, I think you get the picture."

"You don't scare me, Pringle. And I won't ask again. Leave this town and leave the women behind. If you don't, I'll have Stagg arrest you. He'll do it in a heartbeat and take great pleasure keeping you behind bars for as long as he can. The matter can then go to court—be dragged out for weeks—months—on end and only then to determine your prison term. You can bet those young women will have regained their awareness by such point and have much to say against you."

"You're as much a silver-tongued devil as I, Ravenwood. Tell you what. You're more than welcome to attend tonight's presentation. No donation required, unless you're feeling generous. That goes for anyone who might accompany you, and I mean the Cherubs, of course. Expose me right in front of them, if you want. It will be a grand duel of psychology and cunning." He grinned. "You accept?"

"I do. Just know that tonight's performance will be your last."

There came a knock at the door.

"Pringle—I have the contract." Staint knocked again. "I'd like to seal the deal, if you don't mind."

"As would I, Mr. Staint. Do come in."

Staint entered and glared at Ravenwood before handing a sheet of lined paper and pen to Pringle. Pringle scanned the "document" and with a flip of his wrist, signed.

"And so tonight our dueling will come to an end, Ravenwood." He returned the sheet to Staint with a firm snap. "That will make tonight historic, for nothing beyond it should henceforth matter. It will prove the be-all, end-all conclusion, just as you wish, just as I wish."

Ravenwood turned on his heels and headed for the hall.

Staint's crew—a dusty, grimy lot of reefer-puffing men and strippers—regarded Ravenwood several feet away. He paid them no mind, slipping straight past into the auditorium in hopes of getting a better view of the light grid. Unplugging even a select string at the heart of the show could topple Pringle's credibility.

He entered from the stage and sprung off it, his eyes aimed at the hoisted bulbs and taped strands at the far wall. That's when a pale shape caught his eye, rising near the auditorium's entrance—Gwendoline.

As she straightened her posture, her sheer cloth slipped, rendering her naked, her bosom heaving in contrast to her reticent pose.

"Miss Cherub," Ravenwood muttered, his eyes locking with hers, unnerved yet aroused by her unwitting inhibition. "What are you doing here?" He headed toward her. "Does your, uh, captor know you're wandering about?"

She remained silent.

"I suppose he wouldn't care about your state of undress, would he, now? He'd more likely encourage it." Ravenwood again watched her breasts heave. "Are you upset, frightened?" He paused, hoping to read her mind, but the attempt proved in vain. "Do you want to get out of here—away from Pringle? I'll give you my jacket. We'll move quickly. No one will be the wiser."

Her lids quivered, insinuating a blink. Had he reached her?

He unbuttoned his jacket. "I'll get you straight home, right to your mother, your family. I promise—"

Her features softened, and this time the blink became distinct. However, from the side, the ghoulish man appeared, dressed in casual attire, looking flustered, and next to him was the violinist, in more-or-less the same stately attire as the night prior, his gaze calculating.

"Gwendoline," the ghoulish man whispered, extending his hand. "Do come here, dear."

"Yes—come to us," the violinist added with a snap of his fingers. "We'll take you back to your room, so you can be with the other girls."

The ghoulish man snatched the sheer fabric from the floor and draped it over his arm. "Now be a good girl, Gwendoline. Do as we say."

"She doesn't want to go," Ravenwood scolded. "I'm taking her out of here."

The ghoulish man held his ground. "I doubt that, sir."

The violinist swayed next to his friend. "She stays here, sir. You're the one who's leaving.'

Ravenwood raised his fist, his eyes flecked with enraged green. "You'd be wise not to test me, gentlemen."

The ghoulish man laughed and grabbed Gwendoline, wrapping his arms under her breasts as he tugged her toward the doorway. The violinist, meanwhile, fluttered his fingers, daring Ravenwood to make his move.

Ravenwood leapt forth and landed a jujutsu chop to the man's shoulder, knocking him to the floor, while the ghoulish man continued to carry Gwendoline beyond the threshold.

"Damn it," Ravenwood growled, stepping over the whimpering violinist, intending to pounce his next foe, but the ghoulish one had already fled his view, merging into the dimness, where another pack of Staint's smoky associates loitered.

Ravenwood realized it would be foolish to pursue at this point but assured himself that if he had reached her once, he would do so again. Besides, it might be more beneficial not to replace Pringle's confidence with any more contempt. If the fool went into the battle confident, he would fall all the harder.

Ravenwood returned to the auditorium and watched the violinist crank upward. Ravenwood presented the side of his hand. "Like another?"

The violinist cringed and like a frightened puppy darted away.

This allowed Ravenwood to scrutinize the high-propped, modified projector and below, the fine strips of black velvet and blending tape that concealed its adjoining wires. It would not take much to tear away that fabric and disrupt the grid. In fact, if timed right, a few basic tugs would achieve the incapacitating deed.

Ravenwood then exited the theater, swaggering into the brisk air, inhaling in a way that, despite the whispering odds, accelerated his vim. Whatever

"Yes, come to us."

followed would prove a challenge, but one way or the other he would undrape "the naked truth" for all to see.

"You're tense," Sterling stated, as he watched his employer standing before the Nameless One's door.

"Tense? Not at all," Ravenwood's eyes were a pensive baby-blue. "However, I do wish to get matters underway."

"In preparation for Pringle's encore?"

"Of course, and the sooner, the better." He shook his head and laughed. "I daresay, I sound rather like Mrs. Cherub."

"*Anxiousness is fine*," the Nameless One stated, "*as long as it's kept in check. His arduous aura could puncture your psychic prowess, if your step is not nimble.*"

"Why not enter," Sterling interrupted, "and converse face to face?" His eyes twinkled. "That is, why all the telepathic tomfoolery?" He turned toward the door and raised his voice. "A genuine guru—a considerate one—would get straight to the point."

"Our exchanges are fragmented for good cause," Ravenwood rebutted, nudging Sterling back. "Pieces often come in stages, manifesting gradually, through atmospheric ebb and flow. In other words, we don't necessarily need to look at each other to get to the point. We pause as soon as it manifests."

"Whatever you say, sir. In any event, may I accompany you on tonight's venture? I know that Inspector Stagg will be present, but he can be rather cumbersome at times, whereas I'm more inclined to stay inconspicuous."

Ravenwood nodded. "I was about to ask if you might come along. I and Stagg will stay in Pringle's prime view, but you could enter among the shadows, and upon my signal, complete a vital task."

"Signal, you say?" Sterling paused. "Vital task? I suppose it would depend, sir, if I were, indeed, to remain inconspicuous."

Ravenwood consumed the Nameless One's avid approval. "Yes, a signal and tactic, simple but essential, which only one of your inconspicuous constitution could administer." He gestured Sterling onward. "It'll be fine. Let's get a bite to eat. I'll explain."

After they had finished their coffee and sandwiches, Ravenwood and Sterling headed to the theater, content and assured.

Stagg waited a few feet down the line, rolling a peanut about his tongue, as people headed toward the facade.

Ravenwood caught Stagg's eye and waved him toward them.

"So, what's the big deal, Ravenwood?" Stagg asked as he sprinted over, looking from side to side, as if someone might overhear. "The Cherubs aren't here—aren't coming, or so I learned from the lady of the house. You told them to stay away, eh? I'd have thought they'd work to our advantage to get Pringle back on the defensive." He coughed on the nut, before forcing it down. "I hope we haven't let an opportunity slip."

"Who says we won't have him on the defensive? Trust me, I have a plan, Horatio. I even brought Sterling along to help."

"Great—your butler. Looks like he's ready to serve tea. My confidence is brimming."

"I'll have you know, Inspector," Sterling remarked, wiggling his fingers, "I'm more than capable of clandestine maneuvers."

"Bet you are, buddy." Stagg rubbed his brow. "I sure do hope this isn't a waste of time. If I had my way, regulations or not, I'd have strong-armed that bum into a cell hours ago. No one would have been the wiser. You said you visited him earlier, Ravenwood. The two of you chatted like a couple of genuine gents to arrange some silly challenge. You probably boosted the joker's confidence, you know. Watch—he won't budge at all now."

"Again, Inspector, I know what I'm doing."

It was, however, pure instinct that Ravenwood rode on. There were still a thousand things that could go awry, but he focused on one logical passage.

"What's the first step then?" Stagg cocked his thumb back to the theater. "You want to warm him up with more chitchat? Be my guest. In the meantime, maybe the butler and I can flit with Pringle's gals." He nudged Sterling. "You in, stuffed-shirt?"

Sterling groaned.

"I'll supply a little donation, if only to ensure a casual appearance," Ravenwood explained, "and you and I will take our seats, same vicinity as last night. Sterling will head in just prior to show time and station himself at the rear. For now, that's all you need to know."

Stagg laughed. "Brilliant, Ravenwood—real sharp."

Ravenwood ignored the disdain and left Sterling behind, so that he and Stagg could proceed.

As they entered, the ghoulish man froze, pressing his bowl close to his mooned-strewn chest, prepared to turn. Ravenwood skidded before him and with a bow, deposited the dollars. Stagg contributed a few pennies, and from there, they took their seats.

"Lot of the same people," Stagg recognized, twisting his neck about, as the hypnotic lights began to fan. "I guess Pringle has them hooked."

"There are more seats filled, as well," Ravenwood observed, "the evident result of word of mouth."

"Damn fools. Who knows how many pockets this guy will pick by the time he's through? If you listen hard enough, you'll hear Houdini rolling over in his grave."

"I concur, Inspector."

The violinist clicked to his mark.

Stagg rubbed his hands. "Here we go and even a trifle before schedule."

The violinist swayed as he played, though there was no appropriation or fear in his expression, even when his eyes fell upon Ravenwood. It was as if he were engineered by another, one who had no doubt pumped his puppet with adequate bravery.

It did not take long for the lights to strobe, the curtains to retract. Though his chair was nearby, the horned host stood silent next to it, with arms folded over his chest, his face menacing, albeit obscured by the glow. The violinist finished and gave Ravenwood a wide smile before prancing off.

"A bit different tonight," Stagg remarked. "Not that I'm complaining. It's good to have some variance when it comes to any encores. Crushes possible boredom."

Ravenwood concentrated on Pringle's form, watching his face grow sharper, adapting full command, for once he seized it, he could then deepen it. His illuminated countenance drew gasps among the new attendees and satisfied sighs from those who anticipated his devilish glint.

Pringle gave a bow and scoped the vicinity where Ravenwood and Stagg sat and then jostled his gaze outward.

"He's looking for them," Stagg deduced with a snap of his fingers, "the Cherubs, that is. He's ruffled because they aren't here. Clever, Ravenwood. Real clever."

Ravenwood was pleased that Stagg had picked up on his intent and focused further on Pringle's expression, conveying to it, "*The Cherubs no longer care. Your point is lost, Pringle.*" It was hard to tell if his transmission registered, and so pressed harder. "*This show—this charade—is all for naught, a foolish waste of time—a waste of all of our time. Capisce, Pringle?*"

Pringle raised his arms, his cloak swooshing and falling.

"Contrary to adversarial hope," Pringle exhorted, sensing Ravenwood's subliminal shove, "my presence is not for naught nor will it fade." He forced a grin and widened it. "I see there are more of you here tonight. I am pleased, and to show my gratitude, I will again conjure symbolic images from the symbolic past, so that you may understand the present and future and come to believe—

believe, above all else—in the raw urges you have so foolishly suppressed."

"Such prodigious propaganda, but I'd expect nothing less from a deceitful deity. Go on, Pringle. Dare blind them to the ostentatious hilt."

The lights, meanwhile, fanned farther, paving way for the crystalline dinosaurs, which sprung within an instant blast. Spectral splashes devoured the twinkling sand at their clawed feet. Then pillars protruded among them like giant stems, and before them, curvaceous, sheer-swathed ladies appeared, backs pressed against their disjointed columns. The entire, colloidal kaleidoscope moved so fast that it caused the previous night's progression to pale in comparison.

"The past and the future," Pringle cackled, lowering his hands, as the light cascaded around his horns like fireworks, "are rolling into one, served before your very eyes, for my name is Mortimer Pringle, and these devilish delights are the fruits of my tantalizing trade and labor." He spread his fingers, his nails slicing the garish air. "Go on—behold them. Devour them. Make them your own and perhaps, just perhaps, you will see as I see, know as I know."

Household contrivances bobbed by—spectral sinks, chairs, sofas—the demonic dinosaurs cutting through them, jaws snapping, necks and tails whipping. The objects burst into glittery puffs as the creatures chomped, birthing another parade of status-symbol contrivances and therefore, more morsels for the gossamer monsters to ravish.

"This is nuts," Stagg wiggled about his seat, almost appearing afraid. "Too much at once. I don't like it. I don't like it one bit."

As the monsters furthered their assault, the maidens moved from their pillars, Gwendoline in the maddening forefront, the others swirling like expressionless imps.

The violinist reappeared below the stage, stirring another discordant tune, his puppeteered eyes falling once again upon Ravenwood, but the stalwart Stepson of Mystery concentrated only on Pringle, tracking his every twitch.

"This is the world that once was and is," Pringle avowed. "It will be forever constant, forever an anchor, but only if you wish it." He yanked his beard and sneered. "Do you want it? Do you embrace its drabness?" He pointed to Ravenwood, elevating his challenge. "Or do you want the succulent freedom that only unshackled passion brings?"

Ravenwood restrained a reply, opting for focused stability. The longer he sustained it, the stronger his stance.

Pringle's brow furrowed, his horns seeming to protrude. To counter, Ravenwood raised his hand, as if to scratch his ear, and through this subtle gesture, signaled his valet, who was shadowed toward the rear.

The illuminated images continued to shift, adding extra vim, the beams intersecting, and then in a virulent swoop, it all fell dead, leaving only a bland glow.

Pringle stiffened, looking to and fro, as did the violinist. The ladies' movements slowed to a stumbling halt. Gwendoline dropped to her knees, her bosom heaving hard, her eyes bulging. Her companions followed suit, their poses and expressions the same.

The audience yammered and turned about. Staint dashed toward Sterling and grabbed him by the wrist, hoisting his hand to reveal the wires he grasped. "Here he is—here's your culprit."

Sterling twisted free, dropped the wires and then punched the proprietor out.

People continued to yammer and turn, wondering if the disruption was part of the act.

Stagg laughed. "Well, what do you know, Ravenwood? Looks like our goat-headed rube is being served his comeuppance, thanks to that adroit butler of yours."

Pringle scowled and raised his hands and clicked his nails. "Quiet, please—quiet."

Still, the commotion carried.

"Quiet, damn it," Pringle bellowed like a banshee. "Hear me—please."

The audience hushed and looked to the satyr, who drew his attention not to them but rather Ravenwood.

"It matters not that the display has faltered," Pringle explained. "It was but a lesson projected to make a point, with hidden words and psychological incantations to open your minds. But even without the projection, you always fostered an inner truth."

He looked upon the discouraged faces and realizing that his rationale had fallen flat, desperation mounted. He reached out to Gwendoline, pricking her with his nails. It seemed that he wished to make love to her right then and there. That would have been the ultimate shock if only the Cherubs had been present (and a sure-fire way to have won the match), but without the family to mock, his aggrandized intent crashed into lusterless parody, with Gwendoline so frigid that she may have been dead.

"*Oh, yes, the game is over,*" Ravenwood conveyed with piercing vehemence. "*Your zest is gone, Pringle, along with your insolent plan. You can be as offensive as you wish. What does it matter if the intended party isn't here to see? No one else cares. Your warped folly—dead in the water.*"

"You're wrong," Pringle bleated, stepping from Gwendoline as he again smacked his ears and fell to a supplicating crouch. "There's merit and glory in all that I've presented. I've tapped each and every mind, tussled each and every emotion to prove the intangibility of the world. Contrivances come and go, as do pains and worry, but it's a bestial heart that prevails. My dear uncle knew. Oh, how he knew better than anyone." The satyr smiled at the sick, sentimental recollection. "Truly, there's nothing more satisfying than sin without sin."

"Sin without sin?" Ravenwood bleated back. "An unusual idea, but self-indulgence is at best finite. These good people know that. They work hard to do what's right each and every day and night. A guilt-ridden display won't persuade them, no matter how dazzling the illusion or clownish the host."

Concurring murmurs spread, the audience blinking and twitching, as if stirring from a deep sleep. From their auras, Ravenwood knew they had heard his words, that his reasoning had hit a vital, collective chord.

Stagg gave Ravenwood an approving nudge. "You got the greedy devil, now." Stagg regarded the awakening viewers. "Oh, yeah, that's for certain."

"Deny it all you want," Pringle continued, his voice growing shriller, "but every man, woman and child is meant to follow a primal path—my path. Admit it. Each and every one of you is nothing but an aspiring Pan."

Ravenwood snapped on his hat and stood with a tap of his stick. "The sensible see through your veil and recognize its impracticality. They can spot a charlatan a mile away. Regardless of what you claim, Pringle, Pan was an irresponsible clod, and the same goes for you."

The murmurs grew louder, the agitation more pronounced. Ravenwood could feel the slippery slide of the repellent rejection and so could Pringle.

"That's right, Pringle—a clod. A clod who believed he could shock the opposition into submission with carnival fodder. A clod who wished to bring people to their knees, hoping they would buy the hollow notion that flesh is stronger than spirit."

The murmurs warbled into distinct statements, and Ravenwood snatched and tossed them at his startled fawn:

"What is all this, some silly morality play?"

"Whatever it is, it's damn irritating. What happened to the spectacle?"

"Spectacle—oh, pooh. A lot of smoke and mirrors, if you ask me."

"And a wasted donation, at that. I want my fifty cents back."

Ravenwood gave his stick a hardy twirl. "Hear them, Pringle? There's no way you'll win them back." He looked upon Gwendoline, and she upon him. "Your spell is broken. They see through you now."

Further clarity entered Gwendoline's eyes and with it, a twinge of contempt.

Pringle stomped and writhed. "You're as much a fraud as I am, Ravenwood. Your philosophy is flatulent. My philosophy is basic—pure. It holds truth. I'm telling you—the truth and nothing but the truth."

More comments rose:

"He reminds me of a carnival geek."

"A twisted preacher is more like it."

"Indeed, a moral-less fiend for sure."

"There's no chance he'd ever hit the big time."

Gwendoline slid to the right, as her companions reeled past the pillars. They exuded a brush of awareness, and Pringle panicked.

And in that panic, Ravenwood caught a disjointed surge of his adversary's thoughts: a spry priest twirling Gwendoline's pigtails as young Pringle looked on; a cold scalpel carving Pringle's skin to make way for implanted horns in a seedy, south-of-the-border backroom; Gwendoline gliding toward Pringle with open arms and empty heart, entrapped by a beckoning that was both desired and despised; a lecture hall where Pringle listened to a bushy-bearded scholar point with urgency at a blackboard that read "Religion is the Opium of the People", and on and on, each ragged fragment more hounding than the last.

Pringle's brain burned from the spree. Inside him, a rising emptiness formed. In this regard, he wondered if in rebuttal, Ravenwood may not have tossed a subliminal suggestion to stir the prodding process. If so, he had to break it and for self-preservation's sake, toss it right back, but was it at all possible? Did he yet have a chance?

"You've no mastery over me, Ravenwood." Pringle's posture, even while bonded by doubt, remained lofty. "The Cherubs may have evaded me, but not the others."

"Think again, Pringle. It appears these good people have made up their minds."

Much to Pringle's chagrin, the audience had begun to rise, queueing into the aisles.

"Wait—where are you going? Come back. Come back, you hear?" He shook so hard that his horns wobbled, his core of doubt broadening. "Sin is a myth, a lie. Come back, so that I may show you how to embrace your underlying urges. Come back and taste a coveted truth that only I, Mortimer Pringle, can bestow."

"The bastard's losing his mind," Stagg muttered.

Again, the man with no belief tried to pull his prospective disciples inward, twirling his arms and clicking his fingers, but to no avail. "Come back. Come back. Come back." He hunkered, yanking in frustration at his crown, the base of his horns bleeding like melted wax. "Listen to me—please. There is no God. No Devil. No Good. No Bad. There is only you, and only you have the power to carve your path. Turn the cheek now, and you may never come back."

No one turned. No one appeared to listen. When Pringle realized the futility of his incensed petition, he growled and neighed. His body felt stony, evermore empty, as a surge of despair shot through his veins. Blood continued to slither down his crown, curling around his eyes, until one horn popped loose and hit the stage.

"Dear Lord," Stagg gasped. "The damn fool's falling apart." The inspector budged, wishing to dash to the stage, but Ravenwood clamped his shoulder.

"Let him be, Horatio. There's nothing we can do for him now. Let the process run its course."

"Run its course?" Stagg scoffed. "What in the hell do you mean? Can't you see he's in pain?"

"Please, just a moment more, Horatio. Trust me on this."

Pringle's knees buckled, and he collapsed with a reverberating thud, but as loud as the sound was, the exiting audience was oblivious, its members now consumed by a greater draw: an autonomy, cleansed and clear.

The violinist yanked the ghoulish man along, as both gawked in disgust at their shattered leader.

Staint grabbed Sterling's leg and pulled himself upward, just in time to spot his would-be benefactor's second horn pop.

"What—what's happened?" Staint asked, confused by the unpalatable sight. "Say, is this part of the act?" He croaked a laugh. "Yeah, that's it, right? Part of the act. Part of the show. It's got to be."

Gwendoline scampered toward her companions. They reached out and hugged her, as their former master stretched and sprawled, flaccid and defeated in an expanding puddle of blood.

Stagg nudged Ravenwood, who then nodded, prompting the two to head for Pringle. The inspector flung his sturdy frame straight upon the stage, knelt and lifted Pringle's gushing head.

"He's not dead, only unconscious." Stagg lifted and pushed back Pringle's eyelid. "Maybe in a coma, but what do I know? We should have gotten to him quicker, Ravenwood. We should have—"

"It wouldn't have mattered," Ravenwood explained, sauntering over from the steps, past the huddled women. "He had to succumb to his own fate. We'd have only prolonged the inevitable by intervening. What we have here was meant to be."

Stagg gently returned Pringle to the floorboard, yanked out a hanky and wiped his hands. "Maybe you're right. What would a few extra seconds have mattered, considering his mindset?" He looked out upon the auditorium, regarding its empty chairs. "None, most likely."

Sterling approached, as the violinist and ghoulish man moved toward Staint, who now nibbled his nails in the throes of disappointment. "All part of the act, fellas. You two ought to know. You work with him. No one could go down like that. No one."

Stagg squinted at Sterling. "Well, just don't stand there, Jeeves. Call an ambulance." He pointed in Staint's direction. "Ask that fellow you clobbered. He ought to know where there's a phone."

"As you wish, sir," Sterling complied with a brisk turn and approached Staint.

"Mr. Ravenwood," a meek voice whispered. "Mr. Ravenwood, please, if you don't mind."

Ravenwood turned and saw Gwendoline alongside him, doing her best not to shiver.

"So, you know my name." Ravenwood smiled. "It appears you were more cognitive than I sensed. I suppose you know why I'm here."

"To take me home." Her eyes teared. "That's what I want, Mr. Ravenwood. That's what I need."

"We'll get you home all right," Stagg asserted. "That also goes for your pretty companions." He gave the women a wink and though yet disoriented, they mustered the gumption to wink back. "What's done is done." He swatted his palms. "Time to move on."

Gwendoline positioned herself nearer, pushing away one of Pringle's horns with a graze of her toe and gazed deep into Ravenwood's chestnut eyes.

"Thank you for helping me—for helping us." She flinched a tad, only to watch Staint, the violinist and ghoulish man scampering from view. "There are no doubt more of them about, hoping to flee from this. Good riddance. Really, let them find their own way. The soul-searching exercise should do them good."

The siren wailed, as the ambulance zoomed away, Gwendoline, now draped in Ravenwood's coat, remained at his side, while Stagg had snatched some garments from the theater's burlesque stash for the others.

Sterling, who had assisted the ambulance carriers, returned to Ravenwood and Gwendoline.

"It does appear there are more people milling about than not," he interposed. "They seem to have little concern for the night's shenanigans. Pringle was virtually invisible to them in the end."

"The inexorable result of broken influence," Ravenwood explained.

"Another cryptic tidbit from our Nameless One, sir?"

Ravenwood grinned and then spotted a familiar trio approaching from the distance.

Gwendoline followed Ravenwood's gaze and noticed her family pushing through the crowd, her mother in a flower-patterned night cap and robe, her father and brother in disheveled, flannel pajamas.

"Gwen—oh Gwen," Mrs. Cherub cried, picking up pace as she flopped from her fuzzy slippers. "Gwen—are you all right, dear?"

Stagg gave Ravenwood a taunting poke. "Talk about coincidence. I mean, how'd they know to come? Peculiar way to dress in public, too—and traveling all this way by foot, by gosh. Yeah, real peculiar." He poked Ravenwood again. "Why not come clean? Your butler sneaked a call to the Cherubs and got them shaken up enough to dash straight out here, right?"

Ravenwood feigned ignorance, but he knew that the evening's emotions were still running high, moving from many subconscious minds to tug and yank at the air's vibrational strands, but in the Cherub's instance, it was Gwendoline's doing. Her awakened fervor had summoned her loved ones from their slumber. It was all for the best. After all, why sleep on a night such as this, a night when honorable sensibility overturned self-indulgent practicality?

Mrs. Cherub threw her arms around her daughter and pulled her close.

"I don't rightly know what it was," the grateful woman whimpered, "just a terrible, nagging felling, at best, I suppose." She turned to her husband and son, who joined the embrace. "We each felt it, Gwen, as if some great force had smacked us each upon the brow. It was then that we knew the predicament was over and that we would find you, just as you once were." She glanced at Ravenwood. "It truly is over, isn't it, Mr. Ravenwood?"

He gracious eyes confirmed that it was.

"The culprit's been carted off to the hospital," Stagg explained with officious finality. "He had a breakdown right on stage, a pretty messy one at that. He'll be out of commission indefinitely. No doubt of that."

"It's time you good people went home," Ravenwood suggested. "Inspector Stagg will visit in the morning; get whatever further details he requires. Isn't that right, Inspector?"

"Yeah, sure," Stagg consented, pulling a small crumpled bag from his pocket. "Fine by me."

Gwendoline pried her mother away and started to slip from Ravenwood's coat, but he shook his head. "Give that to Inspector Stagg when he visits."

"Yeah, you do that," Stagg played along, tossing a nut to his mouth, only to have it bounce off his cheek. "Damn nuts—think I'll kick the habit and go back to cigars. Easier to chew." He gave Ravenwood a gleeful squint. "I'll give you this, Ravenwood, you're good, real good at what you do, my friend. Someday, maybe you'll spill the beans and reveal all your secrets, if only out of mournful respect to the Great Houdini."

Ravenwood tipped his hat and ticked his stick. "Ah, a good magician never reveals his secrets, Inspector. The Great Houdini would surely vouch for that."

Stagg chuckled, and Ravenwood swaggered away, Sterling at his side.

"I struck a deal with Staint for the projector. I sense he'll not flinch from the arrangement. We'll return in the morning for it. It's a hefty contraption, but the exertion will be well worth the chance to study its mechanisms. Oh, and I also managed to snap a few shots of Pringle before he was hauled off. I'll develop them tonight, before I update the case's narrative. File the backup accordingly, Sterling. One never knows when the content might come of use."

"You suspect you'll encounter more of Pringle's likes, sir?"

"I trust not. Still, in our business, it's best to have all bases covered."

"*A wise habit for certain, my son*," the Nameless One added. "*You were most impressive, in particular when it came to your emotional stream, identifying the danger and shackling it at the core of your instincts. Brilliant performance, really—far more so than Pringle's—and I must say, your faithful valet performed just as exemplary.*"

On the Nameless One's behalf, Ravenwood gave Sterling an appreciative pat, and Sterling reciprocated with an affectionate laugh.

They then headed back to Sussex Towers, satisfied for having solved another mystery, but well aware that many more waited.

"For a moment, I thought he might stir," the nurse whispered, "and his expression—it looks as if he's hatching a plan."

"I wouldn't count on it," the physician replied, "and yet I can't deny there's more to our poor, comatose masquerader than meets the eye. He's lost a lot of blood, but at least those head wounds are patched. We can only hope the catatonia breaks somewhere down the line."

With sorrowful sighs, the two departed, leaving Pringle to continue his furtive pursuit within the cocoon of his metal-barred bed.

He now knew he had worked from the wrong end. Magic did exist and was there but for the taking, but to hell with the bland, sanitized variation. Let the Cherubs have their emblematic Christ. Let Ravenwood bask in his shaman light. He, the great Mortimer Pringle, would bet only on the dark, and through its inky poison, heal.

His crown itched with a hint of horned growth, as a silent guffaw swarmed about his gut.

Yes, he and the dark magic would soon be indivisible—having forged the perfect, demonic pact—for while a man disguised as a devil might seek revenge, only a genuine one could ever attain it.

THE END

RAVENWOOD: MY SECOND STAB

I gained a hankering for contributing to Frederick C. Davis's *Ravenwood, Stepson of Mystery* when Ron Fortier asked me to supply a story for Airship 27's Vol 3. I wrote "Kincaid's House of Altered Cats" as a result and upon its completion, I asked Captain Ron if I might contribute a tale to another volume I'm sure glad he bestowed me the blessing.

For "A Devil By Any Other Name", I wanted to bring Inspector Horatio Stagg into the mix since he was at best namedropped in my previous story. I also came to like the inspector a lot and wanted to present my own spin on him. I believed his interaction with Ravenwood (and others) would be a joy to depict.

The big question was the plot, and a plot is only as good as its villain. I've long had an irksome feel for self-righteous types, in particular those of a secular sort. I thought it might be neat to include an antagonist who despised magic and yet hid behind its cloak to con those he thought beneath him. I also wanted the antagonist to be motivated by revenge due to some great wrong he felt was done to him. As such, Mortimer Pringle was born.

Pringle's persona is in large part based on Pan, a fun character but one I suspect would get on my nerves after a spell due to his self-indulgent nature. With Pringle, snooty indulgence would define him, albeit in a vaudevillian way.

Supporting characters were submitted to bounce off Pringle, including the obliging Sterling and the distanced-but-mindful Nameless One, but the Cherubs are Pringle's adversarial pull. Their daughter, Gwendoline, is most significant in this respect. She's the true core of the action, even if she says (and wears) little.

Well, as it stands, I've woven another Ravenwood yarn. I'm darn proud of that fact and will be forever grateful to Airship 27's generous publisher for giving me the chance to take another stab at Davis' mythology. Thanks, Captain Ron!

MICHAEL F. HOUSEL - In addition to his Ravenwood contributions, Housel has authored the following for Airship 27: *MARK JUSTICE'S THE DEAD SHERIFF, VOL 4, PURITY; THE HYDE SEED; THE PERSONA, VOL 1:*

ENTER—THE PERSONA!; and *THE PERSONA, VOL 2: GREEN-FLESHED FIENDS.*

Housel also contributes to Main Enterprises' pop-cultural magazine, WHAT EVER!, and his work is featured in the Eighth Tower Publishing release, *THE BLACK STONE: STORIES FOR LOVECRAFTIAN SUMMONINGS.* His movie, collectible and book reviews are queued at http://bizarrechats.blogspot.com/.

THE PAST REPEATS ITSELF, BUT THERE IS MORE THAN ONE PAST

by Carson Demmans

Ravenwood stared at the beautiful woman sitting across the table for two they occupied in a fashionable restaurant. He was not a lady's man by any stretch of the imagination, but if anything, that made the time he spent with this blonde goddess in the daring evening gown even more exciting. For one thing, she lied to him incessantly, and for no apparent reason. She claimed to be a member of the rich idle class from California. She must have been rich, judging by her lifestyle and tastes, but nothing about this fascinating creature suggested for one tenth of a second that she was ever idle. She was full of vigor and adventure, and it made him feel alive.

She in turn was fascinated by his appearance, particularly his eyes. The longer they were together, his eyes seemed to shift color from their original dark serious color to pale robin's blue. His eyes were full of a softness that she rarely saw in her own life, and she almost regretted the false pretenses she had used to lure him out for supper. Still, he seemed to be enjoying himself, so perhaps she shouldn't feel guilty at all.

"Tell me what you are thinking," she asked seductively.

"That I am enjoying looking into your eyes more than anything else I have done in a very long time," he said.

"Then tell me what you see," she said.

His eyes shifted in color yet again. They were dark when they first met, but now they were as black as his mood now was.

"So, is that why you pursued me and asked me out for supper?" Ravenwood said coldly. "You want me to tell your fortune?"

"If I wanted that I would go to a carnival," she said bluntly. "You are a fascinating man, Ravenwood. Let me make that perfectly clear. And, I am glad I sought you out here in New York even if I didn't have pure motives to begin with, because I have enjoyed your company. But, yes, I want to know what you see in my future."

"Your mutilated corpse," he said flatly. "I do not know how you die, but your enemies perform every indignity possible on you after you suffer a horrible death of some kind. Your identity will never be determined once the authorities find your body."

"You don't seem that choked up about it," she said with an amused expression.

"Why should I?" he replied. "You knew the answer before you asked me."

She laughed softly as she rose from her chair in a swish of silk that exposed more than enough skin to make her the center of attention in a poorly lit room where people strained to read menus right in front of their faces.

"Anything else?" she asked with a smile.

"Yes," he admitted. "But, I have no idea what it means. It is a proverb, or possibly a prediction. The phrase 'All dominoes must fall' is part of your future."

She laughed again, but this time with such vigor that it echoed throughout the restaurant. She bent towards him and kissed him lightly on the cheek, but then had second thoughts on the subject. She forcefully turned his face with her arms and kissed him on the mouth hard and with a great deal of genuine affection if not passion. He would be the envy of every man in the restaurant that night and for some time to come.

He knew that he would never see her again, which troubled him. He had the power to see the future, but it was something that happened and not something he controlled. It was often like seeing a speck on the horizon several thousand yards away. He did not know what it was until he got closer. Perhaps she did not want to see him again, and perhaps she did but was unable to because of some secret she kept from the world, or she might simply reach her inevitable fate which she seemed to accept if not anticipate with glee. He would never forget her.

"You are a strange woman, Ellen Patrick," he thought to himself as he finished his cocktail alone. When he signaled to the waiter for the bill, he discovered that his companion had not only paid the bill but had paid for a month's worth of meals for him as a going away present. He shook his head in dismay. One day all of this would make sense, but he had no idea when that day would come, or if he would be alive to see it.

The man called Ravenwood had his own secrets. He could see things that other people could not, such as glimpses of the future or realities about the present that were invisible to others. Just as his eyes seemed to change color as his moods did, the world changed around him in ways that others did not see, revealing things he shouldn't know but were so obvious he could not ignore them. A man in the corner laughed heartily while enjoying what would be his last meal before his massive heart attack later that night. A man was crushed as his girlfriend rejected his proposal only to be relieved when she was executed years later for murdering her husband and children for insurance money. With each gesture they made, he could see the ripple effects that they would have on their futures. At least, he thought he could At times, the future revealed that those ripples were actually tidal waves intent on drowning him.

He retrieved his hat and walking stick from the hat check and left by himself, as he always did. At home, there was no wife or children to greet him. There was the Nameless One, the Tibetan mystic who had raised him and had powers far beyond his understanding, and gave him guidance in the form of riddles that often had four or five different possible meanings, some, all or none of which might prove to be true. Also at home was Sterling, the perfect British servant who had wandered into Ravenwood's life years earlier and who had stayed for reasons Ravenwood did not understand. The man was totally out of place in a household shimmering with mystical power, but somehow his sheer ordinariness fit in somewhere in the cracks between premonitions and astral projection.

As he approached his fashionable apartment, Ravenwood was suddenly spun around by an arm that grasped his own arm from behind. Ravenwood grasped his walking stick tightly. It was heavy and more than capable of smashing a skull is he swung it with all of his strength. If that failed, the core of the stick concealed a razor-sharp sword, and his automatic was concealed in a custom-made holster under his left armpit. Ravenwood believed in magic, but he trusted cold hard steel as well.

Before him stood a ruddy faced Englishman holding a tattered newspaper clipping in his hand and who did not appear to be a threat in any way.

"Do you know this man?" the stranger asked as he showed Ravenwood a photo in the clipping.

"Of course!" Ravenwood said with a smile. "That's me! It was taken after I helped the police solve a crime."

"Not you, you silly beggar!" the Englishman moaned. "The man in the background, standing behind you."

Ravenwood squinted and realized that Sterling had wandered into the photo when it was taken in their home.

"My butler," Ravenwood replied. "Also, my cook and dear friend. What do you want with him?"

"To save his life, and mine, and to kill the devil himself!" the man said with great earnest. Ravenwood shrugged and led the man to his home. He sensed no danger from the man and he could easily kill him if necessary. He wanted to know what was going on, and to give help to those who needed it if he could.

Arriving at his home, Ravenwood saw Sterling approaching as he always did when his master returned home. Sterling tried to be the proper servant but could not help grinning whenever Ravenwood returned. The grin quickly turned into a look of pure horror before the tall servant collapsed before Ravenwood and the stranger.

The Nameless One seemed to appear from out of thin air to help Sterling.

The holy man could heal people with a touch so gentle that many travelling evangelists would kill to learn how to do. Ravenwood knew that his friend was in the best hands possible, so he turned to the guest in his home.

"Now that you've seen Sterling and he's seen you and almost died, do you mind telling me what's going on?'

"He will die unless he kills the Red Baron!" the Englishman gasped.

"Kill the Red Baron?" Ravenwood asked in amazement.

"Yes!" the Englishman said with emphasis. "Again!"

"They say that the Red Baron had eighty kills and Billy Bishop had seventy-two Mr. Ravenwood," the Englishman who had identified himself as Alfie, after being assured that Sterling would be okay, explained. "But our Silver killed more than the two of them combined, and he was not a pilot! He was a foot-soldier who did most of his work with a sharpened bayonet and his own two hands!"

"So, Sterling's first name is Silver?" Ravenwood said in amazement. That revelation shocked Ravenwood more than the allegation that a man under his roof was a trained killer.

"I have no idea," Alfie said as he shook his head. "He never told anyone that and I doubt if he knew it himself, God bless him. But we needed something to call him other than Sterling so someone in the regiment picked Silver. He was worth his weight in it, so the name stuck."

The Nameless One grunted as he rubbed Sterling's temples with his skinny but strong fingers. They looked like they would snap if someone shook his hand too tightly, but Ravenwood had seen the old man push one of his slim fingers through a one-inch thick oak plank without even flinching let alone changing his mind about so senseless a venture.

"But what about the Red Baron?" Ravenwood asked.

'There was three of us who went out to where the Australians were holding the line," Alfie said. "I was driving the old man, which is what we called our Captain, James Street, and Silver. The old man was trying to palm Silver off on the Aussies. He wanted Silver dead and had already tried to get him before a firing squad twice. Both times our Silver escaped and made himself a hero one way or the other, always involving a bunch of dead Germans. Anyone else would have gotten a medal, but all he got was a stay of execution. The Aussies were a battle crazy bunch, so the old man figured if he sent Silver to them nature would take its course and he'd be done for. Oh, he was a madman, our Silver."

Alfie's face went white suddenly and he looked over to make sure that Silver hadn't recuperated yet.

"I mean was that he was like a madman, Mr. Ravenwood. He wasn't really mad! Nobody would ever say that about our Silver!"

Ravenwood looked at Alfie with a bemused expression. He was not sure whether to believe Alfie or write the Englishman off as a victim of the Great War. Many veterans had come back more wounded in the mind then they had in the body. But, by the expression on Alfie's face, he seemed very worried about how Sterling would react if he knew his old acquaintance had heard him.

"I have known Sterling for many years," Ravenwood said. "Madman is one of many words I would never use in describing him. Continue."

"Anyway, there was the three of us out heading for the Aussies when we spotted a dog fight in the air. Everyone knew about the Baron and that damn red plane of his. We found out later that he had been chased down towards the ground by Roy Brown, one of the Canadian aces. But, Brown was nowhere around when the Baron went down, you understand? We pulled the jeep over and our Silver jumped out with a .303 and fired. A few seconds after he stopped firing the Baron went down. Us and a bunch of Aussies ran out to the plane after it finally skidded to a stop on the ground and he was dead. Silver had killed the Red Baron."

"After that, a real dog fight took place!" Alfie said with a sigh. "The Canucks said it was their man Brown who had done it, and the Aussies said it was their gunners who done it. The old man kept quiet, but I didn't! I said it was our Silver and as I said it, I looked at the old man. So did everyone else! Everyone could tell by the look on his face that I was telling the truth! But, everyone knew about our Silver and what he was like. He was not hero material. But, this Brown was, you see? Great pilot, loved by his men, respected. Our Silver's reward was that he was sent home. The old man was part of a prominent family, see? His dad was a doctor and he became a doctor himself after the war. We called him the old man, but he really wasn't that much older than the rest of us. He just seemed old, see? So, he pulled some strings and Silver was sent back to an asylum in England."

"Hell," a dreary voice said. "I was sent to Hell."

Ravenwood and Alfie turned to see that Sterling had recovered. The Nameless One was smiling triumphantly and would later claim that Sterling had died repeatedly and that it was only his skill that saved him. Ravenwood never questioned such claims. Even if the ancient man was not telling the truth, he was capable of causing exquisite pain in anyone who questioned him.

"Silver!" Alfie said triumphantly. Sterling winced as he heard the name he was called.

"Alfie," Sterling said gravely. "How did you find me and why?"

"We've all been looking for you!" Alfie blurted. "Everyone left in the regiment has been looking for you. Someone saw your picture in a Yank newspaper and it was agreed that I would be sent to find you. But we're not the only ones looking for you! Barry's looking for you Silver!"

"Barry's dead," Sterling said flatly.

"He's back!" Alfie claimed. " Remember Little Davey? He was a good little lad. He was found dead, shot from above. And when the old man presided over the autopsy, they found that he was full of 7.92 millimetre slugs! Do you remember what shot those, Silver?"

Sterling stared at Alfie but refused to answer the question, even though he obviously knew the answer.

"The devil's Paintbrush! Spandaus! The same machine guns Barry used!" Alfie said.

"But Little Davey wasn't the last! No he was only the first! At least eight men from our old regiment have died the same way. And then the letters started to the newspapers. The papers printed them but they really didn't know what they meant. But our regiment did! The letters said that these deaths were only the beginning and they wouldn't stop until the madman who killed him was dead. And they were all signed Barry!"

"Who was Barry?" Ravenwood asked pleasantly. He still did not know what to make of all this but it was at least as entertaining as any radio program he had ever heard.

"That was what we called the Red Baron," Sterling explained reluctantly.

"But that was what only our regiment called him," Alfie said. "It was Silver who thought of it and we all followed suit, see? But it was only us who called Richthofen that! Nobody else! So these letters were meant only for us, see?"

"So why find Sterling?" Ravenwood asked.

"Some of us think Barry's ghost is back and the rest are stupid and think it's just someone who is pretending to be him, see? But we all agree that only Silver can put an end to this. Whoever or whatever the killer is, he's not going to stop until he finds you, mate."

Sterling's lower lip curled slightly. Ravenwood was shocked, He had never seen his butler display so much emotion at once. Alfie hesitated before he asked his next question.

"Did you see him, Silver? Did you see him at the asylum? Your dad, I mean? That was why the old man picked that place you know. Well, plus his dad was in charge."

Sterling nodded slightly.

"I hate to tell you this Silver, but he's passed away now. The old man said to tell you when I found you. I'm sorry, mate. I know he was in a bad way and not much of a dad, but most of them aren't you know? Did he know who you were, at least?"

Sterling nodded again but did not smile at the memory.

"Look," Alife said as he handed Sterling a card, "I'm staying at this hotel. The old man put me up there. The hotel gave me this card to give to people that I wanted to come see me. Come see me, mate. We'll talk in private. You don't owe me or any of the old boys anything, Silver, but I don't think you want us all to end up dead either, do you?"

Ravenwood watched Sterling's face as Alfie left. He could tell that Alfie had hit a nerve with his last comment and that Sterling would go to visit his old comrade.

"Your father has left you his legacy," the Nameless One said in a soft tome.

"My father was a penniless lunatic who died in the asylum he spent most of his life in," Sterling said with more of a snap in his voice than usual." He left me nothing."

"And yet people believe that you inherited something from him," the Nameless One sighed. The ancient man left the room but his feet did not seem to touch the floor as he glided across the floor and back to his room.

"I shall resign at once, sir," Sterling said sadly.

"Why?" Ravenwood said with surprise. "Have I done something to offend you?

"Sir!" Sterling said with surprise. "You have just found out that I have lied to you for years."

"You did not such thing, Sterling," Ravenwood said as he slapped his butler on the back in a friendly manner. "You certainly never told me that you hadn't served in the war or escaped from an asylum, so you never lied at all. You never told me the entire story, but there are more secrets in this apartment than in the libraries of Alexandria and the New York Public Library combined. I always knew that you lived a life before we met. I also knew that when it was necessary you would tell me about it."

"I had no life before I met you, sir," Sterling said. "Before that, I had a miserable existence of poverty in London, the horror of the Great War, and then the living Hell of an insane asylum. When I escaped from it, I made my way to America and tried to establish a new life here. But, when I met you and the old master, sir, everything changed. I don't know why, but being in your presence has always had a tremendous effect on me."

"Like magic?" Ravenwood said with a smile.

"I don't pretend to understand everything you and the old master can do sir, but that doesn't mean that I believe in magic, sir," Sterling said in his most dignified tone.

"You don't have to," Ravenwood said to himself. "It doesn't care if you believe in it or not."

With that thought, a vision suddenly filled Ravenwood's mind. He grabbed the card from Sterling and memorized the address of the small hotel. He was still wearing his hat and gloves, and told Sterling to get dressed as quickly as possible. Seconds later the two of them were roaring down the streets of New York as fast as traffic and the engine of his sportscar would allow. Sterling tried to remain stoic but a million emotions ran through his brain at once. He was embarrassed that Ravenwood had learned about his past, but thankful his employer was going to help him. He was also terrified because although he enjoyed hearing about his master's exploits as an occult detective, he had never wanted to actually take part in any of them.

By contrast, only two thoughts were in Ravenwood's mind. The first was that he and Sterling had to get to Alfie as soon as possible. The second was that no matter how fast he drove, they would be too late.

He parked his car illegally and raced to the room number on the card. Sterling followed and shuddered as he saw Ravenwood kick in the door of Alfie's room. As he entered, he saw Ravenwood standing sadly in the middle of the room, and Alfie lying on the floor in a pool of blood, his heart having been obliterated by a flurry of machine gun bullets that had left a gaping hole behind.

Ravenwood and Sterling stood there, frozen in time and space until a familiar but unwelcome voice snarled triumphantly behind them.

"You're under arrest, Ravenwood!" Inspector Stagg snarled triumphantly as he entered the room. The portly policeman had hated Ravenwood since the mysterious young man had first appeared in New York and solved a case Stagg had been assigned to. Stagg always resented him for it, even though Stagg's incompetence meant that he would have never solved the case in any event on his own.

"You are under arrest for murder!" Stagg clarified as he moved to put Ravenwood in handcuffs. Sterling instinctively put himself in between Ravenwood and the policeman. He knew that his master did not need his protection, but the sheer repulsiveness of Stagg made him want to keep Stagg from talking to Ravenwood, let alone touch him. Sterling did the laundry for the household and he envisioned having to use extra effort in removing sweaty handprints from his master's clothes if he let Stagg touch Ravenwood.

"Do you see a machine gun, inspector?" Ravenwood said with a smile. "Your investigator will find that is what this man was killed with, and I left mine at home."

"He's right, inspector!" a burly policeman said. "I was in the war sir. This is what it looked like when the Jerries ripped through our boys with one of those damn machine guns of theirs."

"A Spandau," Sterling said, still in shock.

"Right!" the patrolman said enthusiastically. "That's what they were called! Did you serve overseas?"

Sterling nodded.

"He was in my regiment," Sterling said. "He had just come to see me, and my employer and I were here to see him. He wasn't my friend. I had no friends in the army, but he was trying to be."

"A brother in arms beats having a friend any day of the week, pal," the patrolman said. Two other policemen who accompanied Stagg on his raid nodded in agreement. Stagg hated Ravenwood beyond reason. It was a matter of pure primal instinct bearing no resemblance to logic in any way. To that end, Stagg had intimidated, bribed and threatened bellhops, clerks and support people in dozens of hotels all over the city to keep an eye out for Ravenwood so the inspector would always be ready to pounce on his nemesis if he was seen doing anything remotely suspicious.

"I'll help you avenge your comrade, Sterling," Ravenwood said reassuringly. Stagg guffawed in response.

"You were never in the army, Ravenwood, but I was!" Stagg said derisively. "You know nothing about fallen comrades."

"And you were in the army but not the war," Ravenwood whispered in the ear of Stagg as he approached the fireplug shaped cop. "Do you really want your men to find that out from me?"

This information had suddenly come into his mind, so Ravenwood had no idea if it was true or false. Stagg's expression showed him that not only was it true but something he had lied about more than once.

"You devil!" Stagg hissed back. "Did you break into headquarters and read my file? I wouldn't put it past you!"

Ravenwood smiled as he took a step back from Stagg. Stagg was convinced that Ravenwood was a charlatan who used stage magic tricks to create the illusion that he had mystic powers. Ravenwood himself wasn't sure what powers he had and when he was receiving some sort of assistance from the Nameless One. In the meantime, Sterling was chatting with the patrol men who had come in with Stagg.

"So nobody reported a shooting?" Sterling said in disbelief. "If he was shot with a Spandau, the whole hotel would have heard it."

"You know nothing about fallen comrades."

Stagg suddenly turned his attention on his patrol men, and the attention wasn't pleasant.

"Don't give any information to him!" Stagg howled. "At best he's a civilian, and at worst he's the killer!"

"The deceased is a foreigner, Inspector," one of the patrolmen grumbled. "Mr. Sterling here says he has no family here or back in England. As Mr. Sterling is the only one in the U.S.A. who had a connection to him, shouldn't we talk to him?"

Stagg glared at the patrolman, but knew better than to push his luck. His promotions within the force that had led him to becoming an inspector had been equal parts politics and pure luck. At best, the patrolmen tolerated him and at worst he occasionally heard them cocking their pistols when his back was turned.

"Alright then, Mr. Sterling," Stagg said in a tone that was as close to respectful he could manage, "tell me why your friend was here in New York and why he's dead."

Sterling's face showed a moment of panic, but Ravenwood gave him a reassuring nod, and the butler told the tale. He left out certain details and downplayed his possible role in Richthofen's death, but otherwise he gave them the story as he knew it. Stagg guffawed when Sterling was done. The patrolmen who were veterans were far less skeptical.

"I remember hearing at the time that Roy Brown wasn't responsible," one of them said. "The way I heard it, he hadn't shot at the Baron for at least two minutes before Richthofen went down, and the Baron was shot right through the chest and lungs. Death would have been a lot sooner than two minutes."

"I'm not much for believing in ghosts," another veteran said," but people said the Baron must have had a deal with the devil to be as good as he was. Even if it isn't his ghost, he was a national hero in Germany. Probably some fanatic is taking revenge on the people he thinks are responsible."

"Do you have any proof at all for that ludicrous statement?" Stagg demanded. One of the patrolmen pointed at Alfie's bullet riddled corpse.

"Not a lot of Spandau machine guns in New York, Inspector," he said. "And if there are any, I'm pretty sure they make noise. Do you have a better explanation?"

Stagg's reply was a hasty exit.

"I don't understand," Ravenwood sighed as he sat cross-legged across from the Nameless one in their apartment. "I want to help Sterling, but I don't know where to start."

"That is because you are looking at the sky," the Nameless One said. "You must look at the ground instead."

"Why the ground?" Ravenwood wondered aloud.

"That is where the dead are buried," the Nameless One said with a smile.

Ravenwood stood up suddenly and got dressed. He never left his apartment unless he was wearing gloves and carrying his walking stick. He liked to project the image of an aristocratic scholar, as it was that image that allowed him to make a lucrative income as an author, lecturer and consulting detective. He raced to his sports car and then drove at top speed to the morgue where Alfie's body was being kept.

Back at the apartment, the Nameless One laughed at the actions of the man he had raised since he was a boy.

"He is making progress quickly," he said. "It is too bad it is in the wrong direction."

Ravenwood had helped the police on many occasions and was no stranger to the morgue. The men who worked there knew him and knew that they would not get into trouble if they told him everything they knew. In return, Ravenwood told them what prophesies he knew that affected them. On more than one occasion he had done them greater favors than they could ever do for him.

"There wasn't much in the dead man's possessions," a morgue attendant told him. "His pockets were full of junk, and his wallet was undisturbed, so we don't think he was robbed."

"Did he have any cash?" Ravenwood asked.

"A couple of British coins," the morgue attendant said. "Worthless here."

"Then how did he pay for his room and food in New York?" Ravenwood asked. The morgue attendant was speechless. He went back and looked at the Alfie's belongings.

"Good catch, Mr. Ravenwood," the morgue attendant said. "There are receipts here for the room and food at the hotel, but they aren't made out to the deceased. A Dr. James Street was paying his way and signed for everything. I know all of the doctors in New York, but I don't know him."

"That's fine," Ravenwood said as he left. "I know someone who does."

"The old man is in New York?" Sterling said. He was obviously in shock. "I suppose that makes sense. Alfie was as close to a friend in the army that I had, so he was the logical choice to be sent to find me. But, because he was a friend of mine, the old man wouldn't trust him as far as he could throw the Tower of London. If he was paying Alfie's way, and that is the only way Alfie could ever come here, he'd come along to make sure he wasn't being taken advantage of."

"I take it your commanding officer didn't rely on the love of his troops to command them?" Ravenwood asked.

"He hated us," Sterling said bluntly. "At best we were a bunch of working-class men, and at worst a few of us were in the army to not be in jail. The old man came from old money. His family ran that damned asylum and called it a work of charity. If that was their idea of charity, I'd hate to see what they did to people they held a grudge against."

"How long were you there, Sterling?"

"I don't know. Weeks? Months? Time has no meaning there. There are no clocks or calendars. Most of the time you never get to look out a window or go outside so you have no idea what time of day it is. If my father hadn't been truly mad he would have never lasted in there as long as he did."

Ravenwood closed his eyes. It was longer than a blink but not so much that most people would have noticed.

"Rascal," Ravenwood said.

"What?" Sterling said with surprise. "That's what my father used to call me when I was a boy."

"And he did again when you saw him there?" Ravenwood asked.

"He did," Sterling admitted. "He knew me. Most of what he said made no sense, but he did call me that."

"And what else did he tell you?" the Nameless One asked. Even Ravenwood was shocked by the ancient man's sudden and silent appearance.

"Lots of things. Nothing. It was hard to tell with him. He was better when I was younger, at least at times. Mother said he took spells. It was more like he was under a spell. He'd start raving about whores and thanked God that my mother wasn't one. He loved her, I think. He never laid a hand on her or me, for that matter. But, we were the lucky ones. He'd brawl in the streets with strangers or break into the neighbor's place and wreck it. He'd end up in jail at first, and finally it was the mad house. He made me tell him about all of the men I killed in the war. He was never a soldier, at least that I knew of, but those stories seemed to make him happy."

"He was proud of you," Ravenwood said reassuringly.

"Did the dead man know your father?" the Nameless One asked.

"Of course not," Sterling said. "I never spoke of him, either."

"Then how did Alfie know so much about him?" Ravenwood asked.

"I have no idea," Sterling admitted. "The old man must have told him, but I don't know why he would."

"If your old commander is here," Ravenwood said, "perhaps that is who we should talk to next. He would be the only other person in New York with any knowledge of the danger you're in."

"His family had property here, of some kind," Sterling said. "They had property everywhere, for that matter."

"Then that is where we'll look for him," Ravenwood said. He and Sterling found an address through a call to one of Ravenwood's contacts at city hall and left together. As soon as they reached the street, they were attacked by a gang of men.

There were four of them, young and in fighting shape. They pushed Ravenwood aside and focused on Sterling, which was their first mistake. In doing so, they pushed past Ravenwood, and this meant they had their backs turned to him.

Ravenwood's walking stick had been hardened by an ancient Tibetan method that was now lost to science, but that was extremely effective anyway. It was as hard as steel, and the two men Ravenwood hit in the head with it went down instantly. The third man tried to pull the stick from Ravenwood's grasp, but only succeeded in pulling the wooden shaft off of the steel blade it concealed inside. The thug yelled, and the words made Sterling go white with fear. The thug used the hard wood to block Ravenwood's sword as it tried to bisect him. The thug was taller than Ravenwood and managed a high kick that landed in the center of Ravenwood's chest, knocking him to the ground. The thug then turned to help his comrade against Sterling. Sterling was struggling with his first attacker and was overwhelmed when the second one joined in. The man with the stick brought his arm back to swing the walking stick at the butler's head. Ravenwood was back on his feet by that point and pulled the man's arm back further, knocking the thug off balance and allowing Ravenwood to flip him over his hip and onto the sidewalk. He retrieved his walking stick, and now held it in one hand and his sword in the other. The last attacker reached into his pocket and pulled out a pistol. Moving faster than the eye could see, Ravenwood dropped his weapons and pulled out his own pistol, a modified Luger, and fired. The criminal's gun went flying as Ravenwood's bullet knocked it from his grasp.

Sterling was in a rage for the first time that Ravenwood had ever seen, and it was not a pretty sight. The butler grabbed Ravenwood's sword from the sidewalk and rushed the remaining criminal. He would have run the man through if the other thugs had not recovered slightly. One of them tripped Sterling and the other two knocked Ravenwood down long enough for all four of them to make their escape.

"Germans1" Sterling panted. "They were all Germans! I recognized their language!"

"Do you speak German?" Ravenwood asked.

"Not at all," Sterling admitted.

"I do," Ravenwood said. "Why would they have been screaming questions about where the train station, museum and a good restaurant were?"

A frantic Sterling and a confused Ravenwood made their way to the Street family's New York home. On the outside, it appeared to be simply a large house in a decent neighborhood. Inside, it resembled an English Manor. A suitably aloof English butler looked at Sterling and Ravenwood with disdain, and paid no attention to Ravenwood's calling card other than to make sure it landed in the garbage bin he had aimed at. Sterling told the servant to announce that Private Sterling was requesting to see his commanding officer, and the servant reluctantly relayed the message to whoever was in the study that was off of the front entry of the home. He returned and pointed them on their way, making sure to insult Sterling as he passed.

"Imposter," the servant hissed. "If you're truly a butler, I'm the King of Scotland!"

"That would explain your horrible enunciation," Ravenwood said with a smile. The servant backed off and Ravenwood stepped aside to let Sterling lead the way.

Ravenwood entered the study in awe. Ravenwood's penthouse was quite lavish by New York standards, but the Street house put it to shame. The high ceiling was supporting a huge chandelier, and the walls were covered with shelves of leather bound books or hunting trophies from African safaris. There were a few sitting chairs and coffee tables, but one wall was dominated by a massive desk. It was obviously ancient but was so highly polished it almost blinded anyone who looked at it. Ravenwood noted with some satisfaction, however, that the front of the desk had recently gone through some sort of repair or modification. The Streets furnishings were as old as their money was.

Dr. Street sat behind the desk on a chair that could only be described as a small throne. Ravenwood saw why he had been called the old man by his soldiers. The doctor was not much older than Sterling but looked at him with the disdain of a nobleman looking at a street urchin.

"So, you've gone from pretending to be a soldier to pretending to be a gentleman's gentleman, eh Sterling?" Dr. Street said.

Sterling blushed at the insult but Ravenwood did not even blink an eye.

"If by pretending you mean he has succeeded at both, then you are right," Ravenwood said with a slight edge of sarcasm in his voice. Street looked at Ravenwood for the first time, and the firm upper lip of the aristocrat trembled slightly.

"Are you Sterling's son?" Street asked, obviously with some fear.

"Proud employer," Ravenwood replied. "I would be even prouder if I was his son."

Sterling allowed himself to smile slightly for a second but forced his face to go blank again when his former commander looked at him gruffly.

"I sent your friend Alfie to find you, and he ended up dead," Street said. "What do you have to say about that?"

Sterling said nothing in reply. Ravenwood answered for him.

"How did you know Alfie was dead?" Ravenwood asked. "It has not been in the newspapers yet."

"The hotel contacted me to demand further payment to clean his blood up," the doctor said with disdain. "A mercenary society, you Americans. No respect for anything. I can see why you came here, Sterling."

"And did you come all this way to insult him?" Ravenwood asked sharply. "You seem to have put value on finding Sterling and then abuse him once you have done so. Supposedly you wanted to do so to benefit the men who served under you, or is that as much false charity as this asylum I understand your family runs?"

"Do not speak to me in that tone, young man, or I will be forced to come out from behind this desk!" Street growled loudly. Ravenwood was in no mood to be addressed as if he was a spoiled child, which was exactly what he suspected Street would have been once. He walked boldly behind the desk and gripped the Doctor's chair firmly with one hand. Ravenwood was far stronger than he appeared to be, and with some effort he was able to loudly drag the massive chair and its outraged occupant out from behind the desk.

"Men who were once your responsibility are dead and Sterling and I nearly joined them earlier today after being attacked by Germans with limited knowledge of their own language. You don't seem to care about either. I suggest you tell me immediately what your objective is and do it now."

Street tried to show no emotion but failed miserably. Finally, and with some embarrassment, he looked at Sterling.

"I stand by my words, Sterling," Street began, "as you were probably the worst soldier who ever lived in terms of discipline, respecting chain of command and following orders. You were a drunken, brawling criminal. But, you saved many lives in my regiment, and I should have recognized that at the time. Perhaps you were the one to kill Richthofen. The damn story has been told so many times now by so many different people, the world will never know the truth now. I should have found some other way of getting you home instead of having you shipped off to the asylum, but even you agreed at the time that it was better than the firing squad. You were the one who started the course of action that almost led to your execution, not me."

Sterling said nothing, but he also did not disagree with anything being said.

"Men are being killed, Sterling," Street said flatly. "More men are going to die. I haven't the slightest idea why this is happening, but it is. Somehow, you are involved. I am asking for your help. It is time to go home, Sterling."

Sterling looked at a grandfather's clock in the study and confirmed the time with his own pocket watch.

"You are correct, sir," Sterling said with as close to a sarcastic tone that Ravenwood had ever heard the man use. "It is time to go home. I will wait in the car, Mr. Ravenwood so that you can drive both of us back to our home."

Sterling spun on his heel and began to leave the study.

"Your home is England, you traitor!" Street yelled at him.

"In England, I was never discharged from the army or the asylum," Sterling replied. "I am an escaped fugitive and a deserter, and I face the same military charges that could have me executed. You see, sir, I checked. You had told me the charges would be dismissed if I went to the Hell hole your family calls an asylum. Instead, they were only suspended while I was there. If I was ever discharged, the prosecution would continue and I would undoubtedly be convicted and shot. If anyone in this room is a traitor, sir, it isn't me."

Street was speechless as Sterling continued to walk out of the study. Street's butler stepped in the way to block Sterling, but when he looked Sterling square in the eye, he had second thoughts and let Sterling pass.

"Good men are going to die!" Street yelled as Ravenwood turned to follow Sterling.

"Yes, I suppose they could," Ravenwood admitted. "But, Sterling is also a good man, and I plan on doing everything possible to make sure that he isn't one of the ones who will die. You're in as much danger as anyone else, Street. Save yourself instead of ordering men like Sterling to do it for you."

Sterling was sitting in the passenger seat of Ravenwood's sports car by the time he caught up with his butler.

"I did a selfish thing just now, didn't I?" Sterling asked with some guilt in his voice.

"No matter what you did, Sterling, you could end up being shot to death," Ravenwood said. "But we know that the killer is now on this side of the Atlantic and other than Street, no member of your regiment is here in the States. In that sense, by staying here, you are saving the lives of the men you served with."

Sterling nodded. He didn't necessarily agree with Ravenwood's line of reasoning, but he appreciated it that a wealthy man who owed him nothing was standing up for him and trying to reassure him.

Sterling's appreciation of Ravenwood diminished ever so slightly when both of the tires on the passenger side of the car suddenly burst. Ravenwood lost control of the car and it crashed into the back of a parked panel truck. Neither man was hurt but both were stunned. They were stunned enough to not be able to run off immediately but still be aware of the fact that the gang of Germans they had escaped before was advancing on them again, guns drawn.

Ravenwood drew his Luger and started firing. He wasn't even trying to hit anything in particular. He was still dazed after the car accident, and his mind was racing.

"Take cover," Ravenwood said to Sterling. "My guess is that our tires were shot out, and whoever did it is still around."

To emphasize the point, a few ricochets near Sterling's head was enough to make him take cover.

"I can hear the ricochets but not the shots," Ravenwood thought. "Perhaps that's why they thought a ghost was involved."

The advancing thugs were taking their time, and Ravenwood fired another volley of shots in their general direction. They had no idea what he was up to until police sirens could be heard in the distance.

"People still care in New York," Ravenwood thought. "It just takes a few more shots than it used to draw attention to yourself."

The sirens were coming up behind the thugs but Ravenwood was in front of them. They decided to scatter down side streets, yelling in German as they went.

"They say it is a nice day if it doesn't rain. Interesting," mused Ravenwood.

Stagg was the first man out of the patrol car and he raced toward Ravenwood with his handcuffs already out.

"Let's see you get out of this one, Houdini!" Stagg said, laughing at his own joke. He had to. Nobody else found it funny.

"I have a permit for my gun," Ravenwood sighed. "You know that. If you had found the Mayor's daughter's kitten before I did, maybe I wouldn't. Sterling and I were attacked."

"Nice try, Ravenwood!" Stagg gloated. "But witnesses report only hearing one person shooting, and that would be you."

"There were shots from above!" Sterling blurted out. "There was no sound, but there were shots."

"Same as at the hotel, Inspector," a patrolman offered. "If you could solve both of these crimes, it would be a real feather in your cap."

"Meaning?" Stagg asked.

"Meaning we have other leads to follow other than Mr. Ravenwood and

The sirens were coming up behind the thugs.

Private Sterling. Maybe we should let them go. We can always find them if we need them."

Sterling winced slightly at being called private, but the cop was one of the veterans he had talked to earlier. It was meant as a show of respect, and Sterling appreciated it.

"We don't have to find them," Stagg muttered. "They always find me. Get out of here, Ravenwood, but here's a warning for the two of you. Dr. Street has already called in a complaint about the two of you, and he's a powerful man. Apparently he's old friends with the pathologist and coroner for New York, and he's a good friend of the commissioner. Savvy? You're walking on thin ice."

"And you're worried I might fall through?" Ravenwood asked with a slight smile.

"I'm worried that I won't get a chance to drown you myself. Get out of here, and do it now. But, you're walking. Your car will have to be towed off and investigated as evidence."

The two men wandered towards a busy intersection in the hope of finding a taxi.

"Do you own a handgun, Sterling?" Ravenwood asked.

"No, sir."

"Then I'll have to get you one."

"No, sir," Sterling replied. Ravenwood arched an eyebrow in surprise.

"Are you defying me, Sterling?" Ravenwood asked in surprise.

"Yes, sir, I am. I wanted to resign but I respected your wishes and stayed. I now ask that you respect my wishes."

"You need to be able to protect yourself until this mess is over", Ravenwood argued. "Here. Carry my walking stick, at least. Do you know how to pull the sword out of it?"

Sterling pulled the blade out of the core of the stick and expertly looked down its shaft. After admiring its balance, he waved it in the air with a certain flourish and slipped it back into its hiding place.

"It's an impressive weapon sir," Sterling commented as they found a cab. "I have admired it for many years."

As I have admired you, old friend, Ravenwood thought. *As I have admired you.*

When they arrived back at their home, Ravenwood realized it was a good thing that Sterling didn't have a gun, or he wouldn't have a mentor. The Nameless One had used Sterling's absence as an opportunity to experiment in Sterling's beloved kitchen. The entire apartment stunk of burnt herbs, spices and other plant matter.

"You emptied an entire jar of ginger?" Sterling asked in dismay.

"How could I know how much was left unless I poured it all out?" The Nameless One asked innocently.

Ravenwood pulled the old man out of harm's way and Sterling launched himself into a cleaning frenzy that would have pleased any sergeant in the military.

"I need your help," Ravenwood whispered to the Tibetan mystic.

"No, but you want it," the Nameless One said with a smile. "In following every trail you have become lost. Go back to the beginning."

Ravenwood thought for a second.

"Everything began when Alfie found Sterling. He was trying to find him so no more people would be killed."

"Perhaps," the Nameless One said. "But that was not the beginning. It is only when you became aware."

Ravenwood thought hard.

"It began with the death of the Red Baron," Ravenwood mused.

"That pebble was dropped twenty years ago," the Nameless One replied sternly, growing impatient with his pupil's efforts. "It is highly unlikely it is still making ripples in the pond today."

"So, someone wanted to find Sterling, and is using these murders to do it?" Ravenwood asked in a puzzled tone.

"The killer could not find him alone," the Nameless One explained.

"So, he mobilized an army regiment who was motivated to find him to save their own skins?" Ravenwood queried.

"Do not ask questions," the Nameless One said as he glided out of the room. "Find answers."

A vision struck Ravenwood in a violent flash. Just as his eyes changed color with his emotions, the intensity of his visions varied with the nature of what they showed. He saw the horribly mutilated corpse of a woman. The vision burned itself through his brain and into his soul before it faded.

It made no sense. The woman had obviously been killed by a knife and not a machine gun, and all of the current victims were male. He decided to take a chance and talk to Sterling in a guarded fashion.

"Someone wanted to find you, Sterling," Ravenwood began slyly. "Someone who wants to kill you, perhaps for something that you did in the war?"

"I did many things in the war," Sterling admitted. "But it was war. Death was common."

"Then think of something uncommon," Ravenwood suggested.

"Oh my God!" Sterling gasped. "I haven't thought of her in years!"

"Who?" Ravenwood pressed.

"I had been sent out on a suicide mission by the old man to find stragglers left behind in no man's land. I always came back, which always disappointed him. I could hear someone approaching in the dark, and I was close to enemy lines, so I pounced. It was a girl. I have no idea why she was there. Perhaps she was innocent and lost or perhaps she was a collaborator with the Germans. I'll never know. I attacked her in a fury. I was furious with the old man, furious with the war, and with everyone on the planet, for that matter. When I came to my senses I saw what I had done to her. It was grotesque. I had basically gutted her. I was disgusted with myself and ran back to my own base. But, I never told anyone about it."

That doesn't mean nobody knew about it, Ravenwood thought.

"Had you ever seen her before?" Ravenwood asked.

"No, sir, women were few and far between where we were."

She had to be there for someone, Ravenwood mused to himself.

"I'm not like that anymore, sir," Sterling insisted.

"You're not what, Sterling? Human? You were in an impossible situation. You reacted in ways you never would otherwise. "

Ravenwood left Sterling and sought out his mentor. He found the Nameless One standing near a window, staring at a spot on the horizon miles away.

"You healed him when he first came to us, didn't' you?" Ravenwood accused. "Sterling was broken in his mind and his spirit and you healed him somehow."

The Nameless One shrugged.

"What if I did?" the ancient mystic answered. "I could tell the first time that I saw him that he needed help and I helped him."

"Lots of veterans needed help," Ravenwood countered.

"I can not help them all," the Nameless One sighed. "Even my powers have limits. I helped this one. Don't you think he deserved it?"

"And what would have happened if you hadn't?"

"Did you receive a vision of a slaughtered woman?"

Ravenwood nodded.

"Imagine that she is not the most horrible thing you had ever seen, but only the first link in a chain with each corpse more horrible than the one before it."

"And how long would this chain be?"

The Nameless One pointed at the spot in the distance he had been contemplating.

"Somewhere past there. Like my powers, my vision has its limits."

There was a knock on the door and Ravenwood heard Sterling open it. He also heard the door slam instantly afterwards with no words spoken. Curious, Ravenwood opened the door himself and found a shocked man standing there.

He was a stranger to Ravenwood, but obviously not to Sterling.

"I take it you were in the army with Sterling too?" Ravenwood guessed.

"You mean Silver Sterling?" the stranger said in a thick British accent. "I was, sir, I was. We were never friends but I never realized how far from friends we were."

"Then why are you here?"

"The old man has brought most of the surviving regiment here, sir. Strength in numbers I suppose. I was a friend of Alfie, sir. He was the first one sent to fetch Sterling."

"Fetch him to what?"

"I don't rightly know sir. It was the old man's idea. He's a mean bastard, the old man is, but he's not dumb. Silver thought he was sent on those missions because the old man hated him. The truth be known it was because Silver was the only one who could survive them. But, people are being killed, sir. Whoever or whatever is doing it wants us to find Silver. Can you blame us for trying?"

"So, you'd sacrifice him to save yourselves?"

The ruddy faced man laughed.

"A sacrifice would mean that the regiment would have to kill him, sir," he laughed. "Unless our Silver is a totally different man, he'd kill whoever was behind it and a few others for good measure. I may not like the man, but I have faith in him. I guess the old man does too. Why else would he do so much to find Silver? The old man is a problem solver. His dad was a doctor, and he is now too. A doctor cuts out the diseased part with a scalpel so the rest of the body can live. Silver is the scalpel sir, not the diseased part we want removed."

"Where were you to bring him?"

"The old man's place," the stranger said brightly. "Anytime today. A bunch of us are gathering there. It's huge place, I guess. If the old man is inviting the likes of me there, it must be important."

Ravenwood nodded as the stranger left. Once, Sterling may have been the vengeful scalpel that his old comrades were wishing for. But, that man had been forever changed if not erased from existence by the Nameless One. Ravenwood resolved that he would go to Dr. Street's home on Sterling's behalf. He felt responsible for Sterling no longer having all of the skills he needed to protect himself and the other veterans, so he would have to be their agent of vengeance himself.

Ravenwood went to Street's mansion on his own in his second sports car. There was a group of servants in front of the house registering guests as they arrived. Ravenwood signed Sterling's name on the register. The servants were so busy that they did not look up, although Ravenwood thought he noticed one of them make note of his signature and run off once they had done so. Rather than the main house they were directed to a large building at the rear of the property. The first time Ravenwood had been there he had not realized how far the lot extended behind the house.

The out building was large and bare. Perhaps in the past it had been used for large dances or public functions that the owners did not want in the main house. Inside, there was little happening other than confusion. Small groups of men loitered around, waiting for something to happen. It was announced that Dr. Street would be making an announcement soon, and people waited in anticipation, watching the end of the building where a small podium had been set up.

Ravenwood did not understand the source of his premonitions. Perhaps they were from some inherent power within him or they were messages from the Nameless One. In any event, he did know two things about them. Firstly, he didn't always know exactly what they meant. Secondly, when he did understand them, it was best to act on them. This premonition was particularly easy to understand, as it consisted of one simple word.

"Run!"

Although silent, it still echoed inside of his brain. He repeated it by screaming it as loud as he could and then bolting for the door. He tried to push some of the men outside but they resisted. Upon reaching the door, it was blocked from the outside. He took a step back and kicked the door as hard as he could. It took another attempt, but he was able to create an opening large enough to squeeze through. As he ran away, he chanced a quick look back and saw that junk had been piled against the door to prevent exit.

A quick look was all he had time for. The explosion was enough to knock him off of his feet, and he was already hundreds of feet away. The first explosion was followed by others, each in a different part of the building. He waited several seconds before he dared to return to the building, or rather where it had been. Some bodies had been ripped apart from the blast and others were intact but dead. There appeared to be no survivors. The spot that had been the speaker's podium was now a crater. Apparently the podium had contained its own bomb so that Dr. Street would be annihilated.

He looked around but no servants rushed toward the bomb site. Perhaps they had all run off in fear.

Ravenwood sat down and made himself as comfortable as he could on a patch of grass not far from where the building had stood. As he suspected. Inspector Stagg arrived in a few minutes. Some of the same patrolmen were with Stagg that Ravenwood had dealt with earlier.

"Is Private Sterling okay?" one of them inquired.

"He didn't come," Ravenwood said. He found their concern amusing, especially because Stagg found it annoying.

"Damn you all!" Stagg bellowed. "We come upon a mass murder, the only suspect is standing right before you, and you only worry about the whereabouts of a damn butler!"

"Mr. Ravenwood is alright in our books, sir," one of the patrolmen said, and he enunciated the word "sir" so everyone could tell that he really meant "jackass". "He's done nothing but help you and us. Private Sterling impressed the living Hell out of me and everyone else here, except maybe you. He never cared about glory or promotions, unlike some other people who are called public servants."

Ravenwood chuckled at the insult that had been directed toward Stagg, especially because the police officer was too stupid to understand that he had just been insulted.

"Do you see anyone else around here who could be responsible for this?" Stagg screamed.

"There's something new, Stagg," Ravenwood said cheerily. "It's called a time bomb. It's called that because it's a bomb and goes off at whatever time you want."

The patrolmen laughed, and some of them didn't even bother to laugh to themselves.

"I could arrest you right now, Ravenwood!" the Inspector hissed.

"Yes," Ravenwood admitted. "You could. But, it would be completely unlawful, I would be released immediately, and you would be ridiculed if not demoted. I think you'd be almost as opposed to your demotion as your men."

Stagg turned away in anger.

"Some of you men get to the main house!" he yelled. "There were servants there the last time I was here. Interview everyone and find out who was in there and what happened!"

Some of the patrol men reluctantly obeyed. Even Stagg made the right decision sometimes, almost as often as a stopped clock did. Ravenwood gave the Inspector his brief account of what happened, including his premonition. Stagg scowled at Ravenwood, much to Ravenwood's delight. After a few minutes, the patrolmen who had done the interviews told mostly the same story. Registers had been completed of everyone in the building. The registers had been completed by temporary staff who were dismissed as soon as their job was done and the registers had been turned in to the main house. Nobody had gone out to see what the explosion was. Their only concern was the safety of the main house and the location of their employer. The main house was fine but Dr. Street was missing and presumed dead as he had left for the building as soon he had been notified by one of the temporary servants of something that nobody else had heard.

Ravenwood was concerned. Someone had just killed dozens of men, and apparently all as part of a plot to find Sterling and kill him. Sterling was still alive, but Ravenwood was concerned about what lengths the killer would go to rectify that.

Upon returning home, Sterling was shocked at what his master told him.

"All those men dead including the old man!" Sterling gasped.

Ravenwood nodded as his butler sagged into a chair.

"If we were still in the war, I'd understand," Sterling whispered. "But they had all made it home alive. They should have been safe now. That was why we were fighting that damn war in the first place. To be safe."

"Perhaps you should go out with your lady friend," Ravenwood advised. "Something to take your mind off things."

"Perhaps he should be locked inside a small room with no windows," the Nameless One suggested as he seemingly appeared out of thin air. "He is still at risk having his mind put to rest permanently."

"Honestly, Mr. Ravenwood," Sterling muttered. "I don't know why this happening. I'm not that important. I'm sure that I wasn't the one to kill the Red Baron, you know. I'm a rubbish shot. Always have been. I tried that day, to shoot him, but I know I missed. Alfie was the one who decided that I was the one to shoot Richthofen down, and he convinced the old man of it. That damn coward Street was cowering on the ground the whole time, so Alfie was the only witness to what happened, and not a very reliable one. He only got through the war by being drunk the whole time, you know. He didn't deserve to die like that. None of them did."

"This is not about something you have done," the Nameless One sighed. "That much is obvious as even you say that you have done nothing worth killing over. It is about what you might do in the future, and someone trying to prevent it. There is nobody capable of doing more evil that a man who believes that he is doing something for the greater good."

The Nameless One left the room, and for the first time that they could remember, Ravenwood and Sterling actually heard him do it. The old Tibetan was apparently stomping his feet in anger.

Ravenwood sent the butler to his bedroom while Ravenwood retreated to his own room. The answer was obvious to the Nameless One, as it often was. Ravenwood knew from experience that the ancient man would never answer his questions directly, so Ravenwood had to work with what little he already knew. Someone wanted Sterling dead and was willing to kill whomever it took to find him and kill him. The motive for all of that murder had something to do with a dead woman, or possibly many of them, but had nothing to do with the Red Baron, and possibly not even the war. He concentrated more on his memory of the dead woman he had seen. There had been something strange about her other than her grisly death.

"Her clothes!" Ravenwood said triumphantly. He rushed to the Nameless One's room.

"The woman I saw wasn't killed recently!" Ravenwood said triumphantly. "She died years before the Great War even started."

"Many women did," the Nameless one said dryly.

"But that's where everything began!" Ravenwood said. "That's what you meant before. This all started years ago, probably before Sterling was even born. But, it has only been revealed recently, and Sterling is somehow affected by it."

"And how do you find out what "it" is?" the Nameless One asked.

"I haven't the slightest idea whatsoever," Ravenwood admitted. "But I don't think that matters. Someone with a connection to Sterling has come over from England and is trying to kill him, but tried feebly to make it look connected to the Red Baron. Those supposedly German thugs who attacked us were just spewing the contents of phrase books written for tourists. Judging by their accents, they were from the Bronx. They must have some connection to his old army unit because they knew about the rumor that he had killed Richthofen."

"And as far as you know, everyone in New York who fits that description is now blown up," the Nameless One chided.

Ravenwood stopped smiling as he tried to overcome that last barrier to his theory.

"The butler!" Ravenwood finally shouted after several seconds of thought.

"Yes sir?" Sterling asked as he responded to what he thought was a summons by his master.

"No, not you Sterling. Street's butler. Or someone else in that household. None of Street's staff was on the list the police together of the victims of the explosion. They would have the necessary knowledge of their boss's regiment, came over from England with Street, and had access to the building that was blown up. Do you know anything about Street's staff, Sterling?"

"I did recognize the butler," Sterling said thoughtfully. "But it wasn't from the war. It was somewhere else."

"Somewhere you worked? Somewhere you grew up? A friend of the family?" Ravenwood asked hopefully.

"Family! That's it!" Sterling said triumphantly. "He worked for the Streets at their asylum. He wasn't a doctor but I think he was an attendant of some kind, or Street's personal secretary, perhaps. But, I do remember seeing him talk to my father, or at least listen to him. It was almost impossible to talk to my dad,

"Everyone in New York who fits that description is now blown up," the Nameless One chided.

but he was always talking."

"Then that's the connection!" Ravenwood said triumphantly.

"It is at least a connection," the Nameless One sighed. "You are improving."

Sterling looked at the Nameless One in frustration.

"Sir," the Englishman said sternly, "I cook for you, I clean for you, and I watch how you treat Mr. Ravenwood. If you know the answers, why don't you just say them?"

"Young man," the Nameless One said, amused with Sterling's attitude, "the source of my knowledge comes from places you can not even begin to fathom. It comes from where there are lakes of fire filled with ice that does not melt and skies where lightning strikes while the sun shines and there are no clouds. My powers come at a cost, which is a set of rules that I must never break, or the barrier between our world and that world will cease to exist."

The ancient man glided off as Sterling watched in amazement.

"Is any of that true?" he finally asked Ravenwood. Ravenwood thought long and hard about the answer. He did not pretend to understand his mentor's vast powers or even his own personal limited ones. All he knew was that he depended on both. At last, he turned back to Sterling.

"Do you really want to find out?" He took Sterling's silence to mean "No".

"We must go back to Street's mansion before his staff returns to England," Ravenwood said. "Your name was on the list of the suspected dead because I had registered under your name. The fact that you were registered must have been conveyed to the fiend behind this because a message was sent as soon as I signed your name. But, the place is a fortress and we have no idea what we are going up against other than the fact they could probably level a large portion of the city with explosives if they wanted to."

"Then what do we do, sir? Do we just let them leave and hope that they think I'm dead?"

"No," Ravenwood said. "This must be ended and it must be ended now. The police will help us, especially Inspector Stagg."

"You are going to ask him for help?" Sterling said with surprise. That seemed as likely to him as the lakes of fire the Nameless One had described.

"If we asked?" Ravenwood admitted. "He would never help us in a million years. As long as he does not know that he's helping us, it will work out fine."

Ravenwood walked into the police station as if he owned the place. Enough police men knew him and respected him enough to let him have the run of the place. They paid no attention as he walked up confidently to Inspector Stagg's desk. The inspector pretended to be busy and ignored him. At least, he tried to ignore him up to the point when Ravenwood slapped Stagg in the face with a large portion of his considerable strength. Stagg was stunned as Ravenwood turned and silently walked out through a crowd of policemen who offered him no resistance but who seemed oblivious to Stagg trying to get past them, as they constantly blocked him.

"Find that man!" Stagg sputtered. "Put out a drag net! Follow him! Do something!"

"He left the address he was going to," a desk sergeant said as he held up a piece of paper that Ravenwood had left behind. "Do you want us to start there?"

Ravenwood and Sterling circled the police station three or four times in Ravenwood's sports car before he was satisfied that Stagg had found enough policemen who would actually follow his order and was in pursuit before he started driving to Street's mansion. There was a strong possibility that the butler or whoever was behind everything had some sort of military background. Ravenwood was many things, but a military man was not one of them, and he wanted backup before he invaded any sort of military stronghold.

The fact that he was entering such a stronghold was emphasized as soon as he parked his car in front of the mansion's front doors. Bullets struck the hood of his car although he heard no shots. Sterling was hit, but signaled Ravenwood to continue without him. Ravenwood hesitated, but the wound looked to be minor and the police had finally entered the driveway of the mansion, and Ravenwood hoped that Sterling's new friends on the police force would take care of him. He entered the mansion alone. Shots continued to come from above, but Ravenwood's mystical gifts were giving him enough warning to successfully weave his way through them unharmed.

Entering the front entry of the mansion, Ravenwood ran into Street's butler. The butler was trying to organize the rest of the servants for a hasty retreat to England. There were suitcases and satchels everywhere, but what puzzled him was the presence of several large expensive steamer trunks.

"Begone!" Street's butler screamed at Ravenwood, pointing his finger to the open doors in the most dramatic fashion he was capable of. Ravenwood struck out with his walking stick against the outstretched hand and the butler winced as the hard wood broke at least one of his bones.

"Those trunks belong to your employer!" Ravenwood yelled. "Where is he?"

"Dead!" the butler shouted back. "He died in the explosion along with your butler Sterling!"

"Sterling is alive and well," Ravenwood fibbed. "You can probably see him out the front doors along with a large number of policemen who will be storming this house in the next few seconds. I suggest you cooperate."

The servant replied by striking out with his one good hand. He surprised Ravenwood, but only enough to knock him off balance, not hurt him. But now the other servants were feeling bolder and tried to swarm the occult detective. They had the combined combat skills of a soap dish, but even they knew enough to hold Ravenwood's arms while the butler wound up for a proper punch. He connected with a strong blow to Ravenwood's jaw. Ravenwood saw stars but the screams of the butler told him that his hand sustained more damage than Ravenwood's jaw. The butler was now effectively disabled, and all that Ravenwood had to do now was to dispose of the other servants. He strained with all of his might and then suddenly let his body go limp. He was then able to slip his arms out of their grasp. He did a front somersault to put some distance between him and them as they looked on in bewilderment. A few swipes with his cane was enough to make them back off while he grabbed the butler's left hand in his powerful grasp and squeezed with all of his strength.

Ravenwood's grip was enough to crush a fresh apple and make a normal man wince with pain in an ordinary handshake. With the butler already suffering from broken fingers, he was not a normal man. The butler screamed in pain as he felt himself going the short distance from being injured to being permanently crippled.

"Where is Dr. Street?" Ravenwood asked calmly.

"Dead!" the butler moaned.

Ravenwood increased the pressure he was putting on the servant's hand and the butler groaned in agony.

"Try again," Ravenwood encouraged. "I see an awful lot of clothing being packed for a dead man, and who exactly is paying for all of you to go back to England?"

"Upstairs!" the butler said in agony. "He has a platform upstairs on the roof so he can fire down on people!"

"Triumph!" a voice said from the direction of the staircase that led to the upper floors. "Triumph! The monster is dead! I shot him!"

Ravenwood turned as much as he could and saw the Dr. Street was alive and well. He was less well when he saw Ravenwood and he bolted for the study Ravenwood had first seen him in.

"I've got you now, Ravenwood!" Stagg yelled from outside.

Ravenwood let go of the Butler's hand and turned toward Stagg's voice.

"You'll never catch me Stagg! My gang in here will fight you to the death!"

Ravenwood ran after Street as Street's servants looked at each other in confusion as to what Ravenwood meant. They realized that they were being used as the bait in Ravenwood's trap when the police entered, and under Stagg's direction, were attacked and beaten by the police.

"Round up his gang!" Stagg said triumphantly. "Then get Ravenwood!"

Ravenwood approached the study with caution. He could hear Street struggling with a mechanism of some kind. The occult detective drew his Luger and entered the study. Street was sitting behind his massive desk, with both of his hands under the desk frantically trying to work a hidden mechanism of some kind. He pointed his gun squarely at Street before he addressed him.

"Put your hands up slowly," Ravenwood commanded. "No sudden movements, and put the behind your head and interlock your fingers."

Street looked up with surprise. He had been so engrossed with the contraption under the desk that he had not even realized that Ravenwood was already in the room.

"So I take it you're familiar with the blind German mechanic Von Herder?" Ravenwood asked.

"How do you know about him?" Street gasped.

"The only people who truly believe in occult detectives are other occult detectives," Ravenwood said. "I correspond with Hesselius, Van Helsing, Carnacki, and others. Carnacki's friend Dodgson, in turn, is part of a support group for detective chroniclers run by a doctor in London. He wrote the story of Moran, a London assassin who used one of Von Herder's air gun contraptions. There were rumors that Von Herder had built a machine gun version of his silent air gun, but until now they have only been rumors."

"Von Herder was killed in the war," Street said bitterly. "His silent machine guns are deadly, but he was the only one who could actually build the damn things so they would actually fire. Army intelligence tried to duplicate them but with no success. I managed to get my hands on the prototypes and kept them as souvenirs."

"Obviously you've been killing the members of your own regiment as a ploy to get to Sterling," Ravenwood admitted. "And I take it you were able to use your wealth and influence to have the autopsy reports on the dead men faked?"

"Faked is too strong a word," Street said. "I just had them varied slightly so the official report made it sound like the men were shot from above as if by an airplane. But it doesn't matter now, Ravenwood. Sterling is dead and I will be remembered as a hero!"

"Wrong on both counts, Street!" Ravenwood said with a broad grin. "You wounded Sterling but he'll be fine. And if you are remembered, it will be as a madman who should have been a patient in his own asylum."

"No!" Street said in horror. "Listen to me Ravenwood! You don't understand what Sterling is! He's not who you think he is! He's a monster!"

"Whatever he was when you knew him," Ravenwood said, "He's no longer the same. He's been healed in the mind and the soul by someone with far greater skill than psychiatry will ever have."

"It's not possible!" Street exclaimed.

"Sir, you have no idea what the word possible actually means," Ravenwood said. He could hear a commotion in the hall outside, as Stagg seemed to have finally seemed to have fought his way through an army of unarmed, unskilled servants.

"In here Stagg!" Ravenwood called. "I've captured your killer!"

Ravenwood had not taken his eyes off of Street during this entire exchange in the study, and that mistake almost cost him his life. The enraged Inspector but his head down and charged Ravenwood's back as if he were a demented bull. The Inspector was a squat little man, but not without some physical power. The impact was more than enough to send Ravenwood flying and knock his Luger from his grasp. It was also more than enough to force Stagg's ever present bowler hat down over his eyes. With some effort, he pried it up and pulled his own gun on Ravenwood.

"Don't move!" Stagg hissed. "You're under arrest, Ravenwood!"

Ravenwood stared in dismay at Inspector Stagg. If the man had any powers of deductive reasoning at all, his skill level was somewhere between that of an ant and a rock. The policeman was advancing on him now, gun drawn and handcuffs in his other hand. Ravenwood held out his hands so they could be handcuffed and Stagg gleefully attempted to take him into custody. The attempt failed when Ravenwood's right hand sent the Inspector's pistol flying and his left hand deftly slipped Stagg's own handcuffs onto the shocked oaf. He then completed the task and both of Stagg's hands were handcuffed in front of him.

Ravenwood then turned away from Stagg to find his Luger. Street was back trying to operate the mechanism under his desk, and whatever it was, it must have been deadly. Stagg, unfortunately, also proved himself to be potentially deadly. He threw his handcuffed hands over Ravenwood's head and tried to choke him with the chain that held the handcuffs together.

Stagg was gloating in Ravenwood's defeat when his skull seemed to explode in pain. Sterling, having been bandaged by the arriving patrolmen, had entered the house with Stagg's squad. He had grabbed Ravenwood's walking stick from where his master had dropped it on the floor and swung it with all of the strength that his one good arm could muster. This did not free Ravenwood, but it distracted Stagg enough that Ravenwood managed to flip him over his head and onto the floor. Stagg landed heavily.

"Sterling!" Street screeched. "Die, you bastard, die! You have all of these men fooled, but I know what you really are! I know who you really are! I know who your father really was! He confessed to me in the asylum just before he died! Your father was…"

Street never had a chance to finish his accusation. Ravenwood had recovered his Luger and shot the crazed doctor fatally through the heart. Ravenwood, however, took an unusual amount of care in ensuring that the doctor would never speak again. He continued firing until his gun clicked instead of firing.

Everyone in the room was stunned at Ravenwood's apparent brutal slaying of an unarmed man.

"You're a murderer!" Stagg shouted triumphantly. "You're a murderer, Ravenwood! You'll hang for this and I'll dance on your cursed grave!"

With those words, the front panel on Street's massive desk flipped down. Ravenwood had noticed before that it seemed newer than the rest of the desk. That was because it was a new modification Street had added as a last line of defence. A release system had been rigged so that Street could cause the panel to fall forward, but the mechanism had not been tested properly. It had jammed when Ravenwood entered the room, and had only now finally fallen forward and down onto the floor. It now revealed that Street had two of his silenced machine guns mounted under the desk, and they were mounted on swivels. If the front panel of the desk had worked properly, he would have been able to spray the entire room with machine gun fire.

One of the patrolmen who had befriended Sterling went forward to inspect the previously concealed weapons.

"They're both loaded with Spandau bullets!" he said. "We wouldn't have stood a chance! You saved us, Mr. Ravenwood! You saved all of us!"

The Inspector's jaw dropped in sudden realization. He was now standing directly in front of the machine gun muzzles and he would have been the first to die if Street's weapon had functioned properly.

"He saved me!" Stagg whispered. His voice was tinged with shock and a bit of regret. Ravenwood had just saved his life in front of an audience of reliable witnesses. He had been made to look like the buffoon yet again. The whole charade at the police station, he wrongfully concluded, had only been done to humiliate him. He had never been so angry to be alive in his life.

Ravenwood stood silent and was nearly knocked down when Sterling slapped him on the back.

"Brilliant, sir!" Sterling said with pride and admiration. "Absolutely brilliant!

Your brilliant deductions have saved the day yet again!"

"Will somebody please get me out of these handcuffs?" Stagg pleaded.

"The master put you in those for your own safety," Sterling snapped. "If he hadn't, we'd all be dead!"

"Private Sterling is right, sir," a patrol man who hated Stagg slightly less than the others said. He released the Inspector despite glares from his fellow police men. "Mr. Ravenwood figured it all out and had to trick you into coming here because you would have never believed him."

"Street was obviously insane," Sterling continued. He was rather enjoying his role as a narrator in this adventure. He considered contacting some acquaintances in England about how a proper detective chronicler operated. "He had been locked up with lunatics at his own asylum for too long and he struck out at the men in his regiment, me in particular. He had always despised us as his inferiors, and when his mind snapped, it was his excuse to kill all of us."

"But how did Mr. Ravenwood know that there were machine guns under the desk?" the patrol man asked. "None of us could see them."

"Pure logic," Sterling continued. "The master had already deduced the nature of Street's weapon of choice. Look at them. They're bulky and not easily handled. He must have had an ambush prepared with a unit on a tripod at Alfie's room. As he was paying for the room, the hotel staff would have paid him no heed. He had to have one set up on the roof to shoot me. But, it was not easily moved. As a last line of defence, he had these guns mounted under his desk so that anyone who followed him in here would be an easy target. Do you see how the room was arranged? The desk faces the entire room. Upon seeing Street trying to fire his guns under the desk, the master took the only step that could save all of us, and that was to shoot Street in self defence."

The patrol men slapped Sterling on the back and promised to take him for a beer the following night. They also looked at Ravenwood with new admiration. Ravenwood might have strange methods, but he was obviously one of the good guys despite what Stagg thought of him.

Stagg continued to bluster. He was still convinced that Ravenwood was a fraud, but he would now be muzzled in expressing that as loudly as he used to. If he dared to criticize Ravenwood in the future, Stagg himself would be ridiculed as an ingrate by his men.

Ravenwood still stood silent as men congratulated him and Sterling went on and on about Ravenwood's prowess. He had never seen his butler happier. That was one of the reasons he would never be able to tell Sterling the truth.

Ravenwood had not killed Street in self defence. He had killed him because of a vision he had suddenly had in the study. Perhaps it was his unconscious mind putting all of the clues together or maybe it was a psychic vision. In any event, the truth had suddenly become apparent in a split second. The trigger to all of the events that led to Street trying to kill Sterling had been the death of Sterling's father. On his deathbed, he had had a moment of lucidity and confessed his sins to his doctor, Street. The vision of the dead woman in Victorian clothing had been a clue to the contents of that confession, as well as the Nameless One's cryptic comments that Sterling had once been capable of killing hundreds of women just like her. She had been the one thing that Sterling's father had always commended Sterling's mother for not being: a whore. Sterling's use of a sharpened bayonet as his weapon of choice in the war had been another clue to his natural propensity and what he might have become if the Nameless One had not healed him.

Ravenwood had not killed Street in self defence. Perhaps whatever power gave him his premonitions had known of the danger and gave him what knowledge he received in order to save everyone. At the time, however, the only reason Ravenwood had killed Street was because he had not wanted Street to tell the world that his good friend Sterling was the son of Jack the Ripper.

THE END

INTERIOR ILLUSTRATIONS:

SAM A. SALAS - has a been an artist since the 70's. His first love has always been comics and comic book art. His greatest aspiration was to become a comic book artist with one of the major companies. In the mid 90s Sam and a small band of friends decided to publish his own comics. Thus was born ZUB COMICS. The company published two titles. One was GREAT GALAXIES! A science fiction anthology featuring all original stories with art by Sam. The other title was TELLURIA a fantasy title. In all, the company published 11 books and folded in the early 2000's. Since then, Sam has done various freelance projects for local independent publishers including several stories for a book titled WICKED AWESOME TALES, and a few stories for Ron Fortier. Now mostly retired, he is always ready to take on new projects and looks forward to working with his friend Ron on this new book.

COVER ILLUSTRATION:

ADAM BENET SHAW –Accomplished painter, illustrator, and comics creator, Adam has garnered acclaim across a number of artistic media. After completing studies at the Cleveland Institute of Art in Ohio, the Edinburgh College of Art in Scotland and Watts Atelier in California, Shaw was selected as an emerging American artist to watch by European gallery owners and exhibited in London, England. He has been featured in "New American Painting", selected multiple times for the Arkansas Art Center's Delta Exhibit, and shown at the prestigious "Red Clay Survey" at the Huntsville Museum of Art. His work has also been shown in over 50 group and solo shows in the US and internationally. His figurative paintings are a prominent part of a 140-foot mural entitled "The History of Cotton" at the National Cotton Exchange Museum, St. Jude's Children's Research Hospital, the National Contact Bridge Museum, and a treasured part of private and corporate collections. He has created storyboards for several motion pictures, including Paramount Pictures' film "Black Snake Moan" directed by Craig Brewer, stage design for operas and corporate events, and character illustrations for the gaming industry. His published graphic novel work includes the series "Dead In Memphis", "Bloodstream" for Image Comics, "David: The Illustrated Novel" from Shepherd King Publishing and "Harpe: America's First Serial Killers" from Cave-in-Rock Publishing. He shares his love of art through teaching and workshops at his studio in the Broad Avenue Arts District in Memphis. Recently he has been painting book covers for pulp publishers Pro Se Productions and Airship 27 Productions.

OCCULT DETECTIVES

They battle demons and monsters, hunt ghosts and defend us against the things that go bump in the night. They are Occult Detectives and they've been a staple of pulp fiction since the beginning of those glorious, garish magazines. Now Airship 27 Productions is thrilled to bring you a quartet of tales starring some of the most unique Occult Detectives ever created; three newly minted heroes and one classic master of mysticism.

From the days of the Wild West, Joel Jenkins offers up his Indian Shaman hero, Lone Crow. Then we have Josh Reynold's colorful Charles St. Cyprian, the Queen's own Royal Occultist, followed by Jim Beard's Sgt. Janus, the Spirit Breaker. And we culminate with a little known pulp classic figure, Ravenwood: the Stepson of Mystery as chronicled by Ron Fortier.

Get ready to take on possessed gunfighters, eerie mesmerizing spirits, a bewitching temptress and a legion of the undead as these four brand new tales usher you into thrilling adventures beyond the realm of the ordinary; your guides....the Occult Detectives.

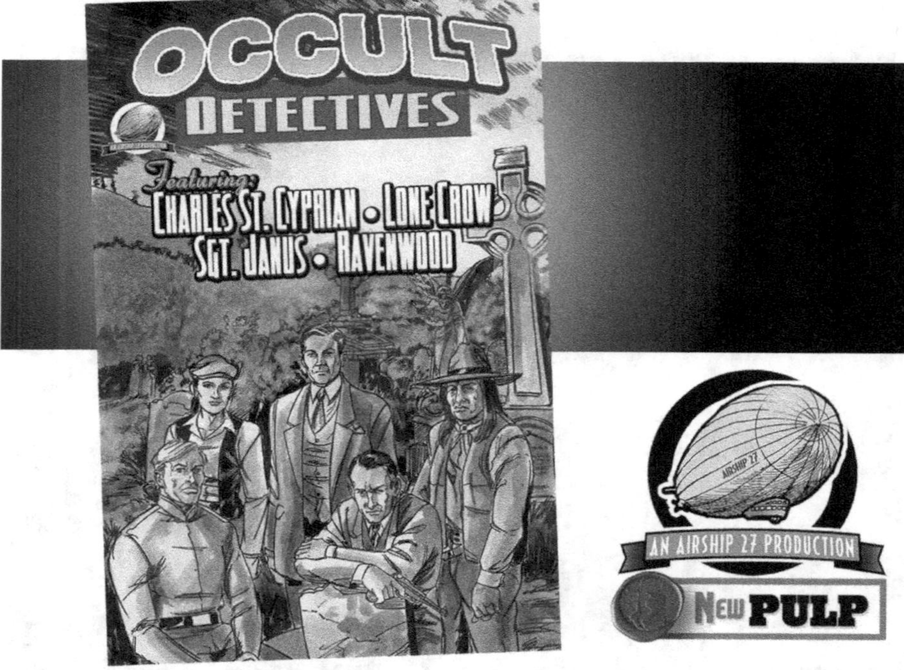

PULP FICTION FOR A NEW GENERATION!

FOR AVAILABILITY INFORMATION: AIRSHIP27HANGAR.COM

www.ingramcontent.com/pod-product-compliance
Lightning Source LLC
LaVergne TN
LVHW010100110826
845155LV00028B/420